The Wind Whispers Her Name

The Wind Whispers Her Name

Mary Irvine

For the island which brought us together

Prologue

An elderly man, with a full head of pure white hair, immaculately dressed, moved painfully slowly down the gangplank of the Dolphin. His right hand rested on a silver-topped ebony cane. A crew member deposited an expensive, well-worn suitcase on the jetty. The autumn sun brushed the fading crest on the case.

The Dolphin left and the old man turned to the waiting taxi, ordered as usual in advance. The same taxi driver, the same moustache, now grey as was his formerly jet black hair. The muscular build long gone, as so many things. He was of an age with his passenger but still proffered a helping arm.

'Welcome, Mr. Kenneth. It's been a long time.'

Kenneth smiled as he waved the arm away.

'Maybe next time, my friend. For now the cane suffices.'

But Kenneth knew there would not be a next time. This would be his last visit. His consultant had advised strongly against this trip. But he had to come. One last time. To feel her presence, to breathe in her essence. Only here could he do that.

'Seven Islands again?'

'Of course. But drive past the house.'

The taxi made its way along the coast road. The bars and restaurants as he remembered them mostly gone, Kostas' Bar, no longer Kostas' Bar. Right, up Horse Buggy Hill, left at Crossbows, no longer Crossbows and so different. The children's playground looked tired and unused as they turned right along the Agia Marina Road, the convoluted turnings he remembered. The taxi slowed as it passed the church on the left.

'Do you want to get out?'

'No, thank you, but stop a while at the gates.'

The dark blue painted, metal gates were set into the wall surrounding a solitary house. Apprehensive of what he would see and how he would feel Kenneth looked first to the right. The hotel was derelict although the out-of-control bougainvillea masked it somewhat. The two floors of the house to the right of the hotel were shuttered, the garden overgrown. But, almost mockingly amidst such surroundings, the vanilla, medlar and damaskina trees sported a display of ripe fruit.

Looking at the gnarled fig tree he recalled fondly the hours of pleasure its contorted branches afforded the three little girls, the middle one invariable hanging upside down, as agile as any trapeze artist. Not one of them had ever fallen, nor were they told not to climb as it was dangerous, only to be careful. Three little girls whose photo he still treasured although the frame had long fallen to pieces. He allowed himself to muse for a while. Where were they all now? Scattered round the world, married with children?

He had never married. How could he? After her. Yes, he had had liaisons but they were ephemeral, a moment's gratification and then, nothing. He had no children, as far as he was aware. He had always been responsible in any sexual encounter, at least in that direction. The non-production of a legitimate heir from the oldest son had caused his parents some consternation but each of his younger brothers had performed the duty Kenneth had so selfishly neglected. There was now male issue aplenty to ensure the continuation of a long and noble lineage. He had no regrets in that sphere of his life.

Thinking of other regrets he turned to the left. The house looked neglected, unkempt, the garden overgrown. A dusty, wheel-less car rested where once the grape vines had flourished. Three motorized bikes of indeterminate age lay abandoned to the left of the walkway, including the red bike that had been there so long ago. A new motorbike lounged outside the main gates as did a sleepy, uninterested dog.

The paint was faded and peeling on all the shutters. The driver watched impassively as his passenger got out of the taxi. With a resigned smile to the driver, who gave an almost imperceptible nod in return, Kenneth walked up to the smaller gate which led to the kitchen entrance. The balcony there had gained an ugly wooden structure around its perimeter. An assortment of boxes cluttered, replacing the once neat border of plant pots. He looked to the right, the side garden, hoping to conjure up a memory. The garden remained mockingly silent. He wouldn't find her here. He returned to the taxi.

'Go on.'

The taxi swept right and left following the curves in the road and drew up outside Kenneth's choice of accommodation.

* * *

Dusk fell. Taking his G&T into the deserted courtyard of the hotel Kenneth closed his eyes to summon a vision of the Ice Queen as he had last seen her. But the picture was nebulous. He couldn't hold it. She wasn't there.

He remembered the night she had thawed. Such a melting. Such passion, such urgency, such need. She had not only taken him to places long forgotten but to heights never known. She had drained him, physically, emotionally. He felt she had taken the very soul of him. After, when they lay quiet he felt a total exhaustion from which he could not believe he would ever recover. He thought he heard her whisper, 'Come back to me, my love.' He didn't know to whom she spoke. Although he might have wished it, he knew in his heart it was not to him.

In the morning she was gone. The place where she had lain was cold. Had she really been there at all? He no longer knew fact from fiction. He heard a car horn. His taxi. He swiftly dispatched the last of the generous drink, more G than T, and stepped out for the journey down to the town.

* * *

Kostas was long gone. The bar had since had several owners but the ambience had not survived Kostas' departure. The first owners had preserved the décor and played the same eclectic mix of music but slowly the atmosphere generated by the third component, Kostas himself, dissipated. Changes had taken place. The highly varnished wooden bar that had been Kostas' pride and joy was now a glaring white. There was a sacrilegious TV up on the wall where the book shelves had once been.

Kenneth gave his order which was received and dispensed dispassionately. He chose to sit outside, carefully gauging his gait across the road to the tables to avoid the through traffic, even more frenetic than his last visit. He sat with his back to the wall from where he could survey all. He saw only strangers, new people. He would not find her there.

He raised an arm as a buggy trotted by. No bell announced its approach and no wild flowers adorned it. The young driver stopped but made no attempt to help the elderly gentleman into his seat. The meagre measure of drink with which Kostas would have been appalled, far more T than G, remained untouched on the table.

* * *

The Garden Restaurant, no longer a garden but a paved courtyard, had a few late season guests as Kenneth re-entered. Some smiled; others gave a friendly 'Good evening.' He acknowledged all with a brief nod. Not wishing to engage in or encourage holiday conversation he chose a table in the far corner where the trees had once been, away from the lights of the main building. A smiling young lady appeared. She lit the candle which nestled in a wreath of cloth roses set in a saucer of smoky opaque glass.

The sight of the homemade roses and the scent of jasmine carried on the night air brought confused memories flooding back. His reveries were interrupted by the young lady. Young to him, as most were these days, but in her late thirties.

'Yes, thank you. I'll have the pork chop with salad, no potatoes.'

'Would you like something to drink?'

'A jug of white, please. And...'

'Yes?'

'The couple who used to run this hotel?'

'My mother and father. They are retired although mama comes to help sometimes. I'll let them know you asked for them. I am Rhea, their daughter. We don't have so many foreigners now. Mostly Athenians who come for the summer or long weekends. Of course we are always full for the Armata. My husband does the cooking now. He is a very good cook.'

Rhea went to attend to the other guests, leaving Kenneth to recall the Armata spent with the woman he had so wanted to be the one to share his life. Why? How? When? Where? The questions remained unanswered as they always had. He watched Rhea go into the kitchen and fill a jug with wine from a barrel. She brought it, together with the small tumbler from which this wine was drunk, to his table.

'From me and my husband to say welcome.'

'That's very kind. Thank you.'

Kenneth took a sip of the slightly warm wine, slowly replacing his glass and politely nodding his appreciation.

'Tell me, Rhea. Do you remember an English lady who lived here about thirty years ago? We came here once or twice when I lived on the island for a year.'

'I remember the English teacher. But I was very young. She always came here after she was alone. I would practise my English with her. She would bring their dog with her. She usually didn't have company but I think I remember you with her sometimes, when you stayed in their old house. I think it's very sad...'

* * *

Rhea returned to the kitchen, leaving Kenneth to ponder the story just revealed to him. The Ice Queen had never mentioned a dog but he clearly recalled the largest of the graves and the Celtic cross. This was one more thing he had never known. And it was 'their' dog. So there had been someone else. Had he ever really known her at all?

He was hardly aware of the pork chop and salad being placed before him or of the 'Kali orexi' that accompanied it as he tried to come to terms with his feelings. Could he, should he, have made greater efforts to find her? Should he have returned to the island immediately after delivering his island manuscript to his agent? That book had been very successful. He had also gone on to write the book his agent had originally expected. Having his amateur sleuth being eaten by sharks had given Kenneth great pleasure but he had never written another book. Finding he couldn't concentrate on a long project he had confined himself to writing articles based on his restless travels. He had never written just for the money. Hadn't needed to. The family trust had seen to that.

Subsequent, spasmodic visits to the island never coincided with hers, although 'just missing her' on occasions. On one such visit he had eaten at a restaurant in the Clock Square, a place he had always liked but to which she had always refused to go - with him. The food was excellent, the service friendly.

It had been a cool, windy evening so he had sat inside. His eyes had been drawn to a black and white photo hanging on the wall. It was a photo of the Dapia, possibly from the twenties. Young men in white trousers, blazers and boaters gazed down on him.

It seemed vaguely familiar yet he was certain he had never seen it before. Argyres had returned with his meal, a platter of seafood with salad.

'Ah, you are admiring the old picture. It was a gift from the lady. Kali orexi.'

The Lady. Kenneth's memory had returned to the oblong shape on the living room wall denoting where a picture had once hung. Photos of different parts of the island had hung on either side. That was what was familiar. All the frames were identical. The picture staring down at him would have fitted the oblong perfectly.

He had finally been told she didn't come any more. No-one had any information so he too had stopped coming. Even Nikki had been unable to help. Although Kenneth knew she held a British passport there appeared to be no evidence of her living in the UK after she had apparently left the island. And she had rarely spoken about her life before she had met him. He had often thought that in her mind she still did live in the past. But on his broaching the subject of her earlier life she had replied there was only the present - the here and now.

After several consultations with specialists he had decided he would return once more to the island to search for her. Although he had not found her anywhere, the wind still whispered her name. He believed she was there, somewhere, and now with this new knowledge he would find her. Tomorrow would decide whether or not he would leave this island forever. He ordered a coffee and brandy.

Diary Entry (mid May - Some thirty years earlier)

What a view. Uninterrupted right down to the sea. Wonder what that is? Another island? Hardly looks big enough. Must say this is quite acceptable, all in all. For a short while. Definitely won't be staying a year. Hardly seems a week since the 'phone call from that ghastly woman.

On the desk a blank sheet of unlined paper, a blotter on which the sheet lay pristine, a monogrammed fountain pen on an oak stand exactly parallel to the top of the blotter. Kenneth stared at the sheet, as he had for several days. There was nothing coming. The telephone, positioned squarely to the left of the blotter, had been calling with annoying regularity. Kenneth reached for the handset.

'Yes?'

'I've found just the place for you.'

Recognising the silky voice Kenneth was tempted to hang up. He refrained, knowing such an action might result in an arrival on his doorstep. His home was sacrosanct. He definitely didn't want the owner of that voice entering its portals. With her he had produced a four volume set of his family's history, no small feat, grudgingly acknowledged by his father when it achieved academic success.

His agent, who had a strong economic eye and with whom he had a fractured relationship, had urged him to break into the popular market of the detective novel.

Kenneth's travels would allow a very authentic backdrop. He had mockingly brought to life Denny Dee.

The first two books regaling the adventures of this singer-cum-amateur sleuth on cruise ships had surprisingly achieved success. How such a banal worm had been well-received by a large section of the public was beyond Kenneth. But several books later Denny was still proving popular. Now his agent, whom he less than affectionately thought of as 'The Bitch', was getting worried at his failure to produce the next. She had engaged a variety of ploys to get him writing but had so far failed. She obviously thought she had the solution.

He vaguely heard 'Greece', 'small' and 'island' being enthused over. All arrangements had been made, a courier was already on the way with details. He could pack whilst waiting. The implications were clear. He wasn't being given a choice.

* * *

He signed for the package and opened it immediately. A brief note informed him The Bitch would see to the flat, utilities, cancellations. She would also send on packages of essentials for his year's stay. Had the woman finally gone over the edge? She wrote she looked forward to receiving the next manuscript a.s.a.p. There was a fat envelope. Inside was an A4 sheet with a detailed itinerary plus an amount of drachma. Other slips of paper proved to be a variety of travel tickets.

The telephone rang. Would 'Sir' please confirm the taxi to the airport, booked to arrive in two hours? Kenneth grabbed the tickets. Five hours to the flight. Bloody Bitch! The itinerary had given Spetsai as the final destination. He had never heard of it.

Where the hell was it? He reached for his 'Times Atlas of the World'. It suggested Spetses as alternative. Turned out to be a small island in the Argo-Saronic Gulf. Pop c.4,000. One main town, Spetses. Original! Looking quickly through other information its greatest claim to fame seemed to be that it was car-free. Something, he supposed.

* * *

He was in a cramped economy seat, no privileged upmarket area on this aeroplane. Another point scored by The Bitch. Her writing was not only on the wall, it was writ large. He had managed to procure an aisle seat so could get up and stretch his legs several times during the flight. A thin, slightly balding, bespectacled man had the window seat and spent most of the time gazing at the clouds. The mountain of flesh Kenneth presumed was the wife overflowed the middle seat.

On being airborne and the seat belt removal sign displayed she had, with a struggle, pushed up the armrest which was Kenneth's only bastion against her physical assault. With a smile that would have made Kaa envious he slowly pushed the armrest back into position. End of discussion. If the lady had wanted or required two seats she should have paid for them. This action also ensured he wasn't addressed by the lady for the remainder of the flight. She did give a running commentary to her presumed husband which is probably why he found the clouds so fascinating.

Kenneth drowsed, vaguely aware of snacks and drinks being sold. No free meals on this cheapy. The Bitch had really thought this one through. But, was he wrong? Could he smell cold chicken? And definitely boiled egg. Kenneth peered through the long eyelashes many women envied, even more finding them sensuously appealing, to see the origin of the smell being waved about by the lady next to him. He wrinkled his nose in distaste.

He consulted his watch - two hours to go. The repast finished, the lady heaved her bulk out of the seat. Pleased to be able to stretch his long legs, Kenneth nimbly jumped into the aisle and, gentleman that he was, bent and pushed both armrests into their upright position to facilitate her passage. During her absence he walked up and down the narrow aisle, moving arms and legs in a way that caused some passengers great amusement. Kenneth cared little, being conscious of the dangers of the inactivity of a four hour flight.

The more than Rubenesque lady having returned to her seat he did likewise, noticing she had returned both armrests to the down position. He closed his eyes until a hand was gently placed on his shoulder. Landing was imminent, seatbelts needed to be fastened.

The lady joined her companion in gazing out of the window. This time Kenneth knew they were not looking at clouds but at the sight of the city below. Athens. He had been several times to Athens to visit his friend, Nikki. He loved the city's night life, felt comfortable there. Had even picked up a smattering of Modern Greek.

But this time Athens was not his final destination. He had a wait of several hours before the next stage of his journey. His friend Nikki lived and worked in Athens but one could hardly pay a social call at two o'clock in the morning, not having been given the time to announce a visit. Night flights were considerably cheaper than day ones. The Bitch. She probably took great delight in imagining him being stuck in the airport with nothing open but the public loos.

* * *

Having passed through passport control - one very bored officer, and a totally deserted customs control - Kenneth collected his luggage and strolled to the furthest end of the airport where buses and taxis for Athens and Piraeus were to be had. There were also coaches waiting to collect package tourists. As he approached the ticket office he saw his flight companions in the queue. He heard them ask for tickets to Piraeus. Kenneth did not do buses. He crossed the road and got into a waiting taxi.

They were straight out into the suburb of Glyfada. The coast road was fairly quiet, it being midweek. Mostly taxis ploughing between airport and ports, buses transporting tourists to their hotels or to the port to wait for ferries to islands with no airport. The lights of bars, restaurants and night clubs, which would glare till late at the weekend, were non-existent but he knew where to look for the beauty of Athens. It was just a brief window of opportunity but he was ready. There she was standing proudly, in ghostly illumination - the Parthenon. A flash and she was gone.

Kenneth heard the driver speaking. He made out the word 'limani' so deduced he was being asked which port was wanted. Coming out with one of his stock phrases, 'Ena leptouli', Kenneth consulted his fat envelope. Yes, he was booked on the hydrofoil - known locally as the Flying Dolphin - which left from Marina Zea. Now he realised why! Zea was totally deserted during the early hours - not even a toilet open. If he remembered correctly there wasn't even anywhere to sit. That was why she'd opted for the Dolphin rather than the ferry. A serpentine smile crossed his face. Another chance to get one over the baptised, confirmed and practising Bitch. He launched into his limited Greek.

'Signomi, to limani megalo, parakalo.'

As he settled back smugly he saw one of the driver's hands being raised into the air. The splayed fingers were thrust heavenwards and the hand appeared to rotate from the wrist, although on closer observation it only turned halfway and then back again. This was the sort of Greek he understood. Again he consulted the envelope, just to make certain.

'Spetses.'

The driver's hand changed shape. The tip of the fingers met the tip of the thumb to receive an enthusiastic smack of his lips, the fingers then snapping open.

'Poli oraia.'

The taxi veered off the main road, taking side streets until Kenneth began to wonder if he were being taken the 'scenic route'. However, they soon drew up at the bottom of some stone steps that reached up to a very large and architecturally ornate church. The taxi driver barely paused as he removed Kenneth's two large valises from the boot, crossed himself - surely the 'wrong' way - and laid his right hand reverently on his breast, which hand then reached out to receive the fare. By the time he'd finished adding on the extras, from the airport, to the sea port, two cases, night charge, the fare was considerably more than the meter stated. Still cheaper than all the other European cities Kenneth had visited.

The ferries to the islands were across the road about two hundred metres down from the church. He crossed the road carefully, checking for stray traffic. At this time of night the traffic lights were switched off to conserve energy. The dockside was totally deserted. The water appeared still, yet the giant ferries swayed gently at their moorings.

Ticket offices were not yet open and the ships had their barriers in place.

He saw the ship he wanted. 'Saronic Express' proclaimed in large letters that its destinations were Ægina, Methana, Poros, Hydra, Ermione and Spetses. It also sported a clock attached above the stern stating it left at 8 a.m. It was just after three. He saw a dim gleam of light past the Saronic ferries. He headed towards the gleam. It proved to come from a small cantina selling tea, coffee, soft drinks, beer and the ubiquitous Seven Day Croissant. Kenneth shrugged.

'Mia beera parakalo.'

His smile as he handed over the money was met with a blank stare. Lady obviously didn't get job satisfaction. Walking back to his ship he settled on a bollard, staring out to sea, waiting for the first sight of Homer's rosy-fingered dawn. But other lights attracted his attention. Dull lights appeared over the boarding areas. The initial quietness and peace were now broken.

Barriers were removed and there was a lot of movement. A closed lorry drew up to his ferry. Bundles of newspapers were transferred from lorry to ship. The lorry then moved on to other ferries. More vehicles began to arrive, a private courier firm, catering companies, private cars. Traffic queues began to build up. The large ferryboats still bobbed serenely, patiently awaiting their human cargoes. The first of these descended on the now-opened, single ticket booth serving all the ships.

The ferries sprang into life. Stern doors were lowered, crews appeared, vehicles began embarking. A trickle of people boarded. Others were buying koulouria - sesame-crusted bread rings, and bottles of water from the street traders who had suddenly appeared. Dawn had arrived without warning. Not Homer's dawn but a lightening suddenly bursting into a surprisingly bright sunlight.

Local people crossed the quay to their work. Many eating breakfast, usually koulouria, occasionally small cheese pies, as they went. He had seen similar sights in Beijing and Shanghai where dumplings were usually the breakfast choice. The hordes rushed to commandeer the 'best' areas on the ferry. Kenneth decided to ensconce himself on the upper deck, under the awning. His fair colouring and strong sunlight did not marry well. He took both suitcases with him despite a crew member offering a 'safe' place to leave them. Donning a pair of Carrera sunglasses to protect his grey-green eyes he sat back to await departure, wishing his Panama hat hadn't been packed deep within a case.

Diary Entry (mid May)
Reasonable sleep. Bed made up with clean, white bedding. Pleased to see mosquito screens in place. No air-con, fans in every room. 'Fridge well-stocked for few days. Will have contemplative day. Get bearings etc. No rush. Have whole year. Ha! No intention of staying that long. Will write up ferry trip. May be of use for that damned sleuth or a travel article.

The slow ferry was aptly named. It had taken more than five hours to fulfil its itinerary before arriving at its final destination. It had also been hot and cloying. Too many people Kenneth thought as he tried to avoid the press who barely waited for the stern door to be safely down.

Once again he caught the nauseous smells and irritating noises that had pervaded his personal space for the journey - garlic, raw and sour, the stale sweat of clothes worn too long, bodies closeted in close proximity, the squawking of live chickens in the confinement of cramped cane cages. At last he felt space around him as the sea breeze mentally and physically revived him somewhat. He felt it refreshingly welcome after the claustrophobic atmosphere on the rather tortuous journey just suffered.

Kenneth, as always, was observant of everything around him. The ferry was of medium size but seemed to accommodate a disproportionate number of people. From the timetable he knew it ploughed back and forth, once a day. For all the islands the ferry was obviously a life-line. It brought everything, mail, food, goods, visitors, tourists.

The unloading of provisions as it made its designated stops provided light entertainment for the initiates on the long journey - organisation and order not being an obvious trait. Kenneth's island was the ferry's final destination. One would just have to become accustomed to the non-urgency so characteristic of this part of the world.

Soon he was surrounded by luggage of all descriptions, smart, matching sets, sports bags, boxes tied with string, plastic carriers, bin liners containing an assortment of items, triffid-like plants, toilet seats, small pieces of furniture and some not so small, hose-pipes, rolls of plaited bamboo, assorted bits of machinery - nothing seemed barred. And the noise which assailed his ears. Incessant talk, indolent chatter to argumentative political discussion, radios, Walkmans, music of all kinds, vying with each other for supremacy, all rising above the not so melodic drone of the engines.

He watched children of all ages, sitting bored, eating, reading comics, some sullen, cowed by fraught parents, others chasing around the decks - why did none of them ever fall over-board - eternally being screamed at by parents fast losing patience. He noted babies, hot and bothered, fractious, sleeping fretfully or suckling with noisy contentment. Kenneth averted his gaze from such intimacy. He felt embarrassed.

A plastic tube of nuts was pressed into his face.

'Fresh, fresh. You like. You buy. Yes, Yes. Very good.'

Kenneth shook his head, but only when he turned his head to gaze seawards did the man go on to the next potential customer. A man selling monthly lottery tickets - selling dreams reflected Kenneth as he again shook his head. He never purchased such tickets. He had no need. And he had achieved success in writing.

His eyes strayed to the make-shift bar now in full swing as passengers bought drinks, alcoholic rarely, mostly bottled water, occasionally cans of soft drinks, more often the iced coffee for which he had never acquired a taste. Snacks were also being purchased even though the prices were exorbitant. People seemed to prefer to stand in the ever-lengthening queue than take advantage of the swarthy waiter who plied up and down, offering the services of his empty tray. Occasionally someone did take pity on him. The pudgy face, set incongruously on a narrow neck atop of a squat body, then became a wreath of smiles. He even grinned philosophically when a puppy, seemingly belonging to no-one, let its presence be felt, visually and somewhat odorously. Kenneth's natural fastidiousness caused his nose to wrinkle as the waiter removed the offending object before retrieving his tray.

He returned to observing. A group caught his attention, different, not indigenous. Their foreign-ness was exotic. All - men, women and children - were possessed of raven black hair which shone, naturally or artificially enhanced. It was difficult to ascertain which, although the former was probably more likely. The men wore standard black trousers, which hugged the hips of the younger ones, flaunting their sexuality. Not so white shirts appeared whiter because of the stark contrast between them and the duskiness of the skins. A variety of multi-coloured, intricately embroidered waist-coats and soft leather, calf-length boots completed the male attire. The colours and embroideries were repeated in the clothing of their women-folk, this time accompanied by swirls of skirts and shawls. The children were miniature clones of the adults whilst babies were swathed in fringed shawls, repeating the colours and embroideries of their progenitors.

All wore gold ornaments with a flair reflecting history and culture rather than prosperity. Their luggage was totally incongruous - modern sports bags instead of the ethnic, hand-worked baskets one might have expected. They stayed together, speaking amongst themselves in a guttural tongue Kenneth didn't recognize. They spoke to no outsider, no-one spoke to them. Their tickets were checked in silence, almost resentfully. Not for them a smile, a friendly greeting. They remained passive and expressionless. Kenneth's eyes moved to another distinct group, their whiteness distinguishing them as holiday-makers, taking a two-week respite from whatever it was they annually escaped. Kenneth was jolted into consciousness by a distinct change in the engine sound and the activity of crew members as they prepared to dock. At last!

Relieved the journey was over it had been, would always be, a memorable one.

Diary Entry (mid May)

Two grey taxis waiting end of jetty. Retrieved note of accommodation arranged by agent, 'Maria and Elias' house', from envelope. Tentatively showed it to drivers. They nodded but said they were booked for next hour. I could wait or take alternative horse buggy taxi. Same price. Decided to wait.

Kenneth slowly took in the scene. The short, narrow jetty, thronged with people arriving, departing, friends or relatives meeting, saying goodbye. Three-wheelers collecting the assortment of 'things' purchased in Athens. The immediate area was crowded with a diversity of two-wheeled vehicles which Kenneth classified under the generic term of 'bikes' - mopeds, scooters, motorbikes of all ages and some that failed to fit any category. All languished in the sun, patiently waiting for owners to return from whatever business it was that had caused this abandonment.

He walked to where the town proper began. The jetty widened into a picturesque waterfront scene of cafés, each with its own distinctive colours of tables, chairs and awnings. Again he became aware of noise. This time of a different character, as the various waiters vied with each other in trying to entice new arrivals into their own establishment. Smiling, targeting foreign tourists, rather than their fellow countrymen, as more likely to have spending power. With fixed smiles holiday reps waited to whisk tourists away to their accommodation. No doubt he would see them around the island before they were replaced in two weeks with a new intake. Hopefully not that couple crossed his mind as he espied a thin, slightly balding, bespectacled man struggling along with two over-sized suitcases behind the mountain of flesh already showing signs of discomfort in the heat of the mid-day sun.

Leaving his luggage at the taxi rank, he sat at the nearest café. This time his 'Mia beera parakalo' was answered with an indulgent smile and a short reply in Greek. Phrase books are bloody useless, he thought. Really no help at all unless the person addressed gives the replies exemplared in the book. He smiled back deferentially, actually feeling rather stupid. The waiter grinned and translated.

'Welcome to Spetses! Large or small beer?'

A quick think. An hour or more.

'Large, please.'

During the twenty minutes it took for the waiter to return with a heavily frosted half litre glass and an Amstel, Kenneth watched the ferry crowd disperse. The beer had begun to warm when he noticed his luggage being loaded onto the back seat of a taxi. It was the stocky young driver who sported a bushy moustache and hair so black Kenneth was tempted to ask him for the dye number, having tried several products with little success. His friends said the touch of grey added gravitas but Kenneth wasn't convinced.

Leaving the dregs of the now undrinkable beer and a tip on the table, he strode to the taxi and got in, the driver having left the front passenger door open for him. They drove past the waiting horses and along the front with the sea on the left and a row of hotels, bars and tavernas on the right, skilfully dodging wandering people, trotting horses and wobbly bikes. Bikes, lots of bikes - but no cars!

Great Moses. Kenneth could hardly believe… Did he really see a family of five on one scooter? Yes, checking the taxi's wing mirror he had not imagined it. Father had a child standing in front, mother was on pillion holding a baby whilst a third child travelled on the luggage rack behind mum. A policeman waved as they rode by, father removing one hand from the handle-bars to wave back. The taxi swerved right, away from the sea road. Halfway up a slope that curved left the taxi met a horse buggy slip-sliding its way down. The taxi slowed. Natural horse power obviously took precedence over mechanical.

At the top of the hill the taxi shot over the crossroads and up another slope which veered left. By this time Kenneth could not have retraced the route, which seemed to be turning back on itself. The taxi stopped. There was no meter so the fare asked came as a shock. Compared with taxi fares in Athens it was expensive. Kenneth paid but added no tip. As he was getting out he realised he had no keys for the house and turned to the driver. In reply to Kenneth's query he said the keys were probably on a hook somewhere on the door frame. If no hook then try lifting the flower pots. He waited until Kenneth had retrieved his cases from the back seat and then rolled away down the slope.

Diary Entry (mid May)

First impressions. Isolated. Dark blue, wrought iron gates. Church to left. Uneven wild garden. Grass two feet high. Five foot wall on three sides. Fourth side a slope ending in dried river bed. Across river-bed a closely shuttered house, air of neglect about it, shutters closed, paint peeling, badly weathered. Noticed large gates (my house) could be locked. Both could be opened wide to admit car. Why? Thought island car-free. Gates noisy opening/closing, better than guard dog. To right three stone steps leading up to cricket length walkway, balustraded both sides. Led to balcony. Lots of potted flowers/plants, plastic table, assortment of bamboo/plastic chairs.

Kenneth approached the door. The bottom half was wood, painted in the same dark blue as the gates and shutters. The top part was frosted glass covered by a wrought-iron grid and mosquito netting. He looked for a hook. There it was and hanging from it, in full view, were three keys tied with string. Two obviously door keys, the third reminiscent of a padlock key. As he reached for them the door opened. Standing there, dressed entirely in black from the kerchief holding her hair in place, apart from a wisp of grey peeping out below one ear, down to the thick black stockings and strong, flat lace-ups, was a plump, middle-aged lady.

She beamed a welcome, almost curtsied. Like being in the family pile crossed his mind. He entered the hallway the size of a small room and put down his cases. There was a table and two chairs suggesting it might double as a dining area. A five-shelved bookcase, with ornaments as well as books, filled the entire wall opposite the front door.

He was ushered into a kitchen to the right. It was large. His gaze fell on a large gas cylinder in one corner. Kenneth raised an eyebrow.

A glass of freshly squeezed orange was thrust into his hand with a nervous greeting of 'Welcome, Welcome.' Kenneth downed the orange gratefully, trying hard to suppress a yawn. The old lady giggled sympathetically. She opened the 'fridge door, indicating the dishes inside were gifts from her by pressing a flat palm with splayed fingers on her chest. To Kenneth there looked enough food for several days. He smiled his thanks with an accompanying mumbled 'Efaristo'.

She led him a few steps across the hallway to a bedroom. She mimed sleeping by placing her palms together on one cheek and closing her eyes. There could be a lot of gesturing Kenneth thought as she pointed at him and then the bed before disappearing through the front door. Although the lady had appeared cheerful enough Kenneth wondered what in her life had caused the sadness in her eyes.

It had been a long journey. A couple of hours' sleep sounded about right. There was a break in the wall between the kitchen and the bedroom. The pipes from a small wood burning stove disappeared through the break. He was curious to see what lay through that break before sleeping. It proved to lead to a bathroom and toilet. Damn, no shower. The wood stove pipes continued through the bathroom and out of the external wall.

'Won't be needing any stove. No intention of being here in winter.'

Kenneth smiled as he realised he had spoken aloud.

Another door led to a second bedroom. He preferred this to the one indicated by the lady, but the bed wasn't made up so perhaps there was some reason why he shouldn't use this room. Too tired to think further he returned to the first bedroom, removed his clothes, placed his watch on the bedside table and lay under a sheet. He was asleep for almost three hours.

When he woke Kenneth felt disorientated. Where was he? He thought he could hear horses. He looked out of the window which overlooked the back of the house. Some scrubland garden led down to a steepish slope and the dried up river bed. No horses that he could see. Must have dreamed it. Beyond lay the house he had noticed on arrival. It was surrounded by high, close growing trees which said 'No entry' as clearly as any written sign.

He turned to retrieve his watch. It wasn't there. He was sure he had placed it on the bedside table as he always did. He looked across to the table on the other side of the double bed. It was there. He had been very tired. He collected the watch and put it forward two hours. It was 5 pm. He slipped into the trousers and shirt lying on a chair, grimacing at the smell of travel.

He would unpack, freshen up and take a short walk. Perhaps he would find somewhere local to have his early evening G&T. Maybe a bite to eat. His bedroom had no wardrobe but he had noticed fitted cupboards in the other bedroom. He would use that as a dressing room. Carrying his valises into the rear bedroom Kenneth took his clothes from the cases and hung them up. They were in a state after their long confinement. Perhaps the lady in black would 'do' for him. He and his family always had people to 'do' for them. He was intrigued by two trunks in the dressing room. They were firmly padlocked so he presumed they belonged to a previous tenant. He would enquire once he was settled.

Kenneth once again removed his crumpled, odorous travelling clothes wondering if the island sported a dry cleaners' or laundry. He shook the creases from his silk, Paisley dressing gown, donned it and walked into the bathroom to check for hot water. There wasn't any, although a large immersion heater hung perilously on the wall over the bath. He also noticed a shower head lying across the bath taps so a shower of sorts would be possible. Apart from the usual toilet and hand basin there was a washing machine in one corner. Kenneth shook his head in disbelief.

He had noticed a niche in the wall by the side of the kitchen with an assortment of switches but decided against any interference until he knew which was which. A cold shower would do him no harm. Hadn't that been the rationale behind his boarding school routine? He was pleasantly surprised to find the water was quite warm. Must be from the sun he mused. He chose a pair of pale blue linen slacks, a Gillie shirt bought in the Highlands, with a darker blue jacket of Oriental design, made specially for him on one of his trips East. A pair of hand-made, dark blue moccasins in soft leather completed his attire. He carefully locked the door behind him. With a quick glance at the hook by the side of the door he placed the keys safely in his inside pocket. As he closed the gates behind him he paused. He had neighbours.

Directly opposite was a two storey house. The windows on the top floor were closely shuttered. The shutters on the ground floor were locked back and there was furniture on the patio. The tidy garden was well stocked with fruit trees and flowers. Kenneth took this as a good sign. It suggested the occupants were caring and responsible people. To the left of the house was a small hotel. A high wall surrounded it but a beautiful bougainvillea grew up the sides of the black wrought iron gated entrance, forming a bower across the top framework. Kenneth thought he heard the sounds of splashing in a pool but could see no sign of such. He turned left. As the wall to 'his' house cornered there were three horses loosely tethered amongst a clump of trees. So he hadn't imagined hearing them. Between the horses and the corner was a dirt path leading upwards.

In view of his attire Kenneth chose to keep to the road. The road turned upwards to the right, towards a long row of houses. Kenneth chose the sharp left. It looked more interesting. It certainly was. After some fifty metres he came across three rubbish bins, inhabited by a colony of cats who watched him with suspicion. He now knew what to do with his rubbish. The track sloped gently upwards, slightly to the left, straightened and ended in a T-junction. He passed scrub and trees on the left. On the right two small hotels. Possibilities for meals or drinks without a visit to the town.

Reaching the T-junction he saw more buildings to the right so turned left onto a tarmac road. There was scrubland on both sides. About two hundred metres along he came to a small plaque with an arrow pointing up another slope, announcing the monastery would be open at the times stated.

Opposite the notice was a very steep slope that looked as though it went up to the heights of the island. Kenneth followed the arrow.

The road led up through an avenue of conifers. Crossing a parapeted bridge over the dry river bed he passed a church on the left. He continued up towards the monastery. It was cool between the trees. The slight breeze was welcome after the heat of the afternoon sun. Several bikes passed him, some with flower-bearing grannies on the back, riding side-saddle - a novelty at the time but a sight which was to become so familiar as to be ignored.

He saw a large, overly ornate building ahead, with stone steps up to massive black doors. About one hundred metres in front and to the right were some slightly rusted wrought iron gates, leading to a cemetery. A number of people were tending graves, washing grave stones, replenishing oil, lighting incense in the holy burners. They acknowledged him. Some spoke, 'Yeia sas'. He nodded 'Yeia sas' in return. He felt he wasn't intruding.

He became aware that although the interred represented all ages there were no burials earlier than five or six years ago. Was there another cemetery some-where, an older one? He also noted there were several foreigners buried there. Photographs on ninety-five per cent of the graves bore witness to people who had lived, laughed, cried. They were important to someone.

The cemetery was on steppes. Looking up to the higher levels, where a small building he took to be a chapel resided, he saw a figure clad in black, gliding amongst the graves. The rays of the dying sun reflected on the nun's spectacles obscuring her eyes and replacing them with two shining orbs. 'The Graveyard Nun'. What a wonderful title for a novel. Kenneth thought he would pigeon-hole that for later use although, at that moment, he couldn't think of a reason for a nun to be on a cruise ship. Perhaps as a ghost? Another thought came into his mind. What was a nun doing in a monastery? He had to check that out.

A second, male, black clothed figure with the tall hat of a priest, made a more determined progress round the graves. Pausing at each one he intoned a prayer for that particular dearly departed. A shake of hands accompanied the exchange of a surreptitious donation. There was something bizarrely calming about the cemetery, but as he left he still wondered about the dates on the headstones.

Diary Entry (mid May)

Discovered monasteria used for both monastery/nunnery. Got info from nice couple where dined. Second monastery with nuns, further up mountain. That one thirteen days 'back'. Must follow Julian calendar. Local one follows Gregorian calendar as most sensible people do. Gave one hotel a miss. Early holidaymakers having a good time! Not averse to that but preferred quieter atmosphere for first evening. Liked little garden place, quite near house. A quieter type of clientele. Called in for G&T. Very pleasant couple, friendly not effusive. Had freshly cooked pork chop/crisp salad with feta.

Complimentary wine served in small jug. Quite acceptable. Finished with brandy and coffee. Certainly patronise this establishment whilst here. Plain food, well cooked, reasonably priced. Don't intend staying year. Will get blasted book finished in couple of months at most. Then back to normality.

Kenneth rose early on his first full day. He decided to have a cup of tea on the side balcony before preparing a full breakfast. There was no fresh milk in the 'fridge but there was a tin of evaporated in a cupboard, next to a packet of Lipton's yellow label tea bags. Putting two into a mug he looked for a kettle. There wasn't one. He half-filled the smallest pan he could find and placed it on the smallest of the three gas rings of what appeared to be an upmarket camping stove. A rubber pipe led to a large, battered, blue 'gaz' bottle. He thought of his camping days with the scouts, which he'd hated. Was this the only means of cooking? Surely not. He replaced the matches thoughtfully left by the lady in black.

A light blue table with matching chairs resided in the centre of the room. The tablecloth matched the curtains at the windows. How very middle class. Kenneth recalled his father always insisting on pristine white linen for his everyday meals as well as for the dinner parties he had hosted before going 'travelling'.

The walls of the kitchen, as in all the other rooms, were painted white. On the kitchen walls hung a variety of posters and objects. A copper fish mould, unpolished and turning black, a knife with a serrated blade and the red handle some sort of sea monster, a poster of three large barrels.

The small poster near the 'fridge attracted Kenneth's attention. He stared at it for some time. It showed a voluptuous lady wearing a low-cut dress and eating spaghetti. A strand of spaghetti had fallen onto her ample bosom. It was not clear how the gentleman bending over her was going to remove the strand. Kenneth found this poster strangely erotic, suggestive, not explicit.

The water boiled in the small pan. He turned off the gas and poured the water onto the tea bags. Leaving the tea to brew he opened the door which led onto yet another balcony, with no provision for shade and only a row of potted plants providing any sort of balustrade. He walked to the right, along a walkway leading to a small locked gate. He thought one of the three keys he possessed might fit but the growth of grass outside suggested the gate hadn't been used for some time. Three stone steps to the side of the gate led down to the rear garden. He returned to the kitchen.

He dispensed with the evaporated milk cutting a slice of lemon from one of several in the 'fridge. Settling on the side balcony he cast his eye over the view. Houses intermingled with pine and olive trees that appeared to reach down to the sea. The arrangement of leaves and branches atop of one tree reminded him of the Manikin Pis. On the horizon the sun, beginning its daily climb to the zenith, shone brilliantly over a sea, the calmness of which he thought impossible. Placing his feet up on the balustrade and taking a sip of the fast cooling tea he observed movement at the house opposite.

The door to the ground floor apartment opened. Three young girls came out each carrying a heavy rucksack. A man and a woman appeared.

The oldest girl - nine or ten he construed - got on to the back of father's moped. The two younger ones shared a motor-bike with their mother, one in front, one behind. Fifteen minutes later the mother returned. Several plastic bags hung from the handlebars.

Removing them she went into the house only to exit it again almost immediately, this time carrying a tray. She bounced down her path and across the road. As she opened his gate she balanced the tray expertly on one hand. Kenneth met her at the door.

'Good morning and welcome. I'm Esther.'

A cheery voice, full of energy, a trace of accent but not Greek. The smell of warm croissants and the heady aroma of orange marmalade were just too inviting.

'Pleased to meet you. Do come in.'

The tray was thrust into his hands.

'Another time.'

With a sigh of relief that his polite offer had not been accepted he closed the door, turned to the kitchen, paused. The sound of a bouncy step and highly pitched la-la-la accompanied her departure. Was she really practising scales?

His breakfast repast over he set off to do some shopping. It seemed logical to go in the opposite direction from his walk of the previous evening, down the slope and past the church. In only two hundred metres there was a T- junction. The left corner sported a large chicken coop complete with duck pond. There were a lot of cats around.

An imposing, fortified house stood at the right corner. A young, dark- haired, muscular man was hosing down two buggy-type carriages. Maybe the horses Kenneth had seen near his house belonged to these carriages. The young man acknowledged Kenneth with a smiling 'Good Morning' in only slightly accented English.

'You must be the writer from England. I'm Panayiotis.'

Slightly surprised Kenneth muttered 'Yes', wondering if The Bitch had arranged a general announcement, just for the publicity. He enquired about the nearest shops.

'Turn left and follow the road but always going down. You will come to the town where you can find everything you want. If you turn right there's a garage two minutes away where you can buy fresh bread and milk. It also sells cigarettes.'

'Thank you.'

Kenneth turned left.

* * *

Kenneth put the fresh milk, bread, fruit and vegetables in the 'fridge. He looked round the kitchen, opening drawers and cupboards. The 'fridge was black but hadn't been originally. A paint job. He explored the cupboards more thoroughly. Plates, mugs, glasses. Everything he would require, including a coffee machine with a large packet of Mocha next to it. Damn. In his haste to pack he hadn't remembered his special brand.

He doubted Blue Mountain was available on the island.

There was a kettle not previously noticed. It carried an adaptor plug so couldn't have been a local buy. And a teapot. A stone sink, with one cold tap, right-angled to the left of the outside door. To the right of the outside door were the gas rings.

Leaving the kitchen he paused to scan the spines of the books in the hallway, Milton, Keats, Hardy, Hughes, McGough, an eclectic mix of poetry. A complete works of the Bard. Classics and more modern novels nestled side by side. No blockbusters he observed. Several dictionaries and a wide selection of reference books. He turned half circle. To his right in the corner was a small table upon which rested a telephone. He lifted the receiver to hear what sounded like an engaged signal. He would need to check whether that signal was what passed for 'line active' here.

He passed through the alcove into the living room. There was a lot of natural light here, three sets of French windows and a casement. All could be shuttered. As a protection against the heat of the sun, and presumably an attempt to deter flying 'things', drapes of muslin hung over each one. One set of French windows which would have looked out onto the main front balcony appeared to be permanently closed and shuttered. A large dining table had been pushed as close as the two chairs behind would allow. Four more chairs were accessible at the front and ends.

The other two sets of French windows opened onto the side balcony, in front of one a large desk. On either side of the knee space were four drawers. Perfect for his writing. Kenneth placed his pristine notebooks in the top left hand drawer except for one which was placed squarely in front of the desk chair. The most important tool of his trade came next. His fountain pen, the kind that took cartridges as well as the 'real' ink Kenneth favoured. At the airport he had purchased several packets of cartridges and he now placed these neatly in the top right hand drawer. The polished oak pen stand, proclaiming his full name and the date of his majority, was aligned with the top of the notebook. The pen was precisely placed on the stand so the crest which announced his lineage was clearly visible.

'I'll start in a few days. Need to get acclimatised.'

In the corner between table and desk, a guitar and two conga drums stood almost decoratively. Forsaken slipped through Kenneth's mind, not knowing why.

Another bookshelf, twin to the one in the hallway, covered the wall between the two French windows. On and under its shelves lay an extensive collection of LPs, tapes, music videos and books, biographies of people from the music world. Music had never played a big part in Kenneth's life, apart from compulsory attendance at charity ensemble performances his mother organised and the country set attended - dutifully. Here music was obviously important to someone.

The casement window opened to the same view as from his bedroom. To the left across the corner a television, a video, a cassette player, a record deck and two other machines, the use of which Kenneth was unaware. Two wires led up to loudspeakers, one fixed directly above the equipment. The other wire led round the wall to the second speaker which balanced alarmingly on a makeshift shelf in the opposite corner. The tangle of wires and extensions all running from one socket left Kenneth feeling bewildered as well as wondering about the safety aspect.

To the right of the casement, in the corner, an open fireplace. Not in use during the summer months it held an assortment of pots of indeterminate age and design.

Hanging above the fireplace were two, round, copper dishes. One had been highly polished and gleamed red. The other was blackened by usage over heat. Kenneth nodded. He saw meaning in the contrast. On the rounded mantel were a variety of brass objects, small candle holders, two small icons, incense burners, a paper knife. Kenneth recognised a Turkish coffee pot and pepper mill.

To the immediate left hung two antique frames. One held the proud head of a Red Indian, the other an equally proud head from the Indian sub-continent. Two fading black and white photos. Both of an age and yet thousands of miles apart. Kenneth pondered the significance before studying the photographs on the wall opposite the bookcase. Some were, he presumed, of Spetses in days of yore. There was an oblong space between two of them, where presumably another had once hung. He wondered what it had been and why it had been removed but the questions were forgotten as he noticed a smaller photograph of a sailing boat with a painter. It was the background that surprised him for he knew it well. He had been there on several occasions. The perennial rivals of Oxford and Cambridge. Whatever was this photograph doing here?

Kenneth returned to the kitchen where he prepared a plate of cheese, olives and fresh bread, followed by kiwi fruit. The unaccustomed heat, plus the wine consumed with lunch, began to have its effect. Kenneth repaired to the bedroom.

'I do believe a siesta is in order...'

As he fell asleep he caught a whiff of Habit Rouge, an aftershave favoured by one of his brothers. He wondered what local flower possessed this scent.

Diary Entry (late May)

Walked into town. About fifteen minutes at leisurely pace. Lots of bikes, small, three-wheeler pick-ups, scooters. Passed some small hotels. Two motor-bike hire shops. Maybe later. Fruit trees/flowers everywhere. Dry river bed alongside main road. Disappeared underground just before town proper. Passed bar on left. Closed but amused by sign 'Full + p/t customers wanted. Apply within.' Looked OK. Will check later. Numbers of tourists, mostly speaking English. Not many children. Narrow street led to small supermarket. Bakery close by. Found good fruit/vegetable shop. Nothing pre-packaged. Very acceptable lunch at restaurant with sea view. Taxi home. Same taxi, different driver. Don't feel at home. All very new/different. Didn't venture out last night. Made medley of vegetables with cheese sauce. Hope lady in black comes back. Don't fancy cooking on regular basis. Fresh fruit. Wine. Found a place selling half-decent French. Ended with coffee and brandy on front balcony. Heard rustling in large almond tree overhanging walkway. Strange/no breeze,

Kenneth woke suddenly. He could hear a swishing sound, vaguely familiar but he couldn't quite place it. He slid his feet into monogrammed slippers, a birthday present from his mother. Hand-made, though not by her. He slipped his arms into the silk dressing gown and padded to the window which over-looked the rear garden. Through the shutter slats he saw a young, fit man wielding a machete. It was this being plied vigorously Kenneth had heard.

Although the sun was still low in the sky the man was sweating profusely. The giant heap of cut grass bore witness to the work already done. Still a lot more to do, mused Kenneth, feeling grateful it wasn't a job he would be required to do. Physical work such as this was regarded by his family as menial, not for their class. Kenneth did visit a gym on a regular basis, wishing to retain the lean athletic body of his youth. He was proud his physique was more than a match for younger men at the gym.

The man seemed to sense Kenneth's presence. He shielded his eyes and gazed up at the shutter behind which Kenneth stood. The man half smiled and then resumed the swishing. Kenneth turned from the window, donned a pair of cotton trousers and t-shirt, exchanged the slippers for a pair of canvas deck shoes and walked into the kitchen where he filled the kettle and switched it on. He took a small bottle of water from the 'fridge and went out into the garden. The man put down his machete. Wiping the hand that had held it down his grubby shorts he stretched it out in greeting.

'Good morning, Sir. I am Bekim.'

Kenneth paused for a moment before taking the hand to return the greeting. The man's English was only slightly accented, suggesting he had more than a smattering of the language. There was something about the man's demeanour that caused Kenneth to reflect on the man's background.

'Good morning. My name is Kenneth. I thought you would like this.'

He held out the water.

'You are very kind, Sir.'

'I'm making some tea. Perhaps you would care for a cup. Something to eat?'

'The tea, yes, I would like. But my wife has prepared food which I have left in the shade for now. I will complete half the garden before I eat.'

Kenneth returned to the kitchen. The kettle was on the boil. As he placed the tea bags in the teapot and poured on the water he realised he hadn't asked Bekim whether he would like sugar or milk. A vision of the family butler crossed his mind as he took a tray from the cupboard. He added a slice of lemon to the tray and carried it out to Bekim who was showering from the hose pipe attached to the outside tap.

'Just the lemon, please. This is very kind of you, Sir.'

Kenneth was intrigued by Bekim's command of English. It was very precise, the tone of education.

'Would you like to join me on the balcony, in the shade?'

Bekim stared at Kenneth.

'Yes, I would. Thank you.

* * *

Kenneth watched as Bekim completed swinging the machete, seeing the man anew in the light of their recent conversation. The grass, seared by the sun, lay in three large piles.

The machete was wiped clean, the remains of the lunch placed in a bag. Both were hung on the battered scooter parked outside before Bekim returned to the balcony.

'I'll come tomorrow for the burn. Early evening. Give the grass time to dry out.

It will need another man for the hose-pipe, unless... '

He gave an inkling of a smile as he raised his eyebrows. Kenneth's first thought was 'no way' as Denny Dee would say but as he looked at Bekim the thought quickly faded. He would enjoy the company of this man. He returned the smile.

'There will be no need to bring anyone else.'

Kenneth watched the scooter rattle halfway down the slope before the engine spluttered into life. He found himself looking forward to the morrow.

Diary Entry (late May)

Just shows. Never judge a book etc. Interesting man. Cultured, educated, knowledgeable. Studied in England. Engineer in his own country. Wrong politics. Had to leave. Now trying to support wife and child. Burning a precaution against possible fires in Summer. Must find out what to do in event of fire. Tried to give Bekim money for work. Refused. Said all taken care of by owners in Athens.

Kenneth looked at his watch. Just after five. He wasn't sure what constituted early evening here but decided he should be ready when Bekim arrived. What should he wear?

Never having done this sort of thing before and certainly not expecting doing any on this visit he had nothing suitable. Sighing he chose a faded linen shirt with slightly frayed cuffs - one he would never wear again in any formal setting but of which he had been particularly fond, being loath to discard it - and a pair of Bermuda shorts, bought in Jamaica. Kenneth allowed himself a smile at the irony implied. Deck shoes and his beloved Panama completed the outfit.

Taking a jug of water from the 'fridge and a glass from the cupboard he went out to await Bekim's arrival. Shortly after six he heard Bekim's scooter struggling up the hill. Kenneth met him at the end of the walkway. Bekim was carrying a bag.

'My wife suggested you may not have suitable clothes for this job so she washed an old t-shirt and shorts but I think what you are wearing will be fine. It's not a dirty job if done correctly.'

'That was very considerate of your wife. Please thank her for me.'

Bekim nodded and replaced the bag on the scooter. He made sure the three piles of dried grass were quite separate. The hose-pipe was already in place, the outside tap being set just under the side balcony. He gave the hose-pipe to Kenneth.

'Once I set fire to the first pile you must keep the edges soaked. I will take care of keeping the grass inside the circle. There is no breeze tonight so there shouldn't be any 'flyers' to chase!'

The two men worked together in silence. A silence broken by the clang of the gate. A lady of frightening aspect was screaming in a torrent of Greek. Bekim approached her, speaking quietly. She seemed pacified as Bekim gently escorted her outside, closed the gate and returned to the burning.

'She was just reminding us of the dangers of setting fire to the entire island with our careless burning. I assured her we were quite in command of the situation.'

'She seemed exceptionally concerned. Is fire a big danger?'

'It can be. Usually in the summer when there has been no rain for some time.'

'How will I know if it's serious?'

'You'll know quickly. All the church bells will ring. If you're in the town you will see the bars being closed and the sale of alcohol stopped. All the men are needed to fight the fire. As a last resort everyone must go to the Dapia where the boats will be used to take people to safety.'

The first pile was quickly reduced to ash. Bekim took the hose-pipe from Kenneth to soak the ashes.

'I think here your shoes may be ruined.'

They moved on to the other piles where the same actions were performed. Bekim gave all the garden a final soaking. Kenneth offered refreshment but this time Bekim refused.

'My wife works at night as a waitress. I have to look after our child. But I do have a favour to ask.'

Kenneth stiffened.

'Oh, nothing intrusive and I will not be offended if you wish to refuse.'

'If I can…'

'Do you have any books in English I could borrow? It has been good to speak English again with a native speaker of culture and education.'

'There are books in the hallway but none are mine. However, as long as they are returned. Do you know Kostas' Bar? I noticed a bookshelf in there.'

'My religion does not allow me to drink, but I have done some work for Kostas. He kindly allowed me to take a book or two. But they were summer reading for tourists.'

Having selected three books Bekim placed them in the plastic bag Kenneth had retrieved from the kitchen.

'Thank you. I will return them soon. If there are any more jobs that you may need during your stay just ask for me around the town. The message will soon reach me.'

Kenneth impulsively proffered his hand which Bekim clasped for a moment. Kenneth watched as the scooter again freewheeled down the slope to allow the engine to kick in.

Diary Entry (early June)

Strange, now garden cleared can see what appears to be little graves out the back, a slightly bigger one with a weathered wooden Celtic cross over it. Why would anyone go to such bother? Lots of broken pottery in one part of garden. A sort of crazy-paved path with assortment of tiles, slabs and flat stones. Some overgrown vines. Lemon tree. Suggests not real gardener. Who? Maybe Esther will know…Garden tools in store under kitchen balcony. Mostly rusted. Box of tools in contrast appear well used/cared for. Supply of logs. Won't be needing those! Continue 'settling in'. Procrastinating re writing. Sit for hours at desk. Even removed top from pen. Not conscious of time passing staring through French windows at sea. Haven't done anything. Don't feel guilty as would back home. … Mystery of graves partly solved (Esther). Previous tenant had lots of cats and a dog. No more info. Went down town to check poste restante. Too early yet. Hope Bitch has remembered to inform people of my whereabouts! Noticed ad in travel agent's window. Day trip to Northern Peloponnesus/Corinth/Epidavros/Mycenae. Seems reasonable. Lunch/English-speaking guide included. Small group of ten. Over twenty years since did tour as part of degree. Could be pleasant diversion. A longish day/hopefully worth it. Must take advantage of opportunity/not planning long stay here.

Dawn had broken as Kenneth walked briskly down to the Dapia. It was the earliest he had been up and about and was surprised there were so many people, apparently on their way to work. Already a small café opposite the town beach was open and doing business. He checked his watch. Quarter to six.

At the end of the mole a small group of people were boarding the 'red-eye' Dolphin, tourists leaving, islanders on day visits to Athens for a variety of reasons, shopping, visiting relatives, often medical appointments Kenneth later discovered. A smaller group were boarding one of the larger moored water taxis. A lady with a clip-board was ticking off names. She saw Kenneth look at his watch.

'Don't worry. You're not late. Just the last to arrive. You must be Mr Graham.' She pronounced the surname in two distinct syllables, making it sound like cooked meat gone off.

'Perhaps you'd like to buy water from the periptero. It's going to be a hot one! Kalimera, Maria.' She waved at a plump, elderly lady dressed in black.

'Kalimera pethi mou. Kalo taxithi.'

The lady with the clip-board pointed to the little kiosk, close to the mooring, where the smiling old lady was already taking a large bottle from the adjoining cooler. Kenneth paid for the water and placed the bottle in the army surplus shoulder bag he carried, where it joined the case containing his sunglasses and his carefully folded Panama for later in the day.

He boarded the water taxi, ignoring the proffered hand of the lady whom he presumed was the guide. A fleeting grin crossed her face as she followed him and took her place next to the driver.

'OK, Apostolis, that's the last. We're all accounted for. Let's go. Good morning, everyone. I'm your guide for today but as this is only a ten minute journey to the mainland, I'll save the introductions for the 'bus.'

Apostolis slowly reversed the water taxi where it could more easily be manoeuvred. He then headed out into open water towards the mainland. The group transferred quickly from taxi to the waiting mini-bus. The guide waved to the taxi driver.

'Thanks Apostolis. See you tonight.'

She climbed into the bus and the door closed. She smiled at the bus driver.

'Kalimera, Panos. Everyone settled? Good morning again but as we're in Greece we should say it in Greek. After me:

'Kal i mare a.'

Oh God, thought Kenneth as the group chanted back. Have I made a mistake with this tour? She sounds like a female version of the cheeky chappie.

'Not quite. You have to stress the 'mare'. Let's try again: 'Kal i MARE a.'

Kenneth cringed as the response was shouted once more. The guide cast a glance his way.

An impish grin played round her lips and he realised how attractive they were.

'I think we have a passenger who knows some Greek, do we not, Mr Graham?'

No reference to rotten meat this time.

'A few words only, Miss ... ?'

'Ah, of course, I have your names on my list but you don't know mine. The people on the island call me Kyria. I know that some of you have foregone breakfast to get here this early so we're going to make a short stop in Porto Heli where you can have a hot drink, maybe a croissant. There are toilets as well. I know you were advised when you bought your tickets to bring a hat or scarf as the sun does get very fierce. If anyone has forgotten there is a supermarket open this early which has a small selection.'

The minibus came to a roundabout. There were some gasps as the driver appeared to go the wrong way round to enter Porto Heli. The guide laughed again.

'A reminder. If you do hire a car during your stay make sure you know the different rules. Here you go right when entering a roundabout and you give way to allow other drivers on! Not that you can drive a car on Spetses. And before hiring a scooter or moped make sure you know how to ride it! Now, Panos has kindly stopped near the café and the supermarket so no-one should get lost. Back in half an hour, please. I'll be just opposite if there are any problems.'

Kenneth allowed the other passengers to alight before moving. He watched the guide walk over to the sea wall where she stood looking out to sea. He strolled towards the sea wall but stopped a little behind her. She sensed his presence and turned round.

'Not having breakfast, Mr Graham?'

Not a suggestion of the cheeky chappie voice.

'I partook early and I remembered my hat.'

He held up the slightly battered Panama recently removed from his bag.

'I did notice, very sensible.'

Kenneth, not usually at a loss for words, struggled to keep the conversation going.

'It's very peaceful watching the yachts bobbing about so gently. Some of them look quite expensive.'

She looked at him without expression.

'Yes. It's time we left.'

How banal she must think me Kenneth thought as he followed her back to the 'bus.

'Now we're on our way I have to admit I'm not an official guide so before you look round each site I'll tell you the most important things to look out for. At most of the sights you'll be able to get a free map outlining buildings and ruins with a brief description. For those of you who would like more information I recommend buying one of the coloured brochures. They also make a nice souvenir and, before you ask, I don't get a commission.'

She laughed and the sound caused Kenneth to tingle.

'The area we're passing through is the Peloponnesus. Its name comes from Pelops who, according to myth, was king of most of this area in ancient times. Two of his descendants were the brothers, Agamemnon and Menelaus. You'll hear more about them when we visit Mycenae. We'll soon be passing the village of Didyma which means twins. Probably referring to the two mountains of Mount Didyma and the Prophet Elias. There's a church to the Prophet Elias on Spetses. It's the highest point on the island. Well worth the climb and reasonable walking ground although I would suggest early morning or late afternoon at this time of the year.'

Kenneth listened intently. Not only did he find the information interesting, he was trying to place the guide's accent. She was quite nicely spoken although he did detect the slight trace of a Northern accent. He'd never had 'a Northern Girl' as a regular companion. He did remember a book signing in Hull. His experiences there had led to a vow of never leaving the south again. He returned to the present.

'Now, if you look to the left you'll see a large crater-like hole. It's called the Large Cave and is best seen from this road. There is also a smaller, more interesting underground cave with two Byzantine churches, one with tenth century wall paintings. There's a beach a few kilometres away. It would make a nice day out but you would need to hire a car.'

Kenneth was almost sure the guide had addressed that last comment specifically at him. He was surprised he was suddenly interested in Byzantine art. A day out with Kyria seemed attractive. And he was a good swimmer, not afraid to display his physique on a beach. Those hours at the gym were worth the exorbitant prices it demanded. He was aware the guide was still speaking.

'Although they are called caves they are something called dolines.' That laugh again. 'I didn't know what they were either. They're like sinkholes. Apparent there is a fault line here. Hope there are no geologists on board...

Our first stop is the Sanctuary of Asclepios, the god of healing, at Epidavros. It was a huge place but is mainly ruins now, apart from the famous amphitheatre with the perfect acoustics which is still in frequent use. If you climb to the top of the theatron - the seats, I'll stand in the centre of the orchestra and whisper a message. You'll be able to hear me although you may not be able to see me clearly as you'll be up in the gods.'

More laughter ensued but Kenneth wondered what the message would be.

* * *

The visit to Epidavros over, the bus set off for Corinth.

'I think you all made the top seats, some more easily than others. What was my message?

Amidst much laughter one passenger offered a reply.

'You cheated! We heard you but didn't understand a word. Was it Greek?'

'Of course it was. What did you expect in a Greek theatre?' Her reply brought more laughter and a few jeers.

'But I think we may have someone among the group who did understand. Am I correct Mr Graham?'

'Well, yes, I think I recognised the piece. A speech from Evripides, if I re-member correctly. You were using the Erasmus pronunciation, I believe.'

'Absolutely correct. But to win the prize you must tell me the gist of the speech.'

'Oh! Come on, Kyria, the man's done enough surely.'

'Be fair. Nobody else knew it.'

'Come on now.'

The passengers were all giving Kenneth friendly support. The guide was smiling, challenging him, but also as though she were certain he would know the answer. How had she summed him up so quickly? Was he so transparent? He returned her smile, holding her eyes with his.

'Was it not part of Hecuba's lament over the death of her daughter after the sack of Troy? The play was actually called 'Hecuba.' There was a moment's silence. All the passengers looked at the guide.

'Well, go on, was he right?'

'Does he win the prize?'

'He certainly does. And as I don't have a cuddly toy to hand there's a drink at Kostas' Bar for him.'

'Could be expensive, love. He looks like a French brandy man to me.'

'And with all the info he gave I reckon he deserves a double. Well done, mate.'

She joined in the general laughter and, although none too pleased to be called 'mate', Kenneth permitted himself a smile.

'We now have a drive of about an hour and a quarter to Corinth. We'll go first to the Canal. It's a short walk to the bridge where you are quite safe to view the canal but please take care as you are near a main road.

The Canal is a very impressive sight. It was opened in 1893. In ancient times, to avoid the long perilous journey round the Southern Peloponnesus, sailors would drag their boats across the isthmus on a series of wooden cylinders, also using some sort of wheeled vehicle, on a pathway called the Thiolkos. Ancient ruts have been identified. Cargoes were usually unloaded and transported by road to be re-loaded once the boat was again in the water. Because of the size of modern shipping the canal is mostly used nowadays for tourism. There will be time for a visit to the toilets before we leave for the short drive to Ancient Corinth.'

* * *

As the bus emptied Kenneth watched the guide enter one of the many nearby cafés and tavernas. She was welcomed by people obviously expecting her. Not the time to try and engage her in more meaningful conversation. He strolled to the bridge. The tourists were snapping away but he took no photo. He had no camera, had never owned one. Photos were the past for Kenneth. Something that could never be recaptured. Why should he fill his life with moments frozen in time? When he returned the guide was counting heads.

She stood back to let him board in front of her.

'Mr Graham makes number ten so we are all here. I hear you were lucky and saw a ship navigating the canal. A chance for some spectacular photos to show back home. On we go to Ancient Corinth.'

The bus pulled away and the guide began her introduction to the next visit.

'Ancient Corinth was once one of the largest and most important cities of its day. The site's been inhabited for over 7,000 years but it wasn't until around 700 BC the city was founded. Destroyed by the Romans in 146 BC, they rebuilt it 44 BC so you see a mixture of Greek and Roman architecture. The Roman toilets are a must, although no longer in use!'

Her spiel was interrupted by laughter. The passengers had warmed to their Kyria, Kenneth noted. For himself he was intrigued. He wanted to see more of this lady, yet he felt he needed to tread carefully. She would not be as easily won over by his charm as others had been. He would need to review both his strategy and his tactics.

'For Christians Corinth is important because St Paul is said to have preached here in the middle of the first century AD. Three hundred years later the city was burned by the Visigoths. That's enough history for now. For me the ruins are magical because you can walk the streets and visualise the hustle and bustle in ancient times. The museum has some excellent examples of everyday objects found on the site. Because there is so much to see we allow two hours here.

And here we are. Please note Panos has to park the bus away from the entrance but he'll return here in exactly two hours when we will be leaving for our lunch.'

Kenneth was strolling round the site when he saw the guide heading towards the museum.

He followed and caught her up at the Atrium where she stood in front of some Roman statues. She seemed to sense his approach for she spoke without turning.

'I have never found the beauty in Roman statues I do in Greek ones. Technically they look the same but there is something special about Greek statues. The Greek sculptors put something more sensual into their work, almost erotic, part of their souls. The first time I saw the Hermes of Praxiteles. I just had to stroke his thigh. I believed it would feel as it looked - alive. You should go into the museum, Mr Graham. See the three statues of important Romans. At least they still have their heads unlike these here.'

She walked away without a backward glance, leaving Kenneth to imagine the fingers of this woman stroking his own thigh. With a heavy sigh he turned to meet the important Romans.

'Thank you all for being back so promptly. I hope you enjoyed the visit. I see most of you bought the booklets of a fuller history of this city. With those you'll be able to re-live a wonderful experience.

Now we have a ten minute drive to the small village of Solomos. It's set amidst beautiful scenery. The taverna we're going to is family run, catering for locals rather than tourists. I came across it purely by chance. The food there is excellent. Lunch will be in the form of a mezethes, meatballs, whitebait, tzatziki, fried courgettes, hummus, village sausage, salad with feta cheese and freshly made bread. If you're not familiar with any of the food try just a little. Jugs of local wine will be on the table. If you prefer beer just ask. I would advise you not to drink too much alcohol as our visit to Mycenae will be at the sun's hottest and the site is very exposed. We'll all be sitting at the same table so will be quite relaxed. And here we are. There's our host, Mr George, to greet us.

'Hiya, Mr George.'

'Welcome, welcome, Kyria. My wife and son prepare your meal now and I bring the wine.'

Kenneth was none too pleased to hear he would be sitting at a communal table but thought he could tolerate it for once. He poured himself a small glass of wine, took a sip and called the young boy over to request a small beer. He remembered Nikki's comment,

'Greek wine doesn't travel well. It can barely make it from the kitchen to the table.'

Amusing as the statement was it was not necessarily true as Kenneth had tasted some quite palatable Greek wines, although still preferring French. From his seat, not next to the guide unfortunately, he had a clear view into the kitchen. A variety of fresh smells wafting from it intensified his appetite - meat, garlic, oil, spices.

There was one lady preparing the food. She turned to speak to the waiter who hardly looked old enough to have the job. Meeting Kenneth's stare, she acknowledged him with the slightest movement of her head, lifting it proudly, almost in defiance. She was very pretty and, although her hair was tied up in a scarf, some strands of the raven black had escaped and were clinging to the beads of sweat glistening on her forehead. Kenneth found it strangely alluring. She wore a simple short-sleeved dress with a large flowery, garish pattern. A voluminous apron was wrapped around her slim waist. He presumed she was the wife of which George had spoken. Had he not been aware of this Kenneth would have thought the relationship that of father and daughter.

The waiter deposited plate after plate of the prepared food, all attractively presented. Several of the group were hesitant, but after sampling they all tucked in merrily. Kenneth was no stranger to Greek food and felt this offering ranked with the best previously encountered.

Soft Greek music pervaded the space and added an appropriate ambience. Kenneth was pleased it wasn't the 'plinky-plonky' music that issued from so many establishments in the tourist areas. The conversation comprised the usual amongst tourists cast together for only a short time. Where do you come from? Is it your first time here? Where are you staying? Kenneth listened, not wishing to be drawn in. When asked direct questions his answers were so non-committal his fellow passengers refrained from taxing him further.

The empty plates were removed and clean ones brought in. George appeared carrying a huge plate of galaktouboureka - a semolina custard in filo pastry, drenched in syrup.

'This sweet was made by my wife. Is a present from us. Kalo orexi.'

Kenneth wondered what sort of life the pretty wife had in this place, trying to picture how she might look in twenty or thirty years' time. It was not a picture he wished to hold. He saw the guide stand.

'I'm sure you will agree Mr. George and his family have done us proud and we would all like to thank them.'

Spontaneous applause broke out and Kenneth willingly participated.

'Now, Mycenae does not have any facilities so I suggest two things. First avail yourselves of the toilets here and secondly stock up on water. There is no shelter there so be careful not to leave your hats and scarves on the bus.'

After everyone, including Kenneth, had followed her advice in respect of a visit to the toilets, the bus set off for Mycenae.

'We should be at Mycenae in about twenty minutes. It's quite a large site, over three thousand years old. It's mostly associated with Agamemnon who led the Greeks in the Trojan War. The walls are famous for their size. Myth tells us they were built by the Cyclops. My favourite part of the site is The Lion Gate. Headless, sadly, but still a very imposing entrance.

Through the gate are the so-called royal tombs. The first excavator claimed one was the grave of Agamemnon after a pure gold face mask was found, but the dates don't fit. If you're feeling energetic it's well worth the climb to the acropolis. The views are stunning.

Take some time to visit the beehive tomb, the other side of the parking lot, referred to as a treasury. As no remains or treasure have been found there we have no idea of its use. Please be back at the bus for a quarter to five.'

Kenneth watched the other passengers go through the Cyclopean gate.

'You're not going in, Mr Graham?'

'Shortly. Can't take in the size of these walls. I felt the same on my first visit. I had read about them, seen pictures but seeing them. I can hardly believe they were built without modern machinery. Such fortifications in the middle of nowhere.'

'And the expanse of the citadel itself. The view from the acropolis shows how difficult it would be for an enemy to approach without the citadel being warned well in advance. I'll walk a little way with you, if I may.'

If she may! Kenneth almost crooked his arm but managed to restrain this urge to make physical contact.

'You spoke of the excavator of these graves. I believe that would be Heinrich Schliemann, who also searched for Troy.'

'That's right. You are knowledgeable, Mr Graham.'

He wanted her to call him Kenneth but he hardly dare ask, feeling sure he would be rebuffed. For reasons he couldn't explain he knew he did not wish to be rebuffed by this woman.

'Benefits of a classical education, I'm afraid.'

'No doubt Private or Public.'

There was no rebuke in her tone, merely a possible statement of fact.

'Both. Yourself?'

'Grammar School. All girls. Look, there it is. Isn't it wonderful, even without the heads? Such magnificence.'

The joy in her voice was palpable.

'Might one ask why this means so much to you?'

'One might ask but one might not choose to answer. Besides, it was all a long time ago.' She smiled at him. 'Go on. I'm going to sit here a while.'

Kenneth reluctantly left, went through the Lion Gate, cast a cursory glance at the grave circle, wandered through the palace, making his way determinedly up to the very top of the citadel. The sun was high in the sky. Kenneth took a long draft from the plastic bottle whose water was now warm and unrefreshing. He was the only person present. He could see for miles in every direction he turned.

He felt rather than heard her approach, but didn't turn round even when he heard her voice.

'There's a real feeling of history here, something special.'

He breathed heavily as her hand slipped gently into his. They stood quietly, enjoying the moment. The hand was removed. When he turned round she was gone. He thought he saw her in the distance and wondered how she had got there so quickly. He checked his watch. There was little time left to the agreed return to the bus. Finishing the last of the water he made his way swiftly down. The others were boarding when he arrived.

'That's everyone. I hope you all enjoyed this visit. Anyone make it to the top?' There was some embarrassed laughter.

'I have to admit I didn't either. It was far too hot for me today.'

Kenneth was puzzled. He tried to make eye contact but her gaze remained firmly on the others. Did she want to keep their meeting secret? That must be it. She must want to keep that moment to themselves. Kenneth sat in uncomprehending silence as she continued.

'Our final stop is the charming seaport of Nafplion, about a thirty- minute drive.

You'll have about two hours to shop or replenish your energy with something to eat and drink. You are safe now to have something alcoholic but please don't overdo it. The fortress there is called Palamidi. It was built by the Venetians in the early eighteenth century, very modern compared to what we've been seeing. It is quite a climb too. But you may think you've had enough culture and history for one day. You were warned it would be a long day.'

* * *

The long day was nearing its close. The visit to Nafplion was over. Kenneth had found a bar with a cool veranda and indulged in a couple of G&Ts. He had thought of asking the guide to join him but hadn't pursued the idea. Her statement that she hadn't been to the top of the citadel perplexed him. Was she playing some sort of game or had he imagined the encounter? He didn't know.

Apostolis' taxi waited for the short journey back to the island. The day was over. Kenneth waited until all the passengers had gone their separate ways.

'That was a most enjoyable day. I think I'll relax by claiming my prize at Kostas. Would you care to join me?'

'Maybe another time. I understand you're here for a year. I have an early start in the morning.'

'Not another classical tour, surely?'

'No. Enjoy your drink at Kostas'. Tell him you earned a double.'

Kenneth watched her walk away. Another time. There was hope. He went off to claim his prize and ponder on that strange encounter.

Diary Entry (early June)

Slept late. Combination of long day/over-indulgence at Kostas'. Must remember larger measures here. Bar full of tourists. Some well into their cups. Only smattering of locals. Latter seemed to drink more abstemiously/more slowly. Enjoyed classical tour. Lot to think about... The tour guide - this 'Kyria'. Wonder if that's her real name? Can't make out that business at Mycenae. Too much sun, mayhap.

Eschewing breakfast Kenneth decided he would pay a courtesy call on the house across the way. Since his first encounter he had not spoken to any of the family except to pass the time of day. Feeling remiss he took the short walk across the road to Esther's door. As he raised his hand to knock, the door opened.

'So you finally decided to come over. I think you are just in time. The biskwits are nearly ready. Come into the kitchen, I have to watch the oven. Sit while I make the coffee.'

The pronunciation of biscuits Kenneth found quite charming. The smell issuing from the watched oven raised hope they would be ready to accompany the coffee, whose smell mingled with that of the biskwits. It was a smell that evoked a childhood memory.

A happy time spent with the family cook in the old fashioned kitchen which had brought hours of pleasure and a feeling of security. He experienced that feeling now.

'I must apologise...'

'No need. You were busy settling in. How are you getting on with the cooking and cleaning?'

'I'm not very good at either. Have been eating out and the house really needs a lady's touch. There was a lady dressed in black when I first arrived. Perhaps she would be able to do for me, two or three times a week.'

'Do, what is 'do'?'

'Cook, clean, shopping, washing, ironing. I've always had someone to do all these things for me.'

'Ah, your wife isn't coming then?'

'I'm not married. I've always paid a lady to do these things. Do you think Mrs...?'

A popping sound announced the coffee was ready. Esther poured the thick liquid into two small cups. She turned to the oven. Donning large, well-used, slightly burned, oven gloves she removed the tray of biskwits and placed them on a cooling tray.

'These are too hot to eat. Don't look disappointed. I have some from the other day.'

She took a tin from a shelf, removed the lid and placed it in front of Kenneth. Sitting down opposite him Esther pushed one of the coffee cups towards him.

'Help yourself to milk, sugar and the biskwits. Her name is Mrs Xanthopoulos but you had better call her Mrs Eleni. That would be polite. I will ask but am sure she will say ok because she is a widow for many years now and has no children.'

'That's very kind of you. These biscuits are delicious. And how much shall I pay her? I have no idea of the wages here?'

'She will tell you. She is an honest woman and won't cheat you. She'll be happy to have someone to care for. She was so young. Her husband was a fisherman. A terrible storm. The worst was the sea never gave his body. More coffee? Biskwits?'

'Thank you, no. I must get on.'

'Yes, you have your writing. I will tell Mrs Xanthopoulos she mustn't disturb you when you are working.'

Esther placed a selection of her biskwits into a tin, thrust them into Kenneth's hand and escorted him to the door. He now knew the reason for Mrs Eleni's sad eyes.

Diary Entry (mid June)
Pleased all settled. Lady in black started within hours. Carried bags of shopping. Busied herself in kitchen. Forgot to ask Esther re tourist guide, another time. Sat at desk pretending to write. Did manage few notes re tour. Useful for travel article. Somewhat distracted by strange, not unpleasant, smells from kitchen.

Mrs Eleni had gone home. It was early evening and the sun, although still bright, had lost the stifling heat of the mid-afternoon. Kenneth decided to explore a little before his evening meal. He walked as far as the delicatessen-cum-mini market. Instead of taking the turn to the town he crossed the road, passing the children's swings on the left, coming to the courtyard of a church, which he had seen from the road. He strode down the stepped slope by the side of the church arriving at a walled circle of flowers. A strong smell of lavender surrounded him as he passed. He followed the passageway between the houses, arriving in an area of restaurants, some stretching out over the water. He presumed the road to the left led to the town and the newer harbour known as the Dapia. Where he was must be the Old Harbour.

He took the slightly winding road to the right and was surprised to see half-built boats resting on trestles. A little further and he was in the Old Harbour proper. There were boats of all sizes and quality, from small wooden fishing boats to expensive, modern yachts. Kenneth paused to watch a yacht entering the harbour. She moved with grace and grandeur, manœuvring slowly and majestically into her mooring, the polished wood and brass reflecting the dying sun whilst the fibreglass yachts bobbed obeisance to her superiority.

Across the harbour were more unfinished boats, overlooked by a row of elevated houses oozing wealth. He would save that for another day. Retracing his steps Kenneth returned to the house. As he unlocked the door he heard voices issuing from Esther's house. He turned to see the three children waving to a figure walking down the pathway to the garden gate. She wore a sleeveless, pink summer dress with a dropped waist, a wide-brimmed straw hat and leather, thonged sandals.

'Bye, Kyria. See you next week.'

The tour guide paused, turned and waved back.

'Make sure you do your homework.'

As she closed the gate she looked across at the house opposite. Kenneth thought he detected an expression of sadness but it turned so quickly into a smile as she saw him he decided he had imagined it. He watched her walk down the slope until she disappeared from sight. Kenneth sighed, opened the door and turned to the kitchen to see what culinary delights Mrs Eleni had left this time.

Diary Entry (late June)

Lots of excitement last night. On side balcony having early evening drink. Saw glow in sky over Old Harbour. Great commotion. Bikes, three wheelers. People running. All heading towards Old Harbour. Decided to follow. See what all fuss was.

Kenneth walked briskly down the hill towards the glow in the sky, now interrupted by plumes of black smoke. It seemed the whole island was rushing to the Old Harbour.

As he came to the koutouki he saw the owner standing in the doorway.

'It's a fire, Mr Kenneth. One of the foreign yachts.'

Kenneth nodded. Quickening his step he walked on, past the mini-market, across the church forecourt, down the steps, through the houses into the main nightlife of the island. Acrid smoke swirled. There was the smell of burning wood.

He watched as an antiquated fire truck fought unsuccessfully to contain the flames. They would soon spread to the adjacent boats, causing an inferno. The fuel tanks would blow. With no heavy rain for several weeks, the whole island was tinder dry. The diesel station was perilously close. One spark and... The decision was taken. The yacht was towed out to deep water, the seacocks opened and the sea did the job the fire truck couldn't. It had truly been a beautiful yacht, the one Kenneth had admired several days earlier. Excitement over, Kenneth decided to eat at the koutouki. He enjoyed the intimate atmosphere as well as the good food. Yani always had room for one more.

'What will happen now? They can't leave the boat where it is, surely? It's a hazard.'

'Oh, they'll lift her in a few days. And then the owner will see about repairs.'

'He's lucky the island has boatyards and experienced boat builders.'

'Not experienced enough for that yacht. I expect he's already sent for Larry.'

Yani placed a bowl of goat stew and a hunk of fresh bread in front of Kenneth and went off to attend to the other four tables, full of locals discussing the events of the evening.

Kenneth heard the name Larry several times. As he prepared to savour the succulence of meat cooked for three days Kenneth pondered on who this Larry might be.

Diary Entry (late June)

Heard some of background of Larry from Kostas. Went to see how restoration going. Finally saw him. Envisaged robust, outdoor type. Not so. Tall, slender, gently spoken, very sensuous. Looking forward to tonight.

The island was famous for its ship-building. Amongst the older men this was very much rule of thumb. The younger ones learned 'on the job' from the older but were slowly adding more modern approaches as they learned how to build boats in colleges on the mainland, in a classroom.

Although there was a lot of experience this boat required an expertise with which few men anywhere were bestowed. Such a one was Larry. He had learned his craft travelling to areas renowned for boat building. In particular the Hebrides, arriving unannounced and asking the boatmen there teach him everything they knew. He would work without pay, needing only accommodation and food. He stayed a year.

Larry could be anywhere in the world at any one moment. How quickly he was located and actually arrived on the island was something of a mystery. He would stay several weeks working and advising until the boat was showing signs of its former beauty - at which point Larry would leave, his especial skills no longer required.

* * *

When Kenneth arrived in the Old Harbour Larry was in conversation with a grizzled, elderly gentleman in well-worn overalls and wearing a woolly bobble hat despite the sun, already strong. His weather-beaten hands and face proclaimed outdoor life.

Kenneth waited until the man had left.

'Good morning. You must be Larry.'

'Yeh, that's me. You are...?'

'I do apologise. I'm Kenneth Graham. I'm...'

'Heard there was an English toff here, a writer. Should've recognised you.'

'Quite. Pleased to meet you. I see the restoration is well underway.'

'Yeh, it's OK. Damage wasn't as bad as first thought. These guys did good to sink her so quick. A good crew.'

'Well, mustn't keep you. Perhaps I could buy you a drink later?'

'Yeh, Ken, that'd be good. I'm playing tomorrow night at George's. Why don't you swing round? Any time after ten.'

'Yes, fine. Until tomorrow then.'

As he walked home Kenneth wondered what instrument Larry played and decided it would be a guitar.

* * *

It was still light when Kenneth left the house at ten o'clock for the short walk to George's. He turned right at the high-walled house, following the road as it curved round to the Atlantis Hotel and Disco Fever, long closed, emerging onto the Agia Marina Road.

He could hear canned music as he approached the club. He saw a couple at the entrance in conversation with a lady who was taking entrance fees. He waited until the couple disappeared through the solid, black, wooden doors.

'Is there an entrance fee?'

'Not for you,' the classical tour guide returned. 'Larry told me to look out for you.

I'll get someone to take over the door and we'll go join him. He hasn't played yet so you've not missed anything.'

Inside there was a fair-sized assembly although the place was by no means full. It was still very early. The crowd would build up after 11pm.

'Hi, glad you made it, Ken. Whatya drinking?'

'A G&T, with lots of ice, please. And, I don't wish to be rude, but I do prefer Kenneth.'

'No prob, Ken...neth.'

Kenneth raised his glass to his two companions.

'Bottoms up.'

'To absent friends,' came the reply in unison.

As the canned music became increasingly louder, and the crowd increasingly more numerous, conversation was impossible. This wasn't the quiet evening Kenneth had envisaged when mooting the idea of a drink with Larry. He was aware of the warmth of feeling shown between Larry and the woman. The touches, the smiles - as though they shared a secret. He became aware the woman had spoken to him.

'Sorry. Didn't catch... the music... too loud.'

'Would you like to dance?'

Kenneth observed the gyrations being performed on the floor.

'I'm afraid I don't. At least not this.'

'Then it's you and me, Larry. Come on.'

He watched them dancing. They looked good together. The music slowed, they moved closer, a closeness sensuous but not sexual. They must have met before. Had they been lovers? Were they still? He felt a twinge of longing, of jealousy. Why? A young man approached Larry and the moment passed. The couple returned to their seats. Larry reached under his seat, pulling out a bandolier with narrow, oblong pockets along half of it. Slinging it across his body, left shoulder to right hip, he went outside. Kenneth looked at the woman.

'He's gone to warm up the harps.'

The canned music faded, the lights dimmed, silence descended expectantly. Larry stepped into the single spot which lit up a small area of the stage. For the next hour Larry played blues, jazz, pop, classical, rock, folk. There was no intermediate applause as he slid almost seamlessly from one genre to another, pausing only to change harmonica.

Kenneth had never realised how emotive and poignant the harmonica could be when played so expertly and with obvious love. He enthusiastically joined in the applause, although not the shouts and whoops that followed Larry as he left the stage to re-join his companions. The canned music surfaced but people began to drift away.

'Must go too. Don't want to sleep in. Can't let the guys at the boatyard arrive before me.'

'Maybe we can meet again, for dinner, perhaps.'

'Yeh, why not.'

The tour guide stood up. 'I've got an early start as well. A pupil at 7.30.'

'May I escort you home?'

'No, thank you. Larry will see me safely home.'

Kenneth took the longer way home, along the main road and then up the slope.

The house was in darkness - a rare night when the sky gave no light. Many times he had admired the clarity of the Spetsai sky at night. He had seen constellations so bright he believed he could almost touch them. Feeling his way up the walkway and crossing the balcony he took the key from the hook and inserted it in the lock. He felt arms encircle his waist from behind as the door swung open. Her arms. He felt breath on the nape of his neck. Her breath. He leaned back against the door jamb, eyes closed, feeling her presence, then her touch as she slowly unfastened his belt, releasing his readiness. Her hands slid down to his thighs as she sank to her knees. He stayed there, savouring the moment. With a sigh he entered the house and felt lonely.

Diary Entry (early July)

Went down to O.H. to see Larry re dinner. Told he'd left. Done the difficult repair. Locals could do rest. Mixture of disappointment/relief he'd gone. Heat wave continues. 38°/40° today. Heard about performances of live plays. Anargyri College Theatre. Visiting group from University of Detroit Mercy. Yearly visit. Could be diversion. Tonight's performance Shakespeare's 'Tempest'. Much cooler. Still somewhat oppressive. Cool breeze from sea. Found College gates easily. Followed people. Quite impressive building. Needs restoration. Am told used as school for senior pupils.

Kenneth followed the stream of people as they veered to the dirt track on the right and up the slope towards the amphitheatre, an early twentieth century copy of the ancient theatres. Bikes passed him, throwing up dirt clouds in their wake. The amphitheatre looked atmospheric. Very apt for 'The Tempest'.

The breeze filtering through the trees surrounding the stage brought the freshness of ozone. A steady trickle of people was arriving. People had obviously been to former productions, coming armed with cushions and blankets as protection against the hardness of the stone and the chill of the night. Kenneth chose a seat halfway up, wishing he'd known about the possible discomfort. Looking round he saw his classical tour guide. She appeared to be alone although several people stopped to exchange greetings. Others waved in acknowledgement.

His eyes swept to the stage, devoid of scenery. He noticed lights positioned in trees, the wires disguised as they wound their way round branches and trunks, disappearing to some hidden power source. It was dusk and the theatre almost full. Kenneth heard the familiar, unwelcome sound of mosquitoes, feeling their touch as they moved in on his face and hands. He brushed them away. A Greek lady offered him half a lemon, indicating he should rub it over his exposed skin. He had seen others doing likewise so presumed, and hoped, it would help keep the mosquitoes at bay. The audience fell quiet as a man dressed in a suit, with collar and tie, took centre stage. In traditional fashion he raised his hands and clapped loudly. Several people left their seats at the rear and moved down closer to the stage. Tradition fulfilled the man left the stage. The play was about to begin.

Diary Entry (early July)

Think more could have been made of the stage. Lots of cloth waving, supposedly representative of waves. Audience appreciative. A pleasant interlude overall. Was very surprised at what transpired afterwards.

The play was over. The audience had shown its appreciation and the be-collared man in suit had thanked them for coming, reminding them there was a performance of 'Œdipus in Colonus' the following night. All would be welcome. As usual the performance was offered freely.

Kenneth watched Kyria leave the theatre and set off down the track to the moonlit road. He paced his step so that he caught up with her halfway down.

'Interesting interpretation, don't you think?'

'Good evening, Mr. Graham. I thought I spied you up there. Yes, it was.'

'I last saw it performed by the RSC but the venue was very different.'

'Not as atmospheric as here, I'm sure.'

They were nearing the road. Kenneth took a deep breath.

'I'm popping into Kostas' for a night-cap. Would you care to join me?'

'I have other arrangements but I'll be here tomorrow night for the Œdipus play.'

She stepped into the waiting taxi and was gone. Other arrangements! Kenneth's mind ran a gamut of emotions but he walked on with the knowledge he would see her tomorrow and that she had instigated the meeting.

Diary Entry (early July)

A different production. No-one aware anything wrong. All seemed to fit the play. Œdipus did die at Colonus. Pity about play's curtailment. Worked out well for me though.

Kenneth showered and selected his outfit carefully. He set off early but when he arrived at the theatre she was already there. She waved and patted the cushion lying on the space next to her.

'How very thoughtful. Thank you.'

'Don't mention it. Does make the performance more pleasurable.'

'Quite. Do you know the play at all?'

'Have never seen it but know the story of Œdipus, of course. I do know this version is by Sophocles.'

'That's right. It's the second play of his three referred to as The Theban Plays.

They are the only surviving plays of a much longer series. He is believed to have written over a hundred and twenty plays, but only seven have survived. He was at least ninety when he died. Oh, I do apologise, I must sound like a lecturer. I do get carried away sometimes.'

'Not at all. I'm interested and it will enhance my enjoyment of the play if I know something about it. I remember you winning the prize at Epidavros.'

Kenneth allowed himself a smile at the shared memory.

'I believe you have some knowledge of the Classics?'

'A smattering only. A friend and I... Wait a minute, there's something going on.

On the raised bit, behind the main stage. They're setting up some scenery. Must be nearly ready to start.'

'It is actually just past nine.'

The play promised to be an interesting production. The raised rear of the stage was set up as an operating theatre, complete with surgeons and nurses in surgical attire. It became clear the body on the table was Œdipus. Intermittent comments such as 'We're losing him', made it clear the surgeons were attempting to save his life. It fitted in so well with the Sophoclean tragedy being enacted at the front of the stage, Antigone helping her frail father to walk, that when the be-collared, be-suited man rushed onto the stage and addressed the audience with, 'Is there a doctor in the house?' no-one thought anything amiss. Even his next request for an ambulance to take the dying man to hospital was not thought untoward, apart from a few smothered giggles as the island possessed neither of these two things. The suit was now desperate.

'This is not part of the play. Œdipus is having a heart attack. We need to get him to a doctor.'

The audience realized the situation was real. It was the actor, not Œdipus, having the heart attack. A pick-up truck reversed into the stage with a dull thud. The tail-board was let down and 'Œdipus' lifted on board. The truck revved off in a cloud of dust.

Kenneth turned to his companion and was shocked to see she was trying hard not to burst into laughter.

'It's really not funny. The man could be dying.'

'I know. I'm sorry,' came the spluttered reply.

Kenneth stood and proffered a hand. Ignoring it his companion got to her feet and picked up the cushions. Still chuckling she nodded 'Yes' to Kenneth's suggestion they go to Kostas'. In the taxi Kenneth tried hard to ignore the snorts and giggles coming from his companion. He felt his own reserve slipping but was determined he would not join her in such inappropriate behaviour.

It was still early so the bar was comparatively empty as Kostas brought their customary drinks to a table outside.

'Did you decide not to go to the play after all?'

'Oh, we did go but...'

The woman's explanation was interrupted by a loud belly laugh. Kenneth winced.

'Was the production no good?'

Kostas looked at Kenneth. By now tears were streaming down the woman's face as she lost control. Shaking with laughter she managed a reply,

'Oh it was quite unique you could say.'

Drawing a deep breath Kenneth proceeded to tell Kostas what had happened. Kostas looked at the woman who was still overcome with apparent amusement at the actor's possible demise. Shaking his head he returned to the bar where customers were waiting to hear the cause of such merriment.

Diary Entry (early July)

Actor didn't have heart attack. Heat exhaustion. Kyria apologised. Said she'd done it all her life. Laughed inappropriately. A nervous thing. Came home alone. Morning found note in Greek on door. Esther translated. Large box arrived from Athens. She would see to delivery. I pay man delivering.

Kenneth removed the delivery notes from the plastic envelope fastened to the tea chest. As suspected it was from his agent. The lid was securely nailed down. He remembered seeing the box of tools in the outside store. There he found a claw hammer. The lid was soon removed, as were the many sheets of tissue paper. The first parcel he opened was a supply of Blue Mountain coffee. A kind thought? A peace offering? Was The Bitch softening? Unlikely. An attempt at placating him?

Another parcel proved to be paper, note books and cartridges. These he immediately consigned to the appropriate desk drawers. Some forwarded mail. Nothing important, apart from a request from a travel magazine. There was a note attached from his agent suggesting he could write something as 'light relief'. She really didn't miss a trick.

A third, smaller parcel held razor blades, the ones he normally used. He had tried an electric razor but soon returned to the more traditional method of shaving. How had The Bitch known which to buy? Of course, the key he always left with his lawyer. She needed entrance to the flat to have the utilities put on hold. It was the first opportunity afforded her. No doubt she would have had a good look round as she had never been invited. Meetings were either in her office or over a meal out.

He was especially pleased with two bottles of Aramis aftershave carefully wrapped in cotton wool inside a wooden box. He loved the combination of essential oils. The soothing, moisturising properties of the oak moss also being a natural antiseptic should he inadvertently cut or 'nick' himself.

He dug deeper. Below more tissue paper he found his beloved Cashmere overcoat. He remembered the day he had bought it. The salesman had tried hard to persuade him to take black but Kenneth had opted for dark blue and had never regretted the choice. It had served him well over the years although he doubted he would have use for it here. After all he wouldn't be here in the winter.

The last wad of tissue paper revealed another garment, brand new and bearing the label of his own tailor in Jermyn Street. A further label described the garment as a driz-a-bone, guaranteed to keep out the heaviest rainfall. Kenneth shook his head in disbelief. What a waste of money to send something like this when there was no way he would be needing it unless the winter in London proved to be particularly wet.

Diary Entry (mid July)

Old 'war wound' playing up. Damned horse. Hasn't bothered me some time. Probably all the walking. Not used to it. Maybe hire bike. Wonder if motorbike in garden can be resurrected? Visited chemist. Offered painkillers. Must get down to serious writing. Get blasted book finished and go home.

Kenneth set off up the hill, the steep slope he had assumed led to higher ground on his first visit to the monastery. But he was not on his way to the Prophet Elias as recommended on the Classical Tour. He was on a more personal mission. The previous day Mrs Eleni had noticed the limp. She had pointed, raised her eyebrows and inclined her head to one side. In answer to her question he had, feeling rather foolish, mimed riding a horse, even giving a quiet abashed neigh. He was thankful the friends with whom he had once ridden to hounds could not see him, nor was it likely they would ever hear of this embarrassing performance. He then mimed a fall, stopping short of actually falling to the floor as being below his dignity. He grimaced as though in great pain, then demonstrated an exaggerated limp. Mrs Eleni nodded.

'Ioanna.'

'Joanna?'

'Nai, Ioanna, her help you, how you call her? Wish woman...'

'Wise woman?'

'Nai nai, wise woman. Her help you.'

She walked to his desk and reached for the hallowed fountain pen. Before she could pick it up Kenneth had provided her with a pencil and a sheet of note-paper. She drew a rough sketch of what was obviously the house. Rows of arrows indicated the route he should follow. Crude it may have been but it was unmistakably where she wanted him to go. X clearly marked the spot.

* * *

Kenneth stared at the map in his hand. A pathway somewhere on the left. Mrs Eleni had squiggled a wavy line to indicate the path he should take, to distinguish it from the straight line which would take him further up the hill. She had told him to look out for rising smoke or the aromatic smell of a fire. Joanna sometimes needed to prepare potions by heating ingredients. Timing his visit was crucial as the wise woman was often out early morning or late at night, optimum times for collecting, depending on what plants she required.

Kenneth wondered about Mrs Eleni crossing herself every time the name Joanna was mentioned. He was not a superstitious man, regarding all religions as irrational nonsense. This had been yet another bone of contention with his father who believed the aristocracy had a duty to support the established church, albeit lip service, setting an example to the people on his estate. Pater firmly believed in pre-ordination. Mater would attend the services but used the time to plan her own affairs, which certainly involved no organised religious group. Of the two parents Kenneth thought his mother to be the more truly spiritual.

He returned to the present with the awareness of someone singing. A sound unlike any he had ever heard. He felt drawn to the sound as Œdysseus had been drawn to Calypso. Then she was there.

Appearing in his path without a sound. Frightening, but not in aspect. A strange wild beauty. For a brief moment he saw his mother again. The moment passed as the apparition morphed into a mortal being with long, straggly, black hair. His mother had been the palest of blondes. The robe this woman wore could only be described as one of which Joseph himself would have been proud. It flowed down to the ground barely hiding the bare feet.

'Why have you come?'

The voice was non-threatening, without emotion.

Her approach had silenced Kenneth, a man never at a loss in the English language. He stood transfixed as the figure circled him. He felt her hands placed gently on his shoulders. Hands that were cool through his cotton shirt but an increasing intensity of warmth emanated from them, releasing tension from taut muscles.

'You mustn't spend so long sitting, looking down. Stand every thirty minutes, stretch. That will release your tension.'

So even she's heard I'm a writer was Kenneth's cynical thought.

'Why have you come?'

Again without inflection. The hands remained and the warmth washed over him, comforting as though he were back in the nursery in the safety of his nanny's arms. Without moving he explained the event responsible for the re-curring, painful limp. As he did so he found himself reliving it. The gathering of the landed gentry, the ritual of the stirrup cup, the baying of the hounds pulling on their leashes, eager to be free to pursue their prey, the call of the horn with its differing signals, the thrill of the chase and then the fall. A hedge taken successfully many times. No-one knew what had caused his horse to shy at the last moment. He could hear the crack of the bone, feel the pain. He became aware of the woman speaking.

'This I can help, but I ask you again. Why have you come?'

The hands were removed and he turned to face this lady. 'I...'

'You are troubled in mind. I can give you oils to help the physical pain but I cannot heal your soul.'

'Mother.'

Another voice. Its owner appeared behind the woman. Straggly hair, even longer than his mother's, with a beard that made Kenneth think of a young Merlin, the image being enhanced by the dun-coloured tunic reaching to the youth's knees. He too was bare-foot.

'Are you all right? Is everything OK?'

'I am. It is, my son. This man is no danger to us. Only to himself.'

The man stared unblinkingly at Kenneth, turned and disappeared whence he came.

'Wait here. I will return shortly with the potion.'

She mentioned a meagre payment and refused the extra Kenneth proffered. As Kenneth retraced his steps down the slope he was troubled by this woman's parting words.

'She can never be yours. There is only one for her.'

'She is wrong. I can make her mine. I will...'

He spoke the words out loud. And the wind whispered her name.

* * *

There had been no arrangement to meet but she saw him sitting alone outside Kostas', waved, went into the bar and returned with her drink to ask if she might join him. He automatically rose as she sat and saw her smile at this politeness. Was she mocking him again?

'I hear you've been seeking supernatural help?'

Was there nothing private on this island?

'One would hardly call it supernatural. Just someone with knowledge of the power of nature and its goodness, utilising it for the benefit of others. I believe, in common parlance, a white witch.'

'One which would have been burned at the stake only a few hundred years ago.'

'Indubitably!'

'And did it help… your problem, or was it problems?'

Kenneth thought he could be as arcane as this woman, though perhaps she wasn't deliberately so.

'She made some interesting observations. I think she is very perceptive, good at reading people - apart from her knowledge of the healing qualities of plants.'

'And did you meet her son?'

'Yes, I did. Briefly. He seemed very protective of his mother. Some sort of apprentice, one presumes.'

'Yes. She also has a daughter, but she left. Said her mother was as mad as a hatter and her brother was going the same way. Think she's travelling… somewhere.'

They sat in silence for some time. She rose.

'Must get the shopping in before the shops close.'

Kenneth wanted her to stay, to come home with him.

'Oh, quite. Thank you for your company.'

He watched her until she turned the corner. She was quite tall for a woman, five eight or so. He had never seen her wearing court shoes. It probably had to do with the terrain and the fact she walked everywhere. In a place where everyone whizzed or tootled round on a variety of two or three wheeled contraptions he had never even seen her as a passenger. On broaching the subject she had replied she only drove vehicles with a wheel at each corner and had been told many times she was a bad passenger on two wheels.

Quite slim on the whole, with small breasts, a narrow waist, fuller hips and rear. Her ankles were inclined to be thick which usually put him off. But it was not her physical appearance that most attracted him, although he wouldn't be averse to a sexual relationship. It was her mind drawing him in. She was intelligent, obviously well-educated, possibly highly so. She had told him Grammar School but nothing more.

What intrigued him most was that, on an island obviously thriving on gossip and rumour, no-one seemed willing to disclose any information about her other than she gave English lessons at all levels, to all ages. It was clear she was valued and respected for her contribution to the island. But there seemed to be something more, a need to protect her - from what? Something in the past? Was it to do with the house? With the music?

With a man? Kenneth felt there was a masculine presence in the house, apart from his own. The owner of the house who had 'gone away'? Who was he and how did he connect with this intriguing woman?

As he walked home he thought of what the witch woman had told him. His leg hurt.

Diary Entry (mid July)

What is it about this woman? Think she likes me but there is a coolness. As cold as ice. Maybe defensive. Why? Something in her past? Am drawn to her. Maybe I could help her thaw... Should go down for early G&T before bar gets busy. Have found Kostas friendly/informative about island. Could perhaps turn conversation to subject of foreigners on island. Pop in a few general questions. Bring conversation round to plays. Go on to the Ice Queen, this Kyria.

It was after eleven when Kenneth got to Kostas' but it was still busy with tourists. No locals for they were still accommodating tourists in their own establishments. It was far too hot to sit inside even had there been room. The windows were open and the air conditioning was trying hard to make a difference. Two of the tables outside had been moved together. Around them, seated or standing, were at least twenty young people.

There were two jugs of coloured liquid from which each filled his or her own glass. Kenneth noted that, although casually dressed, all were sporting the latest brands. There were signs of affluence in the show of jewellery worn by both male and female.

At the end of the row of tables, not the town end, was a small table with a solitary chair. It was never a favourite due to its position away from the lights. As Kenneth sat at the unpopular table Kostas came out carrying another jug for the young people. Seeing Kenneth, Kostas raised his eyebrows. Understanding the question and grateful he would not have to negotiate the crowd in the bar, Kenneth nodded. A large brandy and a glass of iced water were duly brought.

'Busy tonight, Kostas.'

Kenneth tipped his glass towards the young people.

'From the yachts in the Old Harbour. They come every year. This is only a brief visit but they'll be back in August for a longer stay. Good customers.'

Kostas smiled and returned to his busyness.

Diary Entry (late July)

Two o'clock before Kostas had time for a chat. Waste of time in respect of Ice Queen. And re former occupant of house. Kostas isn't a gossip. Got clearer picture of island though. Might be worth recording for use in later writing. A travel article on return to life. Soon!

At last! She had agreed to have dinner with him. He had anticipated this agreement by choosing one of the more expensive restaurants in the Old Harbour. The ambience was perfect for a relaxed, if not romantic, evening's conviviality. But when she had asked if she could choose the venue he had instantly acquiesced.

'Where?'

'Meet me at the horse buggies on the far side of the Dapia, at nine.'

'Shouldn't I book?'

'There'll always be a table for me.'

Again that air of mystery.

* * *

The day dragged. He sat at his desk. He picked up the fountain pen but nothing flowed from that or his mind. He felt desire rising in him as he thought of the evening ahead. He mustn't - as his block-busting hero would say - blow it. A wry smile crossed his face as he acknowledged the sexual connotation of the expression. He replaced the top on the pen, positioning it on its rest so the family crest watched him, mocking him. Ancestors from a past with different values rode through his psyche.

'You want her, My Lord, then take her.'

He decided on a short siesta.

* * *

They were walking hand in hand. The night was perfect, cool, balmy, a strong smell of jasmine. An owl hooted. She drew closer to him and laughed. 'It startled me.' Kenneth released her hand. As he put his arm round her waist the sound of a motorbike approaching broke the magic. She stiffened. 'I have to go.' The woman and the sound merged and evaporated, leaving Kenneth cold and afraid.

Kenneth woke bathed in a cold sweat and entangled in the bed sheet. The sun's heat was waning as it sank lower in the sky. Soon it would drop below the Manikin Pis and enter the sea in a splendid array of colour. He rose to take a cooling shower. He wanted to prepare his attire carefully. A casual approach but he felt she would appreciate an effort - expect it almost. Why did he think that? He chose a cotton suit, the palest of greens, a cream shirt of the finest Egyptian cotton, tailor-made. No cravat. Sandals.

No socks. Kyria had commented socks should never be worn with sandals. Her thoughts or someone else's? Why this feeling there was someone else? Why would he want there not to be? Kenneth pushed the questions away.

He took a last look in the mirror which hung in the niche between the kitchen and the bathroom. A large mirror, six feet high, four feet across, with a carved wooden surround, painted black. The image it revealed pleased him. He cut a trim figure for his age. He saw the Ice Queen at his side. What a handsome couple. No, not at his side, slightly behind and she wasn't with him. She was smiling at someone else, a shadowy figure. He shuddered and both images were gone.

The scent of jasmine was in the air as he locked the door. He paused as the scent reminded him of something. Something hazy which he couldn't quite recall. Too much sun? He must be more careful. He took a leisurely walk down town allowing time for a G&T at Kostas', then made his way along the narrow shop-lined street that led to the Dapia. He nodded to people who now regularly acknowledged him.

'Have a nice meal. It's good food there.'

'You'll enjoy the fish soup. Best on the island.'

Great Moses! Was he the only one not knowing where he was to eat that evening?

On the far side of the Dapia he saw her, sitting on the harbour wall, feet hanging over the water. Again he noticed her thickish ankles. How he wished they would embrace him. She wore a dress he hadn't seen before. Surely not new, especially for him? A Laura Ashley, a fine-cottoned pink with full skirt to mid-calf and a bodice that emphasised her narrow waist. A waist for his hands to encircle.

The clock in the square was striking nine as he held out his hand to help her from the wall. She retained the hand as she demurely swung her legs over the wall, then rose on sandaled feet to brush his cheek with her lips. What bliss. She laughed.

'How very English we are. One slightly early and the other exactly on time.' She still held his hand.

'I thought we'd take a buggy. Is that all right?'

All right? Anything she wanted was all right. She led him to a waiting buggy.

'This is Petros. He knows where we're going.'

So does half the island apparently, passed through Kenneth's mind.

'Hello, Mr Kenneth. We'll have a lovely drive to your taverna. Help the lady in and we'll be off.'

Petros was all smiles. He clicked the horse into action and began singing. Kenneth noticed Petros was not so much driving the horse as merely holding the reins. To the left of the route were houses, bars, restaurants, the Town Hall, two bars that looked worthy of visits, a slight turn, a periptero, more tavernas and a long row of houses displaying signs of past affluence. Two dogs running free on the flat roof of one of the houses barked as they drove past. Kenneth had seen other dogs on rooftops. He wondered if any ever fell.

The sea and beach lined the road to the right. There were still a few tourists swimming but for the most part the beach was deserted.

'I love the beach at night.'

Must keep that in mind. Her hand still rested in his, softly, seductively. He hardly dared move. Was she aware of the effect on him? Beach and sea disappeared behind buildings - rooms, a mini market, the quaint Spetses Hotel where Kenneth had enjoyed an early evening G&T on the terrace. The beach re-appeared. On the left stood a wooden structure of no specific architectural style. Surely...

The horse stopped. Petros turned and positively beamed. So this was the designated place. Kenneth descended, turning to extend his hand, but she had already alighted. He watched her being greeted by a young couple, the man Greek, the woman exceptionally blonde with a creamy complexion suggestive of a much colder clime.

Kenneth paid Petros the amount to which he was accustomed when utilising a buggy and was surprised when he received money back.

'Special price for the lady.'

The Lady again. So many people on the island referred to her as The Lady. Petros gave a click. The horse swung round and ambled off, back to the Dapia. Kenneth's dinner companion had returned.

'Come and meet Takis and Olga. It's early yet. Better for a quiet meal. I hope you don't mind. I've ordered fish soup, the best on the island. I had to tell Takis in advance as he buys the fish fresh from the morning market.'

Kenneth now knew how the news had spread. She took his hand - again - and led him to the kitchen. The smell of fish, so often cloying and nauseous, wafted gently, enticingly, on the air.

'Takis, Olga, this is a friend, Mr Kenneth.'

A friend. Kenneth closed his eyes as he savoured the moment. A friend. She had introduced him as a friend. Not 'my' friend but he'd settle for 'a' friend. He felt it was going to be a good evening.

* * *

She lay on the bed fully clothed. How desirable a woman can be when fully clothed. Why a rush to be naked? Kenneth traced the circles of her breast with a forefinger, ran it down to where her navel hid below a short denim skirt fastened with a broad belt of curious Red American design - a man's belt surely. No matter. With both hands he stroked down to her thighs till, with pleasant surprise, he felt the slight ridge of suspenders. Kenneth looked up at a teasing smile and a raised eyebrow. His hands left the skirt to slide down the fishnet pattern of her legs, his eyes never left hers. Their eyes were locked in knowing, in agreement. The hands moved upwards, unbuckling the belt so the hem of the black polo necked top could be released. The hands now touched flesh but she still hadn't moved.

As always suspected there was no bra. The hands cupped the breasts and squeezed gently. One finger caressed a nipple. There was an instant response. Not only a physical one but a sigh from lips painted bright red for the occasion. Kenneth bent to taste the beauty of those lips.

The clanging of the goat bell signalled a visitor at his door. His musings had been interrupted yet again. As he donned dressing gown and slippers he remembered his lonely walk home.

Diary Entry (late July)

Stranger at the door. A parcel at P.O. from England. Surprised wasn't informed who'd sent it/what was in it. Turned out to be from agent. Opened parcel after siesta. Two books re Spetses and a further supply of Blue Mountain. Note with reference to drafts. Must get down to putting pen to paper. Tomorrow, maybe.

Kenneth placed the note in a desk drawer and the Blue Mountain in the 'fridge. He turned his attention to the books. 'The Magus' by John Fowles and 'The Jason Voyage' by Tim Severin. His classical background led to his being instantly attracted to the latter by the subtitle of 'The Quest for the Golden Fleece', but he flicked through each to ascertain its content. Further attracted by colour photographs, he chose the Tim Severin. Taking a glass and a jug of water he went to sit on the front balcony, now in shade, only aware of the passage of time when a balcony light was needed.

Halfway through the book he studied the photographs in more detail. Portrayals of the Jason story on ancient shards, men working on building a wooden ship, pictures of the Old Harbour, a priest blessing a completed ship and a small photograph which drew Kenneth's attention. He peered closely, then stood to place the picture in the dull beam of the naked light bulb. He had seen this man before. The woolly hat was the clue. It was the little man who had worked with Larry on restoring the fire-damaged yacht. He was described as 'Vasilis Delimetros, the master builder of Spetses, who built *Argo*.'

Noting the page at which he had finished reading Kenneth placed the book on the coffee table. In the kitchen he prepared a plate of cheese, olives and bread. He poured a small measure of gin over two cubes of ice into a tall glass, topping it up with tonic. Taking the repast out to the balcony he recommenced his reading. It was the early hours before he closed the book, the reading completed.

He fell asleep at once and dreamed of being Jason. As he led Medæa to the marriage bed he turned and smiled. The face of Kyria smiled back. Kenneth's body warmed as he saw the promise in her eyes. The eyes became two burning orbs that turned the warmth to fire. He woke to feel the mid-morning sun streaming in through the shutters he had failed to close before retiring.

Looking at the watch that gleamed in the sun's rays he was appalled at how long he had slept. He was not the 'lying in bed' sort. He rose and went straight into the shower without switching on the hot water. He was now used to the water being warmed by the sun.

He dressed in a long-sleeved, white cotton shirt which hung loosely over matching trousers and slipped his feet into pair of soft leather moccasins. He turned back the cuffs of the shirt twice. He decided he needed to re-visit the Old Harbour and see it with new eyes, with new knowledge. Breakfast could be morphed later into brunch.

There was a slight breeze, which softened the heat somewhat. As he approached the boatyards he heard the sounds mentioned in the book - 'the distinctive whine of electric planers, intermittent hammering, the buzz of drills and the noise of bandsaws'.

Kenneth felt he hadn't paid attention before. He walked slowly past the men at work. Some nodded but didn't pause in their labours. He couldn't see the man he now knew as Vasilis. What he did see were large numbers of cats. Where the harbour rounded he saw a few people leaving a fishing boat bobbing at its moorings. They were carrying bags of fresh fish. The fisherman shrugged as Kenneth approached.

'Sorry. All gone. Come early tomorrow.'

Kenneth smiled and nodded. He watched the fisherman spreading his nets, checking them for tears that would need repairs before venturing out again. This time the fisherman was lucky. None were needed.

Kenneth walked on, leaving the fisherman to dry his nets in the sun and wash down the boat. He realised that, although he had been on the island three months, he had never gone beyond these boatyards. He followed the curve of the road to where it straightened to the lighthouse. On his right, slightly elevated, was a row of houses each individually designed. He noticed a lady on a balcony and raised his Panama in greeting. A slender arm was raised in acknowledgement.

There were more boatyards on the left. Men working but no sight of Vasilis. Kenneth noted more cats. Houses and boatyards gave way to scrubland and scattered greenery on the right, the sea on the left with two large vessels straining at anchor chains.

Possibly cargo although Kenneth's nautical knowledge was sparse. His experience of boats being confined to rowing for exercise and romantic assignations whilst at Oxford.

The harbour continued out to the sea. There were swimmers despite a run on the water. Young boys, barely in their teens. Kenneth caught his breath as he saw one boy dive. He did not re-appear for what seemed a long time to Kenneth but the other boys conveyed no concern. They swam round to the other side of the boat just as their friend popped up having dived under the hull of one of the large boats.

Shaking his head at this folly Kenneth moved on until he came to the first of the statues he had, so far, only seen in the distance.

Diary Entry (early August)

Interesting set of statues. Quite impressed. Suit the setting. Liked way spread out. That mermaid, looking out to sea, keeping watch over island together with Barbatsis. Hero of battle against Turks, so informed by Rania. Hoped I'd be here for Armata, re-enactment of battle, beginning of Sept. Could stay to see that and then leave.

Some days after his visit to the statues Kenneth started on the second of the books sent by his agent. He was finding 'The Magus' a little hard going, difficult to follow at times. Was it the mind of the author or the mind of his protagonist. At times he thought he had entered another dimension. Were there some pages missing? Had he nodded off and skipped pages? None of these. Kenneth noted the page number, closed the book and decided to take a walk to Seven Islands for a G&T.

Being early evening the garden was empty apart from one lady sitting in the corner near the roadside hedge of geraniums. She was expensively dressed, almost flamboyantly, yet Kenneth observed and admired the stylish ease with which she wore the outfit. She returned his stare. Did he detect a twinkle? As she reached to take her glass the sleeve slipped back to reveal the slender arm that had acknowledged Kenneth from a balcony. Courteous as ever, Kenneth smiled and approached the lady.

'May I buy you a drink?'

'How very kind. A G&T please, one ice.'

A pleasant well-modulated voice, the English perfect. So perfect Kenneth thought the lady was not a native speaker, yet there was no trace of accent.

Kenneth returned with the drinks. Placing them on the table he introduced himself before sitting down. The slender arm which Kenneth found so alluring stretched out towards him. The hand was cool.

'My name is Rania and I'm very pleased to meet you.'

She raised her glass.

'I hear you are planning an extended stay on Spetses.'

It was a statement, not a question.

'Not really. I intend to leave shortly. Do you live on the island?'

'No. I live in Athens but I have a house here so we come for weekends or celebrations.'

'And is a celebration the reason for your visit this time?

'We're here for my name day. A big day here in Greece.'

'Rania?'

'No, there isn't a Saint Rania as far as I'm aware. My middle name is Mary.'

'I see. What is the date exactly?'

'August 15th'.

'Ah, yes, the Assumption. That would be your house in the Old Harbour, where I saw you?'

'That's correct. I presume you were on your way to see the statues? What was your opinion?'

'They were… interesting. I was particularly drawn to the mermaid. Most impressive, especially when viewed from behind and she is set against the skyline. I expect the animals and their bells cause amusement for the children.'

'Not only the children. I have seen many older people have a little tinkle!'

'Quite. Who was the sculptor?'

'A very famous Greek sculptress, Natalia Mela. The Bouboulina statue on the other side of the Dapia is one of hers. She had a house here on Spetses.'

'The island does seem to have a special attraction. An atmosphere. Can't quite put my finger on it.'

'So you've felt it already…'

'This may sound rude but your English? It's so correct. The inflection so pure.'

'I've spent a lot of time in England. I love the people, the language, the culture.'

'To be so immersed. Would you by any chance have read 'The Magus'?'

* * *

Kenneth returned from the evening encounter. The night air was refreshing. He found he could write for a while after these walks. Two plastic carrier bags were hanging on the door handle. One contained the books Bekim had borrowed with a short note thanking Kenneth, saying how much he had enjoyed them. Kenneth felt somewhat disappointed he had been out when Bekim called and wondered why. Was he feeling bereft of male company? Perhaps he could leave a message in the town suggesting Bekim call and borrow more. The other bag contained fruit. No note. Kenneth wondered who had left that bag. Surely if it were Bekim he would have made some mention of it. He would need to ask Mrs Eleni.

As he switched on the living room light he detected a sudden movement from one of the pictures. In a flash, whatever it was had disappeared. He thought it looked like a gecko but maybe the shadows were playing tricks. Something else to ask Mrs. Eleni?

Diary Entry (early August)

Rania. A charming, cultured lady. Incisive wit, quite subtle. Keen observer of life/people. Most pleasant evening. Pity she refused - most graciously - offer of dinner. Pleaded prior engagement. No mention of 'another time'. Suggested I stay for Armata. Puzzled re her cryptic comment on Magus discussion. 'Be sure you are not drawn in as Nicholas was.'

Had strange dream, mermaid with face of Ice Queen beckoning. A figure - a blue-eyed Poseidon - coming between us, threatening me, an invisible force around me to protect me. Mixture of day's events, nothing really strange. Nothing to worry about.

Kenneth rose early, showered and dressed. He took his breakfast on the balcony so he could see Mrs Eleni arrive. This morning she arrived side-saddle on the back of a very antiquated bike that surely would never have passed any MOT. The handlebars were adorned with several bags. The driver had very long grey hair, with the biggest walrus moustache Kenneth had ever seen. He watched Mrs Eleni descend from the bike and retrieve her bags. The bike chugged off in a cloud of dust and fumes.

Kenneth met Mrs Eleni at the end of the walkway, divested her of the bags and stood aside to allow her to precede him into the house. The bags being deposited on the kitchen table she began to unpack. She stopped when she saw Kenneth was still there.

'Yes, you want?'

Kenneth indicated the fruit that had mysteriously appeared the previous day.

'You buy? Why? I have.'

'No, I didn't buy. On door, in bag.'

'Ah, thora, present.'

'Present. Who?'

Mrs Eleni shrugged her shoulders.

'Someone. They like you. They bring present.'

That mystery was solved, at least in part. Kenneth still remained, embarrassed.

'Ela! Ti theleis? What you want?'

'The other room, last night, behind picture, gecko.'

'Gecko?'

Kenneth mimed something small moving quickly. Mrs Eleni watched patiently.

'Small, long tail.'

'Ah, micres savras. Yes. Ok. No problem. They lucky.'

'They?'

'Are two.'

'Two?'

'Yes, two. Boy, girl. They OK. No worry.'

She returned to her unpacking. Work tops were now spread with ingredients for the several days' meals. Pans and other pots were being noisily assembled. Kenneth had been very definitely dismissed from her domain.

* * *

After leaving his breakfast tray with Mrs Eleni Kenneth decided to walk down to the Bouboulina statue for a closer look. Lifting the Panama from its peg near the door, he left the house and strolled down to the town. Bikes loaded with shopping whizzed by him in both directions. By now he had learned to keep to the side of the roads trusting in each rider's ability to avoid him. He had learned there were few accidents on the island. It was tourists, many unused to bike riding generally, in particular the style of riding on the island, who caused accidents. He had considered hiring a moped or bike but had decided he preferred the walking.

Passing his bar of choice he waved a greeting to Kostas who was inside taking stock, in readiness for the evening - a daily need in August when the bar often didn't close till the early hours. The two bars opposite the Agia Mama beach, who offered English breakfast, were doing well. There were several couples and families already ensconced on the beach. Some newly arrived, judging by the pinkness of their skin. No doubt they would 'overdo' the sun worship and suffer in consequence.

Other people were wandering along the shop-lined street which led to the fish market where the locals were scrutinizing the day's catch. Today there were some octopuses drying on a line strung between two chairs. The usual group of feral cats hovered, hoping for some cast-offs. They were rarely disappointed. Kenneth hurried through the market. At least the smell was fresh.

He walked by the picturesque wooden cafenion which only seemed to accommodate men although being assured by Kyria women were not banned. Indeed she herself had, in the past, frequented it on winter nights. She no longer chose to go there. Why, she did not say. He walked up the steps, between the coffee shops and restaurants on the left and their tables on the right, overlooking the harbour. Prices were higher here. Locals laughing as they said it was to pay for the view. Turning slightly to the right he arrived in Bouboulina Square where important events took place.

The tired-looking hotel to the left reminded Kenneth of the grandiose Victorian style. A notice at the entrance advertised a classical piano recital that evening. Free entry he noted, making him ponder on the price of the drinks. Going to such a concert on this island seemed like a novelty. As it appeared to be a local performer he thought there was a good chance the Ice Queen would be there.

Having made that decision he went on to inspect the statue of Bouboulina. Made of bronze it depicted an ornately dressed, delicate figure of a woman, shading her eyes with a hand as she gazed out to sea. It didn't seem to fit the character of the woman Rania had described. He had pictured a more robust, stronger figure. He wondered how true to life it was or did it depict the ideal of a local hero. As far as the craft wrought in sculpting the statue Kenneth admitted it was a fine piece of work.

He consulted his watch. The tiny diamonds that served in place of numbers gleamed in the mid-day sun. He strolled on, through the area of Kounoupitsa with its bars, restaurants and the taverna on the beach. On to the Spetses Hotel where he decided to go in for a pre-lunch drink. Threading his way through the foyer of the hotel he arrived at the beach bar. Disappointed there was no free table from where he could sit and watch the sea, he left and walked on.

His destination was the taverna where he and Kyria had had their first meal together. There were only a few tourists eating so Kenneth had no difficulty in finding a table. He didn't recognise the waiter who came to take his order but saw Takis busily cooking in the kitchen. He ordered keftedes, tzatziki, a portion of haloumi, a cabbage salad and a small beer. Takis saw Kenneth, waved and smiled, wiping his forearm across his forehead to indicate how hot it was in the kitchen. Halfway through his meal the waiter brought another beer. 'From Takis.' Although Kenneth would have preferred no more beer he did not wish to insult Takis so raised this second beer in thanks.

As he left the taverna a taxi was approaching. Kenneth gratefully hailed it. He needed a siesta before preparing for the recital he had seen advertised.

* * *

Kenneth thought smart casual for the recital. Mindful the evenings could be humid he opted for a pair of cotton trousers in what his tailor described as dove grey but he thought of as off-white. The shirt presented a problem as he wished it to contrast with the trousers but complement the dark navy deck shoes he proposed wearing. He finally decided on a rough linen shirt only a tad different in shade from the shoes. Long sleeved but the cuffs could be turned back for coolness. The shirt had been a gift from a former lady friend. A lady with impeccable taste, class and breeding. She would have been very acceptable to the family had he been inclined to introduce her. The relationship had been fine from Kenneth's point of view until she began suggesting possible changes in his flat, maybe even looking for a larger one. That heralded the end of that relationship.

Taking a final look in the large mirror he left the house early to take a pre-theatre drink at Kostas'. He would ask Kyria to take dinner with him after the recital. He was sure she would be there.

And she was, talking to a girl, late teens, dressed in a simple black cotton sheath with black velvet, ballet flats, her hair in a neat chignon. Kyria was wearing another Laura Ashley. This time in powder blue, a plain top with boat shaped neckline and a flared skirt. The thongs on her sandals were also blue. Her hair hung loose.

There was quite a crowd assembled. Most were already seated. Some stood at the back, others dressed as though just come from a day on the beach. Kenneth breathed hard at this. He saw it inappropriate apparel for a recital even on a holiday island. The lady in black approached the piano and lightly ran her fingers over the keys without actually striking them. Kenneth looked for a seat.

'I thought you might be here. I've saved you a seat.'

Taking his hand Kyria led him to two seats on the front row. Leaflets left on the seats gave them information about the pieces to be played. Kenneth noted there was quite an assortment of composers. As silence crept round the assembly the girl with the chignon began to play.

* * *

Kenneth and Kyria walked along to the pizza restaurant on the Dapia. Although this was not what Kenneth had in mind, he was more than pleased she had agreed to have 'a bite to eat'.

'That young girl is very talented. Do you know her?'

'Oh, yes. She was born and brought up on the island. Her parents were sitting just to the right of the piano. She's been with some of the greatest teachers in Europe.

Everyone says she has a great career as a concert pianist in front of her.'

'Of that I have no doubt. I do think there should have been more of a sense of propriety. One really shouldn't come to such an event in shorts and t-shirts.'

'Don't be so pompous. Those people probably had no plans to come, having just spent a day on the beach, so obviously weren't dressed 'appropriately'. Now, what sort of pizza would you like? I want the hot and spicy one.'

Diary Entry (early August)

Enjoyed concert. A varied selection of pieces. None too heavy. Hope pianist successful in life. Withdrew from potential disagreement with Ice Queen/ still think I was right re dressing appropriately. Can't believe I put up with eating what passes for pizza anywhere outside Italy. Obviously popular place though. Offer of drink at Kostas' refused, politely. Claimed early morning lessons.

The night was hot, sultry, sticky. Kenneth was suffering severe discomfort. The single fan rotating slowly did little to cool the room, merely circulating the stifling air. He lay naked under a cotton sheet. The windows and shutters were open with the mosquito frame in place. One mosquito had managed to negotiate its way into his bedroom. He watched it circling, its buzz hypnotic. Remembering male and female buzzed, a courtship performance, he tried to remember which one delighted in biting anything with blood. He believed it was the female. No matter, he would probably find out in the morning, if he ever fell asleep long enough for the mosquito, should it be female, to bite.

He heard the sound of a motor-bike struggling up the slope. It stopped near the church. He reached for his watch which lay on the bedside table. There was a full moon and the light penetrating the mosquito net intensified the luminous dial which showed just after three. Too late for visitors. Perhaps Esther's husband had had a late night with his friends. Didn't sound like his bike though.

The sheets were damp and smelling of salt. He rose and showered. He wrapped a towel around his waist. By the time he returned to the bedroom he had no need of one. The hot air had done the job of the towel.

He removed the crumpled sheets, replacing them with crisp dry ones. Maybe a Courvoisier would help him sleep. The towel now became a sarong, reminding him of time spent in the Far East. Savouring the smoothness of the drink he walked barefoot down the balcony through the suffocating perfume of the jasmine.

He was conscious of a heat spot emanating from the right. He descended the three steps to the garden and looked at the red bike entangled amongst well-established bushes. The tyres were flat. No-one had ridden this machine for a long time but it was from here the heat came. Kenneth slowly stretched out his hand and touched the engine. He quickly withdrew it. The engine was hot, as though ridden hard. He finished his brandy in one swallow and returned to his bed to dream of faceless men riding red bikes. The Ice Queen was riding on all the bikes.

Diary Entry (mid August)

Another missed opportunity. If only I'd set off an hour later she would have come to the house to give me invitation. Prepared to come to house. Always made excuses before.

What's changed? Not keen on kaiki idea. Don't think am a worrier. Just like to be organized. Have to adhere to arrival/departure times. Always liked choice in any situation. Leave when I want. Don't like being 'trapped'. As long as am with her will put up with almost anything. Why her? Why now? What is it with this island? Credit side she called me Kenneth again. Just Kenneth.

Kenneth had just finished arranging for supplies to be delivered. He had been surprised no delivery charge was made; just tip the person delivering the goods. These were often 'dropped off' on an employee's way home. Considering Kenneth's house was somewhat out of the way he suspected many detours were probably made. He was deciding whether to have lunch down town when he heard his name being called.

'Hi, Kenneth. I want to ask you something. Come and have a coffee. My treat.'

Kyria led him to a coffee shop giving a view of the sea near Agia Mama.

'What would you like?'

Kenneth thought of telling her just exactly what he would like. He resisted the temptation. Having a finely tuned palette as far as coffee drinking went he asked for a fresh orange.

'That's a good idea. I'll have one too.'

The order was given and surprisingly quickly delivered in frosted glasses, decorated with slices of orange and lemon, along with two glasses of iced water.

'I'm pleased I bumped into you. I thought I might have to come up to the house. It's this celebration on the fifteenth. I don't suppose you know about it?'

'Have heard it mentioned. Something to do with a name day, I believe.'

'Only the most celebrated of the year. It's the Feast of the Assumption. Sometimes called the Day of the Panagia, the Virgin Mary. I would say it's the biggest celebration after Easter. The island will be buzzing. Extra ferries coming. Everyone celebrates but especially those named Panayiotis, Panayiota, Maria, lots of Marias on this island, Marios and Despina.'

She paused to take a sip of her orange juice. Kenneth began to wonder what the point of all this was. He reached for his glass.

'Despina?'

'A form of the word for an unmarried woman, but also a name. I've been invited to a beach picnic down at Anargyri. I thought you'd like to come along.'

Kenneth carefully replaced the glass, trying to maintain his composure. She, this woman, was inviting him to join her on a picnic. Although wary of what it might involve he did not wish to lose the chance to spend time with her.

'That is very kind of you. I'd love to come.'

'Good. That's settled then.'

'How will we get there? Do we have to buy tickets, contribute in some way? Bring food or drink?'

'Oh, Kenneth, do stop worrying. I've invited you. You are my guest so all you have to do is turn up and enjoy the celebration. All the arrangements have been made. We're travelling by kaiki to Anargiri, leaving from the Dapia at ten.'

'And when would we be returning?'

'You are a worrier, aren't you? Possibly early evening... sometime.'

She drained her glass and rose.

'Must dash. Lots to do. See you on the fifteenth, Dapia, at ten. Don't forget your swimming togs. And shoes for a short walk. I have a surprise for you.'

Kenneth saw her hand over some money to the waiter and watched her disappear amongst the tourist throng. He finished his orange and wondered what her surprise was. He suspected it was not the surprise he would wish.

Diary Entry (Mid August)

Delightful day. Surprisingly enjoyable. Even boat trip. Enjoyed watching impromptu dancing. All locals, the indigenous/foreign inhabitants. All ages, families/babies to aged. Good food. Plenty to drink. Decided non-alcoholic as was going swimming. Kyria didn't swim. Said she had fear of open water. Why choose to live on island. What brought her here? What makes her stay? Asked me about my writing, interested on present project. (Wasn't totally honest there!) Maybe could ask her to help. Give me background. Shall watch for opening to broach subject. 'Enjoyed' surprise.

It was mid-afternoon when the sun was at its highest. Many of the merrymakers had repaired to the shade of the palm trees which formed a backdrop to the beach. Kenneth returned from a swim to where Kyria sat in the bright sunlight.

'Should we move into the shade? It's very hot now.'

'No, it's time for your surprise. No need to dress but put your shoes on.'

She led him from the beach, through the trees along a well-worn path. It was cool, refreshing, with a strong smell of pine. Kenneth perceived an air of intimacy.

'The smell of pine is quite exhilarating.'

'Yes, the island's former name is Pitoussia which means pine-clad.'

'A much more romantic name. Tell me, are you celebrating today?'

'I'm not Orthodox so don't celebrate name days and I gave up celebrating birthdays some years ago.'

'Any particular reason?

'Just thought it was time. How are you getting on with the writing?'

Kenneth noted how adept she was in veering away from a topic without being offensive or giving explanation. How often she didn't give direct replies when questions of a more intimate nature were posed. Once more she had deflected him from the personal.

The path led downwards and trees gave way to rocks. Up ahead Kenneth saw an opening. A fissure, just large enough to allow the passage of one person.

'This is my surprise. If you go through the opening you'll arrive in a cave of strangely shaped stalactites and stalagmites. The water is so clear you'll feel obliged to swim across to the small sandy beach. It's a magical place. Take some time there.

Feel the calm. Think about your heart's desire and it may come true.'

'Are you not coming with me?'

'No, I went once, a long time ago.'

'And did you achieve your heart's desire?'

'Go. I'll wait here.'

Again she had not answered the question. He turned and entered the cave.

* * *

It was not until he looked at his watch on emerging from the cave that Kenneth realised he had been gone over an hour. Kyria remained seated where he had left her.

'You look like Ægeus after his visit to Æthra. Only the seaweed is missing.'

Kenneth made no reply.

'Are you all right? You look worried.'

'Yes… yes… I'm fine. It's the time. I thought I was only in the cave for a few minutes.'

'The cave often has a strange effect on people. Come and sit by me. I'll tell you its story. There are many myths surrounding it. I don't know which one is true. The first is straight from a fairy tale. A hermit named Bekiris goes to live in the cave. A seal comes every day to feed him. A second story comes from the late eighteenth century. Some Spetsiots hide in the cave from marauding Turks. A man called Bekiris betrays them and they are killed. A third story comes from the Second World War. Some andartes - guerrilla fighters - from Crete are hiding in the cave. The Germans line up the population on the Dapia threatening to shoot all the men unless they hand over the Cretans. There are two slightly different endings. One is the Spetsiot men are shot. The other is a German lady living on the island pleads for their lives and no-one is shot. The Cretans escape.'

'Surely a shooting of such a large number of people would be recorded somewhere? Wouldn't there be a mass grave? A monument?'

'Yes, that's why I went to check out the island archives. They had nothing on Bekiris' Cave and no written records of the war years at all, with nothing to prove the Germans ever occupied the island, although it is accepted that they did. Only oral history and urban myths. But, as so often with myths, there may be some truth there.

I do wonder about the last version because I once saw two elderly men dressed in traditional Cretan dress arrive on the island carrying a wreath of leaves with blue and white ribbons. I have a photo of them laying the wreath at St Nicholaos'. They left the same day. I was told they'd come to pay their respects to Spetsiots who went to Crete to fight with the andartes but never returned. The archives were equally silent on this. For me there's a semblance of truth in this story. Why else would two Cretans do this? Maybe they were two of the andartes in the cave.'

'Possibly. I must say I have enjoyed today, especially your company. Perhaps...'

The end of Kenneth's sentence was lost in the call of a harsh siren.

'It's the boat. They're ready to leave. Come on, Kenneth. It's a long walk back.'

She rushed off down the pine-clad path. Kenneth followed wondering why fate was playing him so cruelly.

Diary Entry (late August)

Seems to be 2/3 islands worth day visit. Need to check timetables to see if possible. Spoke with tourist in Kostas'. Quiet chap. Came on honeymoon 12 years ago. Now here with wife/child. He's done three islands, recommends all of them. Start with Hydra, nearest.

Kenneth stood in front of the Dolphin office double checking the timetables to ensure he could get to Hydra and back in a day. He had decided that would be his first island visit. Kenneth knew from his studies of Herodotus the original name of the island was Hydrea, a reference to the natural spring on the island. Nothing to do with the Hydra of myth as many might think. Kenneth smiled wryly. Another benefit of a Classical Education.

The approach to Hydra was impressive, the rocky crags and fortress battlements with cannons facing seawards imposing. The Dolphin slowed to enter the harbour. The engines cut out altogether. An announcement informed passengers there would be a slight delay due to port congestion. Kenneth frowned.

He had been told it was a small island. It looked small. Just how big was the harbour? While the Dolphin bobbed and waited a big ferry slowly reversed out of the harbour. Was it really four months since he had been on that ferry?

The Dolphin could now enter. The mystery of the port congestion was solved when he saw a smaller boat advertising itself as a 'One Day, Three Island Cruise'. That, with the big ferry, had commandeered the berths available. Several donkeys, with unbelievable heavy-looking saddles, and their owners were waiting to transport goods and luggage.

This island really was car free. Looking at the shape and general terrain, how could it be otherwise? As Kenneth stared up at the mountainous backdrop he saw a bin lorry winding its way down a tortuous road. An obvious exception.

The Dolphin delivered its passengers, collected new ones and reversed out of the harbour into open water where it could safely manœuvre before continuing its journey.

There was a buzz about the harbour. The area proliferated with small shops, café-bars and restaurants. Lots of people, tourists by their garb. Far more than the island he had just left. Kenneth thought the majority Scandinavian by their appearance. He certainly recognised Swedish but also heard German.

On the far side of the harbour he saw teenagers jumping from rocks into the water. There appeared to be no beach. He wondered just how safe such activity might be.

The small harbour housed many small craft, fishing boats, kaikis and water taxis. Kenneth could see no mainland. How far and how much crossed his mind. Needing to get away from the press he turned down a small passageway. Steep steps led up, away from the harbour. The height of the buildings on each side shaded the sun but the air was hot, unpleasant. The buildings were mostly residential with an air of uniformity, white framed windows contrasting pleasantly with the stark grey of the walls.

A notice announced further steps led to the old city with several churches and monasteries, extolling the wonders of their old wall paintings. Kenneth turned aside and followed another narrow passageway. He was pleased when he came to a more open area with the ubiquitous shops and tavernas. He observed the prices displayed at the latter were considerably cheaper than those on the front. As on Spetses sea views cost a lot.

He chose a small taverna, taking a seat in the shade. The table was spread with a paper cover, indicating it was an 'eating' table. A slow-moving waiter deposited a glass, bottle of water and plate of toasted, garlic bread. He also produced a menu. Kenneth ordered a small beer. The menu was geared to tourists, chips with everything. He thought of the play which he had seen in his student days. The play was highly acclaimed but Kenneth had not been impressed. His only contribution to the discussion that ensued being he saw no plot. A comment met with much heavy breathing and shaking of heads.

The beer arrived. Kenneth decided to order the coq-au-vin, with a green salad in place of chips. The salad was fresh and tasty but the coq-au-vin was not as expected. He wondered whether this was the Hydra version or a general Greek one. However, if he thought of it as chicken cooked in tomato sauce it proved palatable. He finished the beer, paid the bill and continued his wandering.

Coming out of the narrow passageways he found himself back in the harbour which was now empty of any large vessels. To his right was a large, impressive building.

He strolled towards it. A free leaflet revealed it as the Church of the Dormition, founded 1643, destroyed by earthquake 1750, rebuilt by Venetians. Once used as a prison, now housing historical documents, artifacts, icons, Byzantine and modern. There were also technical details of the architecture. Kenneth folded the leaflet and placed it in a pocket. Another travel article might be got from this visit.

Removing his hat he entered the church and relaxed in its coolness. Kenneth appreciated the architecture but experienced no feeling of spirituality. It was too ornate, too ostentatious. He returned to the courtyard where several statues were displayed. The majority, according to attached inscriptions, were heroes of the uprising against the Turkish Rule in 1821.

Kenneth looked at his watch. He returned to the main port area choosing to sit at a gelateria from where he could see the approach of his return Dolphin. He had no desire to miss it. Not wishing to risk the coffee he indulged in a banana split. What arrived was amazing. Two bananas, three large scoops of ice-cream, pistachio, vanilla and chocolate so dark it was almost black, a variety of fresh fruit, a selection of chopped nuts, topped with honey and a sprinkling of chocolate whirls. It was served on a large plate and accompanied by a complimentary glass of water with mint encased ice cubes. It cost as much as his earlier repast but was much the better value. Kenneth wondered if he had time to finish this feast as he espied a dot on the horizon.

Diary Entry (late August)

Another scorcher, windows open all night. Thank the lord for mosquito netting/ few around despite dried up river bed. Temp 45/47 yesterday, unbelievable. Wind searingly hot. From Africa. Red dust everywhere. Electric fans worse than useless. Like standing in front of giant hair-dryer. Watched electric storm over Hydra last night. Amazing coloured lightning. Reminded me of Caribbean. Told hottest summer on record, following coldest winter. How cold is winter here? Won't be here to find out. Hope it's cooler tomorrow for my trip to Ægina.

It was a slightly longer journey to Ægina. The harbour there was different from that of Hydra. A less spectacular approach but a wider aspect. Again the colour and vibrancy of the shops were obvious but this, to Kenneth, had a more leisurely feel, not so hectic.

He strolled down the jetty to where the town began and was drawn towards an establishment that declared itself 'The Yacht Club'. He had noticed a long balcony overlooking the sea front. It would be relaxing to sit there, watching the world of Ægina go by whilst sipping an ice cold beer.

There was a young Greek man, also enjoying a beer, sitting at the table adjacent to Kenneth's.

'Good morning. I hope you are enjoying your visit to my island. I'm Angelos.'

A strong, cool hand was extended.

'My name's Kenneth. I'm only here for the day so won't have much time to appreciate its obvious beauty.'

'That's a shame. Perhaps I can recommend what you should see to remember the best of Ægina.'

'That would be most kind of you. May I compliment you on your English? It's very good.'

'Thank you. I had a very good teacher. I was on the island of Spetses for a while and had lessons with an English teacher there.'

'I too am staying on Spetses for a few months. The teacher you mention. Would that be Kyria.'

'Yes, that's the lady. Do you know her?'

'We have met once or twice.'

'Please tell her Angelos sends his love and hopes she is happy.'

'Most certainly. Now, what can you recommend?'

'Well, of course, it all depends on your interests. The most famous feature of the island is its temple to Æphæa. It's the only remaining example of a two storey temple and well preserved. The name comes from a Greek word meaning someone who vanishes into thin air. Great views of the Saronic Gulf. On a clear day you can see the Temple of Poseidon in Sounio and the Acropolis of Athens. In ancient times this had religious significance, these three temples forming a sacred triangle.'

'And how would I get to this site?'

'The sun's getting hotter so I suggest a taxi. Not all the drivers want to go to the temple and wait but I know one who is willing and speaks English. There's a short dirt track which the taxi can't negotiate but Fotis will wait there while you walk the rest of the way. I notice you are sensible; you have a hat with you. If you want he can tell you a little bit about the temple.'

'Not too much or too technical.'

'I'll let him know…'

Angelos led Kenneth down to the harbour where several taxis idled in the sun. He spoke with one of the drivers and then returned to Kenneth.

'I've agreed a good price for you. Pay him when you come down. I've taken the liberty of telling him to take you to the beach taverna over there.'

Angelos pointed to the right of the harbour. 'It's quite atmospheric. You feel as though the sea is lapping round your feet.

The fish is so fresh you'd believe it'd just jumped out of the sea. I'll call and let the owner know you'll be along later.'

As Kenneth got into the taxi he turned to shake hands with Angelos.

'And in case you're thinking it, I don't get a rake-off.'

'Did Kyria teach you that expression?'

'She certainly did, amongst others. You'd be surprised how colloquial I can be.'

I probably wouldn't Kenneth thought as the taxi took him to the Temple of Æphæa. On the run up the driver revealed the legend. How she had escaped from sailors bent on having their wicked way with her, running up the mountain to disappear into thin air.

'She was mountain hunting goddess. She take care for virgins, like Athene do. Before many years Ægina very important ship island so she take care for sailors.'

'A busy goddess. Why haven't I heard of her before? Are there other temples dedicated to her?'

'No. Maybe something with Cretan goddess but different name. I wait here. You take time. No problem.'

The short path up to the temple caused Kenneth little effort. Grateful to escape the story of the Cretan connection, he had been interested to hear of the uniqueness of this temple's architecture dedicated to a busy lady. The cella had two rows of columns supporting another level of columns that reached the roof. Kenneth strolled round the ruins. There were few visitors. Most came early in the morning. When it was cooler, he had been informed by the knowledgeable taxi driver. Kenneth considered he had spent enough time being suitably impressed by this gem and returned to a dozing driver who woke instantly on hearing Kenneth return.

'She very beautiful, no?'

'Oh, very. Yes, very.'

'I take you to have nice meal by the sea. Cool there. Very good fish.'

Angelos had been quite correct. The ambience of the taverna was without question in keeping with eating fish. Kenneth chose Greek cod with a garlic paste, a plate of horta and a large beer. As he watched the sea lapping towards his table but never quite reaching it he thought of Kyria, wishing she were here to enjoy the tranquility.

After being pleasantly surprised the bill was not overly expensive he saw the dot on the horizon. He left the money on the table, waved his thanks to the waiter and set off to the nearby harbour. He stood a little aside from the small group waiting to board.

'Did you enjoy your day on my island?'

'Angelos! Yes, I did, very much. The meal was especially enjoyable. Are you also leaving?'

'No, I just came to see you off. It was pleasant meeting you. We're like ships that pass in the night.'

'Another expression from Kyria?'

'Of course. Have a safe journey.'

The siren sounded its last warning for boarding. Kenneth strode quickly up the gangplank. The manœuvres to the open sea safely completed the vessel continued its journey. Kenneth watched the figure of Angelos, arm raised in farewell, disappear much as Æphæa must have done.

* * *

'I hear you've been island hopping Kenneth.'

'In a manner of speaking. As I'm only here for a comparatively short time I thought I'd take in a couple of the nearby islands.'

'Which have you been to so far? Hydra, I expect, it's the nearest.'

'Quite. It seems very popular.'

'You know Leonard Cohen has a house there. Often comes over, wrote one of his most famous songs there. 'Bird on the Wire'. You'll find it on an LP in the house.' Again her knowledge of music and of the house. He was sure now there was a very definite connection. He decided to check it out before they met again.

'No, I didn't know although I have heard of Leonard Cohen. I'll certainly look for the LP.

One of his exes was a Cohen fan and he had listened to what he considered very gloomy songs the lady had insisted on playing. Maybe that was why the relationship didn't last. However, if Kyria was a fan of Leonard Cohen he was more than prepared to give the gentleman another chance.

'Where else have you been?'

'I went to Ægina. A little less crowded. I met an ex-pupil of yours. A very pleasant, polite young man called Angelos. He spoke most highly of your skills as a teacher. He sent his love and hopes you are happy.'

'Oh, yes, I know Angelos. A lovely young man. One of my better students. Are you thinking of anywhere else before you leave?'

'I think Poros. It seems I can get there and back by Dolphin although I will only have a few hours there, unless I stay overnight.'

'No need to do that. I can take you there by car if you'd like.'

Oh, the politeness of the English language. If he'd like! Dismissing the urge to get on his knees and kiss her hand in gratefulness, he engaged the reserve of his back-ground.

'Well, if it wouldn't be too much trouble. I'd pay for the petrol naturally.'

'Fair enough. I drive, you pay.'

'You said a car. Should we hire one?'

'No need. I have the use of a friend's car. It's old but it goes. It hasn't been driven for a time. I'll get someone to go over and check it out, oil, water, petrol. Be nice to get off the island for a while. No more classical tours for me as they have an official guide now. She wasn't available the time you went. I just stepped in. Just think, we may never have met.'

Kenneth didn't believe in fate but he began to wonder. Was the island exerting its mystery again?

'Any particular day of the week you'd like to go?'

'Well, I'm very flexible. Can always put my writing on hold so I can fit in with your lessons.'

Kenneth's writing seemed to be on permanent hold at the moment. Far too much going on in his psyche and far too hot. He knew he was trying to justify not writing but further excused the lack of by saying he still had the Autumn, less action, a more salubrious climate and still time to be home by end of November at the latest.

'Are you sure it will be all right with your friend?'

'He won't mind at all. The car is at my disposal any time I want. We could go over next Sunday. We'll get the first car ferry at 7.20. The car's just over on the mainland. We'll make a day of it.'

The longer the better, thought Kenneth.

'That sounds very pleasant and I'll leave the itinerary to you.'

'That's arranged then. I'll meet you down the Dapia at 7. Wear stout shoes and don't forget the hat.'

The impish grin told him he was being teased again.

* * *

The god looked down on his sanctuary, thronging with suppliants. He watched one couple strangely out of place. From foreign parts by their dress. They spread a cloth, placing bread, cheese and olives and ate. The other suppliants seemed not to notice them. The dream faded. The sky was still dark as Kenneth woke and reached for his watch.

Early but he didn't want to risk missing the ferry and losing a whole day in the company of Kyria.

Diary Entry (late August)

Told Kyria how a dream had foretold our picnic. As I did realized I was the god, not the man with her. Reflecting own insecurity? Does blasted man follow us everywhere? Rest of day went well.

Dawn had completed its dawning as Kenneth approached the Dapia with a youthful spring in his step. Kyria was waiting. She was wearing a blue, yellow and orange outfit in thin cotton comprising harem style trousers and a long sleeved caftan. A straw hat with fresh flowers complemented the outfit. Were the flowers for him? Instead of the usual toe thonged sandals she was wearing plimsolls with white ankle socks, giving an air of vulnerability she sometimes displayed and which he found so appealing.

There were few foot passengers on this ferry crossing and only a few vehicles, mostly motorbikes. On the Mainland Kyria led him to a dirt path away from the main parking area. There, in splendid isolation, stood a not so splendid car. Underneath the dust was a bright yellow Citroen, a classic in its day but not well cared for of late. Would have been the pride and joy of someone when first purchased. UK plates, a right hand drive, automatic. Kyria looked at Kenneth's astonishment and shrugged.

'It goes. Kenneth, I know I said I'd drive but would you mind taking over? I'll give directions.'

They set off. Kenneth had never looked forward to anything so fervently in a long time. He felt like a young child given a special treat. There was no more conversation until they were approaching Porto Heli.

'Remember, we're turning right so don't need to go all round the roundabout.' Kenneth nodded. Having safely manœuvred the roundabout he was informed he should follow the road to Kranidi.

'We're going to make a short detour for breakfast. Koilada is a pretty fishing village. Fewer than three hundred people live there. It'll be lovely to have coffee overlooking the bay.'

Anything you want was the driver's thought.

'Should I look for a sign indicating the turn-off?'

'I'm not sure there is one. I've only been once before and I wasn't driving then either. But it's the first turning left. You can't miss it!' She laughed.

Kenneth's thoughts raced. Who was driving? Was it in this car? Was it the owner of the car? If so, where was he now?

'Here's the turnoff.'

A few minutes later the village came into sight.

'I told you it wasn't far. Let's park the car here and walk in along the sea front.'

They passed several tavernas offering fresh fish, later in the day, when the boats came in.

'The fish here is wonderful. Maybe we should come one day for lunch?'

Kenneth almost gulped. 'That would be something to look forward to.'

'There's also a cave we could explore. Quite close. Prehistoric remains were found, evidence of humans living there for thousands of years. After all, you do need to get all the experiences in quickly if you're not staying for the winter.'

Teasing again?

Although Kyria had mentioned coffee Kenneth was pleased she took tea for breakfast, with the fresh croissants and honey. Their table was near the sea, overlooking the bay. The air was fresh and smelled clean. For a moment Kenneth thought of his home with its noise and pollution. Would it be such a bad idea to stay here, with this woman? He was aware she was speaking.

'Penny for them.'

'Oh, they're really not worth it. I'll pay the bill and then we can be off.'

* * *

The car was once more on its way.

'We can avoid Kranidi completely. Stay on the main road until we come to a roundabout.' She giggled. 'Yes, another one. Take the third exit towards Ermione. Taking this road will take us round the town, avoiding the hold-ups in Kranidi.'

'Hold-ups?'

'The town was never built for the amount of traffic it now has so traffic jams are a way of life.'

'Don't people get annoyed?'

'Of course they do. But they just sit and toot their horns till the jam clears. We'll bypass Kranidi completely but if you'd like to consider another experience there's always the Thursday morning market. I sometimes go myself.'

Kenneth mentally chalked up a further chance to spend time with Kyria.

'There's another roundabout coming up but we'll need to go straight on.'

The two roundabouts safely negotiated, the road now followed the coast. A busy tourist spot apparently as Kenneth noted several camping sites, hotels and tavernas.

For the next thirty minutes or so there was a relaxed silence. Just like a real couple.

'The area we're in now is Troizeneia. Very important in ancient times.'

'The Theseus connection, I believe.'

'But it was also one of the biggest cities and very important politically. They had a close connection with Athens. After all, Theseus was the founder of Athens. Ah, sorry, I was forgetting your classical background.'

Kenneth momentarily took his eyes from the road to look at her but she was smiling.

'The road sweeps inland now towards Galatas where we can take the car ferry over to Poros.

'Cars are allowed there then?

'Yes. On both the islands.'

'Pardon?'

'Poros was originally two islands. Kalavria, very ancient, is the bigger. Sferia is the small promontory in the south. That's where the capital is. The two are now joined by a very narrow strip of land. Don't worry, there is a road bridge which is quite safe to cross. But we're not going to Poros immediately. As we have a car I thought we'd take in some ruins and have an early picnic lunch there. We'll buy fresh bread, cheese and olives from a patisserie on the way. We'll also need more water and soft drinks.'

There was a pause. Her voice seemed to falter. 'Quite romantic...' Kenneth knew the last phrase was not for him. He wished he knew more of her past.

'We have to drive through Galatas. There's a ten minute drive to Trizina, the new town, and then another short drive to Ancient Troizeneia. We can park the car and wander round the ruins. It's quite atmospheric.'

* * *

Leaving Galatas behind they drove along the road which now led to a small hillside town surrounded by olive and lemon trees, fruit bushes and flowers. They stopped in the village for their lunch items which Kyria placed in a small rucksack taken from the boot of the car. Driving a short way they came to a Y- junction.

'Go left and park the car on the verge.'

'Will it be safe to leave the car here? What about other traffic, visitors?'

'This spot is not on the tourist route so there are no buses and few people bother to come here. Only the really interested seek this out.'

'Or the ones who find it romantic.'

There was a moment's silence during which Kenneth wished he had not made such a trite remark. He watched as Kyria reached for her rucksack and swung it on her shoulder. Kenneth thought better of offering to carry it. Within a few yards they came to a very large boulder. A nearby plaque proclaimed it was the very stone Theseus had lifted.

'Must have been a strong boy.' She smiled.

Kenneth smiled back. He had been forgiven. 'Most people think he used a lever.'

'Just imagine. And long before Archimedes…'

He was enjoying the intellectual sparring. It was going to be a good day and maybe she would thaw a little.

'Where do we go from here? I'm entirely in your hands'

How he wished he were. 'This site was omitted on my first classical tour.'

'From here we walk up to the corner of the road and then follow it to the Tower. Only the lower section of the tower is ancient. The rest is much later. The high position of this place made it a good place to have a fortress.'

For the next hour they wandered around the site, the Temple of Hippolytus, the Sanctuary of Asclepios to which so many came in hope of being healed. They recalled the myths and legends associated with the area. Ghosts of people long dead watched benignly.

'It is said that Phædra is buried here, somewhere.' Kyria spread her arms.

'There's a certain irony in that.'

'This place seems so spiritual.' Kenneth recalled the walks with his mother. 'I can almost believe there is real substance in the myths and legends. Here… they come alive.'

'Look, over there. The beginning of some restoration, clearly showing what a vast place it once was. Sadly many of the stones were taken to help in more recent buildings.'

Kyria slipped the rucksack from her shoulder.

'There is shade among the olive trees. Shall we sit and have our lunch before I take you to the Devil's Bridge?'

'The Devil's Bridge. What…?'

'Don't be so impatient. Wait and see.'

As Kenneth ate his lunch he looked at the ruins, imagining them re-built with modern stones. This would show how it once looked but it would attract the tourist buses.

They would destroy the ambience he now felt.

He was happy Kyria had explained there were no plans for an immediate dig. Apart from comments praising the taste of the cheese, the sweetness of the olives and the fresh bread, they ate their meal in companionable silence. Packing the remains into the rucksack Kyria again swung the bag over one shoulder.

'Let's go. The Devil's Bridge awaits!'

They walked back through myriads of poppies growing out of the ruins. At the Tower Kyria led Kenneth along a rough track, through damp undergrowth and tangled trees. The track became a narrow footpath and suddenly they were there at the bridge which spanned a deep gorge.

'It doesn't actually look like a bridge. More like....'

'Shush. Listen, close your eyes and just listen.'

They both stood in silence with eyes closed.

'What can you hear Kenneth?'

'Only the rustling of the trees and yet there is no wind.'

He opened his eyes. Kyria still had hers closed.

'It's the trees whispering. They are whispering of times past.' She opened her eyes. 'Silly, aren't I? What did you think the bridge looked like?'

'Part of an aqueduct.'

'How very perceptive. It is the remains of an ancient aqueduct. Come on; let's get back to the car and on to Poros.'

* * *

Kenneth took his seat behind the wheel but Kyria turned, pausing for a moment before getting into the car.

'Just saying goodbye to the ghosts'.

Was there any ghost in particular? Wondering about a possible deeper significance of the brief visit to the Devil's Bridge, Kenneth turned the key in the ignition. Ten minutes later they were back in Galatas. Having bought their ticket they parked behind a small queue of cars waiting for the next ferry. The car ferries plied back and forth every half-hour. The kaikis, for foot passengers, could hold pole position for ten and then had to make the crossing whether they were full or not, or so Kenneth was informed.

A ferry arrived, cars were efficiently disembarked and the waiting ones embarked. The stern doors were still rising as the ferry pulled away.

'It's a short crossing. Not worth getting out of the car. Keep the window down as someone will be along to check the ticket.'

The ferry approached Poros.

'As soon as we've left the ferry area turn left on to the main road. That will take us over the bridge to Kalavria. We'll head up to the Temple of Poseidon and the Sanctuary of Asclepios. There are plans to excavate but they haven't started yet so we can roam freely. Poros was important in ancient times. This temple and sanctuary were not only religious and a place of safety and healing but had great political significance.'

'If I remember rightly this area was also the centre of a sort of co-operative of local settlements, before the city states became firmly established.'

'Now, bear left. We have to negotiate a couple of loops as we climb but it's straightish from then on. Should take about ten minutes barring mishaps.'

Kenneth decided not to ask what the mishaps might be.

The site was totally deserted as they parked the car to one side of the narrow road leading to the ruins.

'I was hoping the wild flowers would still be out.'

Kyria drew Kenneth's attention to the carpet of pink, mauve and purple. She bent to trail her fingers lightly over this carpet. Kenneth imagined being stroked in this way by those fingers. She rose.

'The ruins do give some idea of the extent of the place. It was of importance for a long time. Probably from 6th century BC at least to Roman times as some of the surviving bits bear witness. Up to 4th century AD when an earthquake destroyed it.'

'Quite an irony as Poseidon was also in charge of earthquakes. Someone must have annoyed him.'

'Probably. In the Poros museum there is a foot belonging to a large statue, said to be Poseidon. The length of the foot suggests the statue was about five metres high.'

'There must have been other statues in such a large temple. Were no more remains found?'

'Not so far. Rumour has it that people from Hydra helped themselves to stones from here for their own building projects.'

'So re-cycling isn't a new thing, then.'

'Oh, Kenneth you can be so droll when you relax.'

Kenneth had never before been described as droll but was pleased his comments amused his companion. An hour later, their rambling over, they returned to the car.

'Where now, my classical guide?'

'There you go again. We'll make a little detour before going down town. Maybe have a coffee.'

She gave directions. They arrived at a small taverna with a few tables overlooking the steep, tree covered slope leading to the sea. There was no-one else there. Leaving Kenneth to sit at his table of choice Kyria went into the taverna. Kenneth watched her in conversation with the proprietor. She came out smiling and sat opposite him.

'I've ordered a cappuccino for me and fresh orange juice with a dash of lemon juice for you. I know how particular you are about your coffee drinking.'

The coffee and orange were delivered along with a plate of butter biscuits. The man disappeared into the taverna. Kyria pulled a face.

'We really shouldn't as it might spoil our dinner but as these are offered free we have to be polite.'

'Why don't we share one? That will surely satisfy politeness?'

Kenneth broke the biscuit and offered half to Kyria. Their fingers touched, causing tingles in Kenneth. Lost in a brief reverie he realised Kyria was speaking.

'Just through those trees, round the corner, there is a monastery. Just to prove Greece isn't just a land of ancient ruins we'll take a walk. We can refill our water bottles from the fresh spring.'

'Is the water safe to drink?'

'People have been filling their jars and containers from it for centuries and there have been no epidemics so, yes, I would say it's safe.'

They collected the empty water bottles from the car and Kyria led the way through the trees and round the corner.

Kenneth was surprised to see a large edifice imposing in size and its simplicity. The high walls appeared to have no entrances. There were large numbers of loophole niches which gave it more the appearance of a fortress than a monastery. Kenneth turned to his companion.

'How does one get in?'

'There is only one main entrance. We've missed the visiting hours. In any case I think we've done enough cultural activity for one day.'

'Are there any monks living there now?'

'Usually there are only one or two monks in permanent residence although holy men do visit for temporary stays.'

'And the name of this monastery?'

'Zoodochos Pigi.'

'Which means?'

'The spring of life. Some say it refers to the Virgin Mary but I think it refers to the spring where we're going to replenish our water supply. Then it's time to eat.'

'We can leave the car at the ferry car park and walk through the town or by the sea, whichever you like.'

* * *

The car had been parked. Kenneth looked at the throng of people jostling through the narrow passageway with colourful shops on one side and outside café areas on the other. The sound of vendors loudly declaring theirs was the best, menu chasers approaching tourists to claim theirs was the best, the most delicious. The smell of different styles of food, traditional, fast food.

'I prefer the sea side.'

Kyria smiled. 'Good choice.' They walked along, making their way through a small crowd just disembarked from a Dolphin. It made its way slowly down the narrow strait between mainland and island before reaching the open sea and engaging full throttle. The kaiki ferries were doing good business. No empty trips this day. Deserted fishing boats, their work done, were tied alongside, with nets spread out to dry. A few fishermen were selling the remnants of their catch.

Past a square which marked the end of the tourist section. More official or domestic buildings on the left. They had almost left the town proper when they came to three tables overlooking the strait. Their large, blue and white umbrellas not only proclaimed their Greekness, they complemented the blueness of the sea and sky.

'Here we are 'Meze, Meze'. It's shady outside under the umbrellas and we have the cooling breeze from the water so let's sit outside.'

No sooner had they sat than a smiling lady, mid-twenties appeared with two glasses of minted iced water.

'Welcome Kyria. A long time to see you.'

'Hi, Sylvana, time passes so quickly. This is Kenneth, staying on Spetses for a while.'

Sylvana smiled a welcome at Kenneth. She left, returning at once with a paper tablecloth, also blue and white but with nautical knots, a basket of bread which smelled as though fresh from the oven, cutlery and two menus. She gave Kyria one before hesitating.

'Would you like a menu in English, Mr Kenneth?'

'Thank you. I believe my knowledge of Classical Greek may carry me through. If not I'm sure Kyria will help.'

'Don't be too sure. There are times when I have to ask for explanations. Pleased I have on some occasions.'

Sylvana left them to peruse the menu.

'How hungry are you? It is some time since our repast with Theseus and his fellow ghosts.'

Kyria laughed at this levity from Kenneth. He loved it when she laughed.

'Do you have any favourites?'

'I am partial to whitebait and tzatziki. Not averse to fried squid.'

'Fine, I like the meat balls here, spicy. The stuffed peppers are delicious so we'll have some of those.'

They discussed the other mezethes and decided on grilled haloumi, butter-beans, dolmades, and fava as well as their own personal choices. The cold dishes were brought straight away whilst the hot ones were being freshly prepared. They discussed their day.

'I wish to thank you for suggesting you accompany me on my trip to Poros. I am most grateful.'

'Don't be so formal, Kenneth. I've enjoyed it and wouldn't have offered if I hadn't wanted your company. After all, we are friends aren't we, for as long as you choose to stay? And you did say you'd pay the expenses so you can pay the bill and then we'll be off. I have a special treat for you. It's my treat and I'm paying.'

The bill settled and goodbyes said, the two retraced their steps to the town proper. Suddenly Kyria took his hand and led him across the road.

'Now for your treat.'

Kenneth thought it was treat enough to hold her hand. She led him through the press to a gelateria where Kenneth was faced with the widest selection of ice cream he'd ever seen.

'There must be nearly thirty flavours from which to choose.'

'At least. I suggest we get double cones with a different scoop in each cone.'

'I think that may be too much after the big meal we've just eaten.'

'You're probably right. Nevertheless I'll settle for the double cone with pistachio in one and coffee with chocolate chips in the other.'

Kenneth settled for a single cone with raspberry ripple. Crossing back to the sea side they sat on a bench staring across to the mainland. The sun had been replaced by a full moon which shone brightly over a calm sea.

'I remember the last ice-cream cone I had. We had gone to our town house. My nanny took me to the park. She bought me an ice-cream from one of those vans with the silly jingles. When my mother found out she was furious. It wasn't 'done' to eat in public and who knew what germs lay in such a van.' Kyria stood and took his hand.

'We've had a lovely day and we both enjoyed our ice creams. Let's agree to leave all our ghosts behind just for this one day.'

Their hands remained together till they got back to the car.

'Just follow the signs for Spetses.'

* * *

The car safely parked, they took a water taxi across to Spetses. Kenneth held out a hand for Kyria to alight.

'Nightcap at Kostas'?'

'Would you mind if I gave it a miss. I have an early start.'

He watched her walk up the steps. She paused and waved before rounding the corner. Kenneth walked along the front to Kostas' and ordered a Courvoisier. Kostas brought it over to the table.

'Good day?'

'Yes, very good, almost perfect.'

Almost but not quite. Perfect would have been if Kyria had come home with him.

* * *

A field of poppies, the wind rustling trees that weren't there, whispering her name but he couldn't find her. Suddenly she was there with arms outstretched. She was walking towards him smiling. She wanted him. As she approached he saw her eyes. They were looking not at him but through him. She walked through him. When he turned she was gone. No, not gone. Two shadowy figures away in the distance. One a man with his arm around Kyria. The man turned. Even at that distance the mocking, triumphant smile could clearly be seen. The poppies grew to immense heights. They closed in, enveloping him. The smell of the poppies smothered him. He couldn't breathe.

Kenneth woke. The air in the room was stifling. He rose to open the window wide, hoping the morning air would dispel the overwhelming aroma of poppies.

Diary Entry (first week September)

Strolled down town at dusk. Crowd gathering on town beach near Kostas'. Ambled over to sea wall. Children focus of attention - all bearing model boats. Some should surely never be near water! This proved when launched bearing candles, supposedly the masts. Much excitement. Children AND adults. Wonder who actually assembled these constructions! Seemed idea how far boats would actually go. Most sank quickly, candles spluttering. Others managed further. Water reflected flames, very atmospheric. Only one left. One little boy ecstatic. His boat sailed bravely on till it too disappeared. Cheers all round. A few moments everyone gone. Charming, apparently pointless, ceremony. Heard Kostas' voice behind me. 'That's it for another year. Coming in for a G&T?'

He watched her across the bar. Kyria was with another woman, her own age. A woman he'd not seen before. Presumably from the Ice Queen's homeland. She had alluded on one occasion to being English. Although her origins had never been discussed that slight English Northern-ness no longer bothered him.

He rose from his table, taking the few steps that brought him to the two women.

'Might I buy you two ladies a drink?'

'Oo, dun't you talk posh. G' on then. Mine's a lager and lime.'

The blonde girl giggled. Kenneth cringed, inwardly. The Ice Queen looked amused. Kenneth subdued, he hoped, his antipathy at the pronunciation of lager and lime.

'And for you?'

'My usual, thank you.'

Kostas had heard the exchange and was already preparing the drinks as Kenneth turned to the bar, an action that involved no steps. Implacable as ever Kostas made no comment as he recorded the drinks next to the appellation 'The Toff'.

'There you are, ladies. May I join you?' With no dissent forthcoming he sat down.

'Kenneth, this is my friend Cathy. We were at university together. She's here for a short break to see the Armata. Cathy, this is Kenneth, a writer. He's staying on the island for a year, writing a book.'

More giggling ensued from the blonde. 'Din't know you knew anybody like 'im. Is 'e yer bloke?'

Kenneth cringed again. He wondered how the two had become friends and why their speech differed so greatly. Kyria did occasionally slip into a full pseudo-northern accent but he was never sure whether that was merely to mock what she perceived as his prejudices. Kenneth always protested no such prejudices but often displayed a belief in a North-South divide and would have to admit he had never 'dated' a Northern girl - but not from choice. He just hadn't met any. Not quite true he mused. He had done a book tour which included several Northern towns. No, he had to be honest, not towns as such, universities, when he had written the final volume of the quartet - a history of his own family from the Norman Conquest. The women there were certainly on his intellectual level and there had been the occasional one-night. He couldn't claim deep knowledge of any of them, often failing to recall names and faces.

'No, we've merely met socially, once or twice.'

'Oh, aye!' Cathy giggled, giving an exaggerated wink.

This is going to be a fascinating evening thought Kenneth as he raised his glass.

* * *

As Kenneth escorted the two friends back to the house for 'a convivial brandy and coffee' his brain raced. Would this be the night? The night the Ice Queen melted. He had managed to lay in a supply of Courvoisier and The Bitch continued to send regular supplies of Blue Mountain - probably thought it would inspire his writing.

Kenneth allowed himself a brief smile as he re-called the raised eyebrows on leaving the bar with an attractive lady on each arm. And the conspiratorial wink from the island drunk. The clarity of the night sky was striking. The singular lack of light pollution meant Kenneth was seeing stars more brightly than ever before.

'Admiring our beautiful sky, Kenneth? We see more stars without a moon but the moonlight is so romantic.'

Kenneth wondered if she were flirting with him. Who knew with her? Before he could reply the friend struck up with a slightly out of tune rendition of 'By the Light of the Silvery Moon'. The moment was lost. They walked on.

Diary Entry (first week Sept cont)

Friend not my type, blonde, buxom, exceptionally 'jolly'. Coffee/brandy on balcony. Lied re no ice when friend asked. Really, ice in brandy. Might help local sort, but Courvoisier! Conversation surreal. Friend's incessant spiel re benefits of living on Greek island. Interrupted by Ice Queen asking for 'Red, Red Wine' by Neil Diamond. Noted in previous conversations she possessed eclectic knowledge of music. Found track. That could have been the moment. Eyes closed, wistful smile on her face. Looked vulnerable. Can't believe friend. 'Like UB40's version better. You can dance to that'. I could have danced to Neil Diamond's version - with Ice Queen in my arms. Another moment lost. A night to remember indeed. Expected friend to react favourably. But what to make of Ice Queen. What a response. So cool about it all. Not to mention her friend. Might use episode in future novel - or maybe not... Not sure which I enjoyed most, anticipation of being the filling in the sandwich or the Ice Queen as voyeur - totally unexpected. Wonder what The Bitch would think of that. Surprisingly friend quite the whore, exceptionally inventive. Ice Queen watched seemingly impassive to antics. Some point she left. Found her later, sitting in dusty earth of back garden. That Golden Shower business. Not used to my ladies holding out so long. Great Caesar's ghost! Is she mad or just trying to drive me mad. What do I have to do?

Kenneth stared down at the buxom figure lying beside him, her mouth slightly open, her breath coming in little snorts. He felt nothing. Pulling on trousers and shirt he slipped his feet into a pair of moccasins and left the house.

The moon had disappeared behind a single cloud but the stars shone clearly over the back garden where he found Kyria staring out to sea. She didn't turn but must have sensed his approach. She raised a fragile arm, pointing, 'Can you see Peter Pan?' She was pointing at Kenneth's Manikin Pis. How vulnerable she looked. Why now? Here? Why had he never noticed this before? She spoke without turning her head.

'Have you ever performed a golden shower?'

He was stunned, not certain he'd heard correctly, but the question was repeated, almost sadly.

'Well, I, I… Would make rather a mess… of the bed, you know…'

'Not if it were done here…'

A whisper now. Before he had chance to make any response she had turned. With a bright smile and in a pleasant voice she spoke quite normally.

'Is Cathy ready to go? Thank you for a most delightful and entertaining evening.'

* * *

The next morning Kenneth woke late. He looked at his watch, eight thirty. He decided he would shower, stroll down to the Old Harbour and have a croissant and coffee at the taverna over the water. He found the early morning smell of the sea clean and invigorating. On arrival he found the boatyard a hive of industry. Foregoing his breakfast for the time being he went over to ascertain what all the activity was. He found Kostas, leaning on a pedal bike complete with front basket, watching the activity.

'Good morning, Kostas.'

'Good morning, Mr Graham. Didn't expect you to be up and about so early.'

Kenneth decided there was no innuendo intended so took the comment at face value.

'I did rise somewhat later than usual this morning. I have become accustomed to rising early as I find my writing is at its best then. Might I ask what is happening here?'

'They're building a replica of the Turkish ship for the Armata next weekend. They started a few days ago.'

He went on to explain.

The ship being built was a shell mock-up of a Turkish warship. Well known over the centuries for their expertise in boat-building the Spetsiots, this time, were definitely not aiming at sea-worthiness or any endurance. The ship's only purpose was to be towed to the town harbour where it would be packed with explosives and fireworks to form the impressive, explosive finale of the re-enactment of the 1822 battle. At the appropriate time the fuse would be lit by a brave fellow in a rowing boat, the length of the fuse allowing for his safe retreat.

Kostas mounted his bike and rode off towards the lighthouse. Kenneth watched the work in progress for a while, then made his way to the taverna over the water, only to find it didn't serve breakfast. Not wishing to sit inside the only snack bar that did serve anything approaching this repast he returned home, stopping at the bakery to buy freshly baked croissants. He would sit on his balcony with a cup of Blue Mountain and croissants spread with some of Esther's quince marmalade. Then he would catch up on his diary, maybe do some serious writing, or not, as the mood took him.

* * *

Kenneth was sitting in Kostas' listening to ex-pats giving a brief explanation of the history of the Armata to tourists. The biggest secular celebration of the year, of great importance to all Greeks, celebrating a major sea victory of 1822 during the War of Independence against the Turks. The island heroine, 'Admiral' Bouboulina, didn't take part in this battle. She was busy blockading Nafplion.

What was far more entertaining were the accounts of the years when things went awry, not quite going according to plan. How many were true or even partly true Kenneth had no way of ascertaining, but the anecdotes seemed to improve with each telling.

Kenneth took another sip of his G&T as he heard yet more accounts of previous celebrations.

'Remember when the boat broke its moorings and floated out to sea?'

'Yeh, the water taxis had to tow it back.'

'Did they? Don't remember that. Thought it was the kaikis.'

'Naw, the water taxis.'

'Were you there when the boat blew prematurely? You could see the man rowing for dear life. Very funny.'

'Actually, not very funny.'

'Well, suppose not. But no-one was hurt so we can laugh about it now.'

'I was away for that one but I do remember when there was so much smoke the tourists who had paid to be part of the sail-past couldn't see a thing.'

'Wonder if they got their money back!'

This comment was received with guffaws of cynicism.

'Remember the year when the sea was so rough the Port Police wouldn't allow the 'Armada' to leave the Old Harbour so the tourists dipped out on that one too.'

More laughter. The island drunk now joined in.

'I'll tell you one I remember. The year we had all the fires. Some wanker went online and told everyone the Armata was cancelled 'cos o' the fires. Stopped a lot o' people coming. Caused a lot o' fuss and anger.'

'Someone on the island?'

'Oh, aye. But my lips are sealed.'

'Was that the same year the Mayor said he couldn't afford the Armata?'

'Just the fireworks, I think.'

'Didn't the local businesses step in?'

'The one I liked was the year the 'plane came without the wreath.'

'What was that?'

'The Second World War 'plane that comes on the Sunday morning to drop a wreath. That year it just circled the Dapia and left. No wreath.'

'Naw, don't believe that one. Did you actually see it happen.'

'No but...'

'Well then...'

And so it went on.

* * *

Kenneth had a shower and dressed casually. He took a large G&T to the side balcony where he sat, watching Peter Pan, as he now thought of his Manikin Pis, waving gently in the breeze. The drink finished he strolled down to the town.

The Dapia was packed. Tourists came from wide and far to see this historic event celebrated. All the coffee shops, bars, restaurants, with views directly over the harbour had been pre-booked for weeks. For most of them this was the last big chance to make the money necessary to survive the winter. Booking a table meant buying a meal afterwards, not that any place serving food would be short of customers this night. The only time of the year, Kenneth had been told, that every room from the prestigious and expensive Spetses Hotel down to the room-only establishments would be full, many booked months in advance by Greeks not only from Athens but all over Greece.

Kenneth chose to stand on the steps of the Dolphin office from where he had a clear view of the boat representing the Turkish flagship. As he waited for the show to begin, scheduled for 9 pm but already tardy, he wondered if all would go well this year. The sudden blast of martial music issuing from loud speakers scattered around the Dapia signalled the beginning of the show. Kenneth looked at his watch. Not that late by Greek standards.

He listened assiduously as the historic battle was described in both Greek and English. He heard how the small fleet of ships attacked the much larger fleet of the Ottoman navy. How Spetsiot hero Kosmas Barbatsis sailed his ship close to the Turkish flagship, setting it alight. The Turkish fleet losing heart and fleeing. The commentary in Greek and English was interspaced by sounds of gunfire, cannon and explosions.

Then the grand finale. A tiny boat could be seen hurrying from the 'flag-ship'. Flames slowly enveloped the ship. They reached the hold packed with explosives and fireworks. The entire Dapia was lit up in a fantastic eruption of noise and colour.

More fireworks and cannon fire joined the extravaganza.

'Oohs', 'ahhs', 'bravos', 'oraios' rose from the crowds as their attention turned from the burning wreck to the display in the sky. A bright blue-white flash lit up a face in the crowd. His Ice Queen was transformed into a child as she laughed with delight at each bang and crackle. But between the laughs, when only the slightest of smiles played on her lips, he thought he detected a happy sadness of a past Armata.

When he looked again she was gone. Vulnerability or childlike qualities? Was this what attracted him? Did he feel protective for the first time in his life? Some great hurt he couldn't reach? He would one day, despite what the wise woman had said.

Smoke and the smell of burnt gunpowder hung in the air as Kenneth strode along the sea front to Kostas'. The bar was full, inside and out, with people standing on the roadway, using the window sill as a table. He saw Kyria sitting in the window seat. She waved.

'Come and sit here. We can move up. Might be a bit cosy, though.'

She gave Kenneth a cheeky grin. 'Demi, Alexandros, this is my friend, Kenneth.'

'The writer from England.' Alexandros extended a polite hand, then waved it at the bar, catching Kostas' eye who nodded.

'Welcome, Kenneth.'

Demi patted the space made when she moved closer to Kyria. Kenneth had hoped the move would have been the other way.

'I'll get a drink first.'

'It's already done. Tonight you are our guest. Demi and me will practise our English. How was the anniversary for you?'

'Celebration, not anniversary.'

Kenneth cringed at this perceived rudeness. The other three laughed. Demi explained.

'We ask Kyria to correct our English. It is good for us.'

'And we don't pay,' laughed Alexandros. 'So, how was the celebration?'

'Well, nothing untoward happened this year as far as I could tell. A decent show of fireworks. Quite impressive, overall.'

The evening continued easily with Kenneth receiving an invitation to visit Demi and Alexandros for coffee one day. They lived in the Old Harbour and Kenneth realized he had passed their house several times. In the early hours the company broke up.

'We'll walk with you to your house, Kyria.'

Kenneth wanted to say 'I can do that' but she had always refused his offer to see her safely home. Once more he didn't want to risk public rebuttal.

* * *

The Armata weekend over Kenneth decided he would take up the offer of coffee with Demi and Alexandros. He had learned that Demi was an art and drama teacher at the local public schools. Kenneth was confused until Kyria explained. Public in Greece meant State, not private! Alexandros was a world-renown art restorer, working mainly for the church. He also gave private art lessons.

Kenneth chose to go in the early evening. An art lesson was in progress and Demi was nowhere to be seen.

'I'm sorry. If this is an inconvenient time I can come back.'

'No, it's OK.' Alexandros indicated an archway. 'Go there. The class is nearly finished.'

Kenneth looked round the room in which he waited. A comfortable room. Lots of artwork about. He was about to check out the signatures when Alexandros appeared.

'Would you like tea, coffee, a beer?'

'Whatever you're having will be fine.'

'A beer, half and half. Demi will be late. She has, how you say, practice with play.'

'Rehearsal?'

'Yes, rehearsal. I hear her bike. She will want herb tea.'

Alexandros filled the very small pan Kenneth now knew as a vreki with water and put it to heat. By the time Demi had parked her bike and climbed the steps to the house her herb tea was waiting.

'Welcome, welcome, Kenneth. Very pleased you came. I had a practice with the children. We are playing a theatre.'

'Oh, is it a play I know?'

'It's 'Peace' by Aristophanes but I have made it more simple.'

'Not Lysistrata, then?'

'They are children, Kenneth.'

'I think Kenneth is making fun, my sweet.'

'And will this play be performed in their school?'

'No, we have a lovely theatre, Kapodistriaki, very beautiful. Everyone will come. You must come.'

Surprised the island sported a theatre Kenneth wondered what it was like. Although he wasn't too keen on the idea of a simplified Aristophanes he thought the Ice Queen would probably be there. Maybe they could go together.

'But you didn't come for the children. You want to see Alexandros' work. You go to look and I'll order souvlaki. I know Alexandros wants two. Kenneth?'

'One will be quite sufficient, thank you.'

'One hour, OK?'

Alexandros led Kenneth to a smaller room filled with all the tools of a serious artist. Positioned to benefit from the light of two windows a table easel held a gilt frame. What it encased was so grimy it would have been totally unrecognisable had it not been for one tiny corner, an inch square. The vibrant golds and reds suggested it was an icon. Alexandros confirmed this.

'That corner took me about two weeks.'

'So just this one piece could take many months?'

'To do good job, yes. If quick, maybe damage icon.'

Alexandros went on to explain the difficulties of working on such old pieces. How he needed to prepare compatible mixtures to match pigmentation.

'One time I was on Mount Athos. Very old paintings on walls. How you call? Frescoes. Very strange place. Didn't feel good there. Wouldn't want to live like that.'

'Why do you live on Spetses?'

'Everyone lives somewhere. I came for love. This is Demi's island.'

The door-bell rang, interrupting their discussions.

'The souvlakia has come. Let's eat. Do you know why I always have two?'

Kenneth shook his head. Alexandros took one souvlaki in his right hand and a second in his left.

'For my healthy. One in each hand. A balanced diet.'

Diary Entry (late September)

Jolly nice chap Alexandros, sense of humour, obviously very talented. That icon, revived, brought to life, cleaning, repainting, repairing, whatever necessary. Came here for love. Could I do same. Why even think it! What is it about this island that draws people?

It was a beautiful balmy evening. He had enjoyed a leisurely brandy at Kostas', savouring the thoughts running through his head. He walked on firmly, deliberately, contemplating what awaited him. The Ice Queen awaited his attention. The restraints may be cutting into her ankles and wrists so he mustn't dawdle. The substitute hood was amusing but the t-shirt worked well. The metal clang of the gate would alert her to the fact that someone was approaching. But would she know it was him? His excitement rose. He opened the bedroom door and gazed at the bed. He closed his eyes and heard a sigh. His own. Pulling the door to he moved to his writing desk. He reached for the bottle to the right and poured two measures into the embossed brandy snifter he always carried with him, a reminder of his heritage. Taking the fountain pen he slowly unscrewed the top, placing it carefully back on the stand. He thought the practice of appending it to the end of the pen passé.

He wrote steadily for two hours, only pausing once to refill his glass. He slowly screwed the top back onto the pen and replaced it on its oak stand. He entered the bedroom, sat on the edge of the bed, removed his shoes and stripped naked before lying down on pristine sheets, hoping he would dream of the night his Ice Queen would lie beside him.

* * *

The next morning Kenneth sat on his balcony re-running his fantasy of the previous evening. He needed to get away for a while. Away from the influence of this island. Somewhere nearer reality. He nodded, drained his Blue Mountain and went inside. He lifted the telephone receiver, dialled a number. A male voice answered.

'Good morning, Nikki. How are you fixed for a short visit from an old friend?'

Diary Entry (early October)

Visit to Athens. The red eye. Seat at front, bouncy. Had hoped for 40 winks. School kids on day trip, noisy exuberance, teachers ineffective. Pleased won't be on their return journey. Overnight case sufficed for 2/3 nights. Met by Nikki at Piraeus. Quite a number of tourists about considering end of season. Ones who waited till schools back. Is it really nearly five months since I boarded ferry here? After this visit will dash off book. Leave before winter sets in.

The beauty of the sunrise, now seen through the bow windows of the Dolphin never failed to bring forth Kenneth's admiration. It reminded him of the early communes with his Mater. The old bird was still that way inclined, even in her late sixties. Prone to long walks in the woods which covered their extensive estate, collecting herbs, plant roots, remedies for her children and the servants. Would never have a conventional doctor in the house with their chemically produced potions. She did her duty by Pater, hosted his dinner parties, entertained when required, produced three sons.

Pater must have married her for her beauty. Probably lineage played a big part. Her family went back to the Norman Conquest, Pater's only to the Wars of the Roses.

Having ensured the family line was secure, the children all safely reaching maturity, Pater went off travelling, disappointed his eldest son and heir appeared to be following in the steps of Uncle Toby, his older brother who 'failed' in his duty and took to the hills to paint whence he disappeared, leaving the second son to carry the burden of preserving the family line. Kenneth didn't mind the comparison as Toby's work had been exhibited in the Royal Academy. Perhaps he could achieve similar heights in literature although, he hoped, not posthumously, as did Uncle Toby.

The drone of the engines slowing brought Kenneth out of his reverie. He allowed the children to disembark before collecting his case.

'Kenneth, over here.'

'Nikki, good to see you again. How's the family and how did you manage to park so near to the arrivals?'

'The family are all fine. Another one on the way. And the parking, old boy, is courtesy of diplomatic plates. Sling your bag on the back seat and I'll drop you off by Syntagma. Should be in time for the Changing of the Guards. Don't believe you've ever had the pleasure.'

'I've actually seen very little of Athens. If you recall, previous visits have all involved a lot of wining and dining more than sight-seeing.'

'Talking of which I've arranged to take you to 'Oroscopio'. Italian restaurant not far from the flat. We can walk there, eat, have a few jars and catch up. Make sure you give yourself plenty of time to shower and change.'

'What about the wife?'

'Come now, old boy, how often do school chums get the chance to meet up? Oh, in the glove compartment you'll find a map of the centre where most of the interesting sites are, a key to the flat in case there's no-one there, and my card which is English one side and Greek the other. Just in case you have a problem with the taxi. Don't forget the water. I see you're still sporting the old Panama. Isn't it time you got a new one.'

'A new one wouldn't be worn in like this one.'

'Quick. The lights are against us. Jump out and watch the traffic. Remember a green man in Athens doesn't mean it's safe to cross, only that you have a sporting chance. The bikes come from anywhere. See you tonight!'

The noise was horrendous. Kenneth dodged quickly between the revving cars as he saw the lights change. He had only once driven in Athens. Never again. He hated the buses, close proximity of people, smells, pick-pockets. He had similar views of any underground transport. Although he had driven on the family estate from an early age he preferred to take taxis in London and other cities. Much more relaxing and convenient.

Kenneth stood in front of the impressive Parliament Building, the first royal palace, where the Changing of the Evzones - the Presidential Guard - would take place. To his left, on the corner, he was attracted by a stall with the most colourful and varied profusion of flowers he had seen since helping his father's head gardener set out the very regimented flower beds.

He strolled over and realized it was not a single stall. At least a dozen stretched along one wall of the state building. They seemed incongruous in the midst of the hectic movement of people and traffic. The stall holders were doing good business and Kenneth was impressed by the deft way flowers were selected and quickly presented in attractive fashion. The heady aromas from the mingling of the various perfumes offered a pleasant, if brief, respite before exhaust fumes overwhelmed them.

He was aware of sudden movements as customers and vendors moved aside so a clear passage was available to one of the most bizarre sights Kenneth had ever seen. Three strangely dressed figures were marching down the street in single file and in a fashion the like of which Kenneth had never before witnessed. Something akin to a goose-step he thought but quickly realized this was not so.

The march was quite slow with the left leg conforming to the generally accepted performance of marching. The knee of the right leg rose to waist height before the bottom half of the leg was thrust out and forward, the foot striking the ground strongly with a metallic clank. As they passed by Kenneth saw the clog-like shoes worn were of red leather decorated on the front with a large black pom-pom. He wondered how the clogs were retained as the backs were very low. How many 'faltered' on the slippery pavements and what punishment would be meted out to any who dared to fall. Maybe the thick, white wool tights helped the grip. The rest of the outfit comprised a white, thigh length, multi-pleated kilt - Kenneth remembered Nikki telling him there were four hundred pleats to represent the number of years of Turkish rule - an exquisitely embroidered, sleeveless, high necked jacket which revealed the voluminous sleeves of a white undershirt, and a red skull cap from which a black tassel hung over the right shoulder to the waist.

Kenneth followed the three and joined the crowd which had gathered to watch the ceremony. Most war memorials or graves of unknown soldiers made reference to modern conflicts. Kenneth was captivated by the large relief which formed the back-drop of the ceremony taking place. This memorial displayed a dying hoplite, not surprising considering the importance and bravery of these soldiers in ancient times. Perhaps also a reminder that war is a constant, mused Kenneth, as his eyes alighted on two plaques, one either side of the hoplite. He recognised the inscriptions on them as quotations from Pericles' funeral oration in Thucydides' play, 'History of the Peloponnesian War'. He smiled wryly, remembering his aging professor reciting the oration with tears in his eyes.

Diary Entry (early Oct Athens)
Beautiful desk Nikki's got here. Solid. Real Wood. Still uses fountain pen. Old habits etc. Mustn't touch that! He'd know. Only takes cartridges. Can use ink in mine. Strange ceremony that guard change. Bit drawn out. Wonder re origins. Popular with tourists. Wonder what young soldier chaps think of it all? Can't imagine it's popular with them.

The large crowd that had assembled for the ceremony began to disperse. The sellers of pigeon food, who had disappeared on the arrival of the soldiers, now moved back.

Children nagged parents for money so they could feed the birds. Kenneth looked at the pigeon deposits on the gleaming white marble area around the memorial. He hoped one day soon laws would be enacted prohibiting purveyors of food that encouraged such desecration by what he perceived as vermin. He had never been impressed by the pigeons in Trafalgar Square.

He consulted the map provided by Nikki. If he followed the main road away from the centre he would eventually come to the Olympic Stadium, used for the 1896 games. He could then walk past the Temple of Olympian Zeus to Hadrian's Arch and across the road to the Plaka - the tourist shopping and eating area.

He could escape the twin assaults of traffic noise and pollution on his health by cutting through the National Gardens. Although somewhat perturbed by the inordinate number of feral cats Kenneth revelled in the temporary escape from the noise of screaming brakes and blaring horns.

There was a slight smell of decay amongst the coolness of the trees and bushes, a smell that mingled and vied with the disparate flower fragrances. The rustling he heard in the undergrowth he discovered was made by tortoises, much larger than the pet shop ones he'd seen. He sat on a bench to enjoy the oasis of calm for a while. Several people passed, joggers, old men with sticks, old women in black carrying shopping, a few young women with prams. An attractive woman smiled as she passed: 'Good morning.' Did he really look so very English.

Moving on he passed a large neo-classical building which proclaimed itself the Zappeion, then followed the signs which would take him to the old Olympic stadium.

Finding the glare of the sun on the white marble too much he took the Carreras from his army pack. He could feel the heat from the seats as he climbed the levels. Staring down into the arena he watched several people running round the track. Kenneth left the stadium and moved on to the statue of Baron de Coubertin outside.

'Kalimera, an impressive statue, is it not?'

'Indeed. And we have him to thank for the return of the Olympics.'

The old man who had engaged Kenneth in conversation smiled and gave an almost imperceptible shake of his head.

'So most people would have you believe! But that's not quite true. It is true that this gentleman was responsible for the creation of the IOC in 1894.'

The old man smiled again. 'I'm sorry I detain you…'

But Kenneth was already captivated by this charming stranger and what he had to say.

'Not at all, please go on.'

'There has been a stadium of sorts here since the 6th century BC, from a simple racecourse to the marble beauty you have just witnessed. But the Modern Olympics were installed… no, no, that is not the correct word… revived, yes, revived, before Coubertin was born!'

The old man paused and removed a Panama hat more battered than Kenneth's.

'If you have a moment perhaps we could sit while I give you a little information?'

'Most certainly.'

Kenneth crooked his arm. The old man inclined his head in thanks and took the proffered help to the steps of the statue which provided a convenient seat. There he continued his story.

'We owe the Modern Olympics to Evangelis Zappas who sponsored his first Olympics in 1859. He bought this site, paid for its excavation and re-birth no, not again. I forget. I'm sorry, my friend. Its restoration, yes, its restoration.'

'Please, don't apologise. I think the word re-birth is most apt as the stadium became alive again.'

'You're very kind. But, please, do tell me if I use a word incorrectly. Now, Zappas actually gave money for marble to be used but this is Greece. They used wood!

The first games were held in 1859 but only included Greeks - from all round the world. Zappas died six years later and left a lot of money for the continuation of the games. It was not until 1896 that they became truly international.'

'Zappas? I passed an exhibition centre in the National Gardens. That was called Zappeion? There must be a connection.'

'You are an observant man. It was money left by Zappas that paid for the building.'

'So de Coubertin began the first International Olympics?'

This time the old man's smile was exceptionally broad.

'Not exactly. He helped but most of the money came from Greek philanthropists. The IOC gave nothing!'

The old man rose stiffly from the steps.

'It has been a pleasure to speak with you. I rarely get a chance to practise my English these days. I used to be quite proficient.'

'The pleasure was mutual, Sir. And your English would put many native English speakers to shame.'

The old man gave a final smile and left with a sprightly walk despite the cane on which he obviously relied.

Kenneth rose and took one more look at the statue, seeing it with different eyes. He braced himself to cross the road. The street down which he walked was obviously some sort of termini for the hundreds of buses which proliferated in the city. To his left he could see, through the iron railings, the ruins of the Temple of Olympian Zeus, a Roman construction. A very impressive sight, recent restoration indicating its original magnificence. Surprised to hear birds singing, he found a small rusting gate and decided to walk through the temple grounds to Hadrian's Arch, hoping, in this way, to avoid the worst of the bus fumes. He noted, as on the Poros sites, there was no charge. Crossing under Hadrian's magnificent arch, he crossed another manic main road and entered a quiet, once residential area, the architecture of which reflected its past glories. Musty trees complemented deserted, decaying buildings.

He walked on. To his left the Acropolis with its imposing Parthenon. He had spent a whole day there during his student visit. He came to an area he recognised as Roman in origin. A plaque told him he was looking at the Tower of the Winds. Kenneth looked at the two thousand year old, octagonal building which was probably the first real meteorological station with its sundials, wind vane and water clock. He smiled, almost fondly, as the building awoke memories of his Oxford days and his visit to the Radcliffe Observatory. Information there had stated James Wyatt had based his design on the very building at which Kenneth was now looking.

Walking on he came to a square. The cafes there catered more for the general tourist than the discerning diner. He opted for a plain omelette and a small beer.

Kenneth suddenly felt weary and decided that was enough for one day. He would go to Nikki's, have a shower, a siesta. He was looking forward to the meal at 'Oroscopio'.

He hailed a passing taxi.

* * *

'Let's sit outside. I think it's quite warm enough.'

Kenneth acquiesced and they chose a table in the corner, away from the road but giving an uninterrupted view of the square. Kenneth was impressed by the number of squares in Athens, the map clearly depicting the large number that dotted the congested centre. Areas of greenery which also bore witness to the culture of Ancient Athens.

Reminiscent of the agoras, it was to these squares families converged in the evenings with each generation enjoying the square in its own way. Sitting on benches recalling days of youth, eating, socialising, conducting business in a more relaxed atmosphere and all watching children, grandchildren meeting with their peers, playing, buying soft drinks or sweets from the quintessential peripteri.

Men with lottery tickets displayed on a notched stick, doing good business, selling hope - they were everywhere. Kenneth had never participated in any games of chance although his father enjoyed baccarat at his gentleman's club. Another disappointment for the family heritage as Kenneth had steadfastly refused to join any of the exclusive clubs to which his father belonged.

'Kenneth!'

'Sorry?'

'You were miles away there.'

'Just watching the children enjoying themselves. Now, what do you recommend?'

'Well, I know you're not a pizza man but for starters I always have the small taster plate of mini-pizzas, each with a different topping. Why don't you try those?'

'Fine. I'll take you at your word. Any suggestions for a main course?'

'I've never had a bad meal here so that's a personal choice. Do you still have a preference for fish?'

'Yes, and I think I'd like to try the red mullet with oranges and olives.'

'Good choice. I'm having the stifado. They make it with the traditional rabbit meat here. Love it but I can never eat it when the wife's around. Says it reminds her of the pet rabbit she had as a child! Ah! Good evening, Andreas.'

The order given and two beers being delivered the two men began their reminiscences of 'Do you remember when?' - 'Whatever happened to...?' - 'Did you hear about?'

Oxford seemed so far away in time and space. He had never gone back. Kenneth didn't do reunions - being polite to peers you never liked and probably who didn't like you. Being all jolly for the annual get together. Nikki was his only link with Oxford. Their friendship had worked - so far. No regular communication and very different paths in life. This visit was different. He seemed to have little in common any more. He felt restless. He didn't want to be here.

* * *

Diary Entry (post 'Oroscopio')

Are Nikki and I growing apart? The old boys' network. Don't remember half of them. Won't take up invite to ski in Parnassus, Use leg as excuse. In any case won't be here for the snows. Funny, don't associate Greece with skiing. That complimentary choc cake with hot choc sauce really finished the meal. Did feel somewhat bloated. Busy day tomorrow. Will walk it off.

Nikki had left for the Embassy a few streets away in Ploutarchou. Jennie, his wife, had taken the boys to their private school in the suburb of Pallini. She would then have the long drive back to join her husband at the Embassy where she worked in the visa section. Kenneth had only once asked Nikki what his job at the Embassy was.

'The usual, old boy. Pushing paper around.'

The reply was sufficient for Kenneth not to enquire further. He placed his cup in the dish washer and picked up his army bag thoughtfully filled by Jennie with two bottles of water, one frozen, two bananas and two apples. How very organised. He walked to the Hilton turning left towards the centre. He passed several kiosks on the way, all doing good business. It never failed to amaze him what they sold. He was particularly intrigued by the daily newspapers hanging up all around, attracting people who paused to read the front page headlines before moving on.

Turning right at the main post office he was now in a busy shopping area. Lots of small shops, a singular lack of chain stores that had mushroomed in London.

He came to a large church. A notice outside proclaimed it to be 'Metropolios'. Unless of great historical significance Kenneth didn't 'do' churches so he wasn't inclined to join the trickle of tourists entering. The church formed one side of a large square. In the corner of the square he noticed a café, the outside seating being shielded from passers-by with a tasteful display of potted shrubs.

As his breakfast had only been a cup of coffee he decided on a croissant and fresh orange whilst planning his day. Hunger assuaged he consulted his map. Seemed quite straightforward.

Leaving the square he entered the Plaka. Although invited to look further inside Kenneth moved swiftly past the assortment of shops, most selling very similar souvenirs. The Plaka, the oldest area of the city. Restaurants, cafes, shops. It appeared to be devoid of heavy traffic although a few deliveries were being made by motor-bikes, weaving in and out of a mass of people. Kenneth's first impressions were of colour and smell. Brightly coloured scarves and shawls, traditional and not so traditional articles of clothing, rugs, both factory and handmade. Lots of pompom slippers he noted.

Smells, compressed lamb or chicken being shaved from spits, coconut from street vendors who had arranged an ingenious contraption on a handcart to provide a waterfall to keep the slices of coconut fresh looking. Not so the sellers of watermelon slices although they did wave little paper fans to deter the flies, not always successfully. Kenneth never bought street food - anywhere.

Tourist shops selling the same items, mass produced. He admired the ingenuity of those shops which considered themselves above the rest by advertising they only sold genuine copies of an original, with a metal tag supporting the claim. Kenneth never bought souvenirs although he had, albeit rarely, seen an artefact he had considered but then realised how out of place it would be in his modern flat in London.

He stopped to peruse an impressive array of gold jewellery in a small shop that would not have been out of place in the smarter echelons of London.

'Oi right mayt? Ow bin ya?' Kenneth looked round, thinking he had misheard. A Birmingham accent - here? The man standing in the shop doorway enjoyed Kenneth's puzzlement for a short while and then continued, this time in quite standard English.

'Thought that'd surprise you. Bet you're thinking Brummie. Near enough. I was married to a girl from West Brom. Lived there over twenty years. Why don't you come in and chat for a while. I'll even make you a cup of tea - the English way!'

Almost on autopilot Kenneth followed this man into the shop. The man indicated a chair.

'Won't be a minute. I'll put the kettle on. A real kettle and teapot. Brought'em myself when I came back. Ta-ra a bit.'

He disappeared behind a gauze curtain through which Kenneth could make out a small kitchen area. He looked around the shop. Small, spotless, tasteful, but reflecting money. Genuine gold. Kenneth knew enough of that to be sure. A voice came through the gauze.

'Milk and sugar?'

'Just a spot of milk please.'

The proprietor came out through the curtain carrying a tray.

'That's the tea made. Leave it for a bit before pouring. My name's Pandelis.'

Kenneth stood up, hand extended.

'Kenneth, pleased to meet you.'

'I take it you're not from the Midlands, not with an accent like that.'

* * *

Leaving Pandelis and the cup of well-made tea behind Kenneth walked on down the street. Contemplating his surreal encounter he was hardly aware of the tourist shops or the proprietors trying to tempt him into their establishments. He came to a large square which he recognized as the one close to the Tower of the Winds. Instead of taking the exit he knew led to the Tower he took the exit next to the metro which led to Monasteraki. The stall and shops he now encountered must be the famed flea market.

An eclectic mix of antiques, genuine, quasi and downright fake, more tourist shops, bric-a-brac, furniture, an assortment of household goods, much busier than the more exclusive part! Locals looking for bargains, tourists looking for something different. Kenneth paused several times but moved quickly on when any approach was made encouraging him to buy or go inside to look. He eventually came to a T-junction. The metro line ran along the cross of the T behind a wall. A variety of spasmodic tables and chairs his side of the wall. The cafes to which they belonged lay across the road that proclaimed itself 'Thissio'. Here were also a long line of shops.

This area was not as claustrophobic as the flea-market proper. Loud music issued from one small shop. Music Kenneth recognized. He'd once had a fan of Chuck Mangione as a girl-friend. The music he now heard reminded him of their last date. She had insisted they attended a showing of 'Children of Sanchez'. As he passed the open door of the music shop he noticed a number of racks of LPs being avidly searched through by people of all ages.

There was little in the way of traffic so Kenneth decided he would partake of some refreshment. He strolled along checking each table, selecting one which seemed the most salubrious. As soon as he sat down a young boy came across the road to place a clean cover on the table, then returned with bread, water and a menu. Kenneth opened the bottle of water.

After a lunch of stuffed vine leaves and cabbage salad, washed down with a small beer he was surprised to be presented with a complimentary dish of Greek halva, served with an ice-cold glass of water. Although a little on the sweet side for Kenneth he found the syrup eased the grainy consistency down very well.

He watched people passing, noted how many couples there were. Suddenly he felt lonely. He thought of the visits spent in the company of Kyria and wanted her here, now, by his side. He paid the bill, walked to a main road and took a taxi back to Nikki's.

Jennie was cooking tonight. Kenneth couldn't wait.

* * *

Diary Entry (late Oct Athens)
Strange I find myself talking to people I wouldn't at home. They approach me, wouldn't happen in London. Here strangers are treated as guests/temporary friends almost.

Paths that cross for a brief moment of time, strangers may be gods - still in Greek psyche. Jennie's dinner predictable as always/her signature menu - smoked salmon/scrambled egg starter, steak pie (real suet topping), selection of fresh veg/creamed potatoes, apple pie/cheese, coffee - Nikki thoughtfully provided Blue Mountain. Jennie clearly just waiting for Nikki to return 'home'. Children at 'English' school etc.

The next day Kenneth decided to leave. He no longer felt in tune with Nikki. They had chosen different paths. Their previous connections were in the past and not standing the test of time. Nikki would understand. But Kenneth did question whether he was looking for an excuse to return to the island.

He took his coffee and croissants on to the balcony from where he could see the heights of the prestigious Hilton. His eyes moved to the left, down towards the centre.

Athens, the most beautiful, the most wondrous and, sadly, possibly the most polluted city in Europe. From the balcony of Nikki's house in the suburb of

Pangrati Kenneth could clearly see the pretty, pink cloud, hanging over the city, signalling high pollution.

He knew Athens rested in a bowl surrounded by mountains. As most Athenians did, he also hoped for a strong wind which would temporarily clear the pollution. Nikki had told him of Government measures to reduce the threat posed by the pollution, creating more green areas, restricting traffic so car owners could only enter the centre on alternate days. The latter failed as people merely bought an extra car. Traffic was certainly the biggest problem as far as Kenneth was concerned, the rule of thumb seeming to be if there were no free parking spots, use the pavement. He remembered his first visit with Nikki to the National Museum. Unable to find a parking spot Nikki had left the car across a corner, hoping his diplomatic badge would preclude the heavy and instant fines that seemed to have little effect anyway.

Kenneth's attitude towards Athens was very ambivalent. He loved it in so many different ways, the way the city had sprawled its way outwards, the mixture of old and new, the night-life, the hustle and bustle, the taxi drivers, the bus drivers who managed to remain sane through it all, the cosmopolitan atmosphere. In so many ways like his home city of London but with something more. He couldn't quite explain what it was but there was a sort of romance about this city.

Yet he found himself wanting to leave this city with its vibrancy, its life. He felt confused. He wanted, needed to return to the island. What drew him? The Ice Queen or was it the island itself? A cold wave passed through his body. He packed his bag and wrote a short note thanking his hosts. He closed the door behind him and dropped the key into the post box as he passed through the foyer. He called into the nearby florist and arranged for a bouquet to be delivered. His next call port of call was the liquor store next door. He paid for a bottle of Johnny Walker Blue Label to be delivered to the same address.

If he took a taxi he would make the first Dolphin. Striding to the main thoroughfare he crossed the road to stand on the other side of the road which led to the port, remembering in time Athenian taxis didn't do u-turns!

* * *

Kenneth approached the Dolphin office. He felt light-hearted, happy to be returning to the island. There was no queue at the office. He looked towards the Dolphin bobbing at its mooring. There was no gangplank in place and no crew members in evidence. A notice on the window of the deserted office informed him there would be no Dolphins that day due to bad weather but the slow ferry might be going.

Kenneth did not wish to stay in Athens any longer so strode to the ferry office and purchased a ticket. Although he would have preferred an outside seat all the passengers were being firmly directed to the inside lounges. A crew member was busy telling people to place all luggage on the floor so others could sit. Kenneth found a seat at the end of a curve of seats, pleased he wasn't so hemmed in as he might have been. Not as pleased there was already so much wafting cigarette smoke.

The journey from Piraeus to Poros, via the usual intermediate stops, was uneventful, with no sign of the bad weather foretold. People had disembarked at Poros but the ferry had not moved. An announcement, first in Greek, then in English, told passengers for Spetses to disembark and find alternative travel as the sea was very rough from Poros onwards. It was unlikely the ferry would be able to dock at Spetses.

No-one moved. The announcement was repeated. Several men stood, shouting. Among them Kenneth recognised Apostolis, the water-taxi driver from the Classical Tour.

'Ah, Mr Kenneth. Stay, sit. Another water-taxi man has gone to the captain to tell him his job. If the ship can reach Hydra it can go on to Spetses. Or maybe go to Ermione. Easier for Spetses there.'

A second announcement caused Apostolis to grin.

'Now the captain knows what to do.'

Everyone settled back as the ferry made its way through the calm waters separating Poros from the Mainland. The sea outside the strait was choppy. The choppiness increased. Luggage slipped from one side of the ship to the other as the ferry was buffeted by ever increasing winds. Old women began wailing, calling on the Panagia. Some older men crossed themselves. Parents clasped their children close. It seemed the ferry was making no headway but there, on the horizon, was Hydra. The sea and sky were both black.

Another announcement caused a mixture of relief and annoyance. The captain had decided it was too dangerous to continue. The ship would return to Poros and then go back to Piraeus. Kenneth turned to Apostolis.

'So....?'

'We have a long taxi ride to Kosta and then a water taxi over to Spetses.'

'What if the weather is too bad for them to come?'

'They will come. They always do. For their own.'

There was more wailing and crossing of breasts as the ferry went through its manoeuvres to turn. Kenneth braced himself against the back of his seat and grasped the front. Apostolis laughed.

'In case you were wondering, the life-vest is under the seat so your hands are in the right place.'

The ferry arrived at Poros once more. Taxis were waiting but Apostolis walked by them.

'We'll take the car ferry over to Galatas and get a taxi from there. It's cheaper. We go half and half.'

Apart from driving rain the road journey was uneventful. Several water taxis were waiting at Kosta, knowing from experience the Spetsai people would get home this way. Apostolis acknowledged all the drivers but chose a smaller taxi. The sea was choppy and the water-taxi bounced down hard as it made the short journey across to the island. Kenneth reached for his wallet but the driver waved away the offer of payment.

'Apostolis is my cousin and we are pleased you are both safely home.'

As Kenneth approached the house he wondered about what the cousin had said, 'both safely home'.

Diary Entry (mid October)

A most fortuitous meeting. Discovered she once lived in Athens. Said it was a long time ago. How often she hides behind that phrase. Her full programme explains recent lack of contact. Must ask Kostas about 28th.

'Hello, there. I hear you had a rough crossing back from Athens? You were lucky you made it by all accounts. The Port Police closed the port just after you got back. Ten minutes later and you'd have been stuck in Porto Heli.'

The day was bright and warm - an Indian summer. He had decided to walk along the pathway he had noticed behind the monastery. He had no fear of getting lost. As Kostas had once said, 'If you turn right or left on the main road you will eventually come to the town. Only a matter of distance!'

He had met no-one and the path had led to the main road. He turned left, having worked out that by keeping the monastery on his left he would eventually come to the garage. Several bikes passed him, some slowed to offer a lift. These he politely refused with a shake of his head. He felt reassured he was walking in the right direction when he came to a beach he recognised. Paradise Beach was obviously popular with tourists as it had always been full whenever Kenneth had walked that way. Now he thought there was a certain beauty in its deserted aspect and stood to enjoy the rustling of leaves and the lapping of water. His thoughts turned to all he would be leaving behind - soon. He thought he heard Kyria calling him. Did she want him to stay? Would he? Stay?

'Kenneth, up here. At George's.'

He turned. He had not imagined it. Kyria was beckoning him to join her.

'It was rough. Surprised how quickly it blew up. Is that a regular occurrence?'

'One of the joys of island living. You just get used to it.' She paused. 'If you stay long enough...'

The innuendo was not lost on Kenneth but he made no comment.

'How was your trip to Athens?'

'Fine. I met some interesting people.'

'I loved living in Athens... but it was all a long time ago.'

The conversation was interrupted by the arrival of an assortment of mezethes and a large jug of wine.

'Were you going to eat all this yourself?'

'Of course not. Yani saw you walking along and assumed you would be joining me.'

The smile told Kenneth he was, once again, being teased. But were they now being regarded as a couple? They began eating and the conversation revolved round his trip to Athens. It was a relaxed meal and the sun was setting as they left George's, Kyria insisting on paying as she had 'invited' him.

They stood to watch the sun complete its setting over Paradise Beach. Kenneth thought he was indeed in Paradise, if only for a brief time. They walked along the road until the turn-off that took Kenneth home.

'Thank you for your company. I must get on. Now the children are back at school I have a very full programme. But let's meet up for the twenty eighth, have lunch together.

Before Kenneth could reply or ask what was significant about the twenty eighth a bike had drawn up, Kyria had jumped on and was now being carried away from him. With a sigh but also a feeling of hope for the twenty eighth he returned to a lonely house.

Diary Entry (late October)

Must get on with writing if to be home for Christmas. Keep an eye on the weather. Have to prepare for the celebration - yet another. This one 'Ochi' day. Looking forward to lunch.

After breakfast Kenneth showered, shaved and dressed. He chose his outfit carefully, not too formal but displaying respect for the occasion and in consideration of the weather - a dreamy, bright autumn day. And also for the expected lunch with Kyria. Although he hadn't seen her since their chance meeting at George's he felt certain she would be there, waiting for him.

After checking his appearance in the big mirror he left the house, carefully locking the door and hanging the key on the hook provided on the left jamb. He flicked the goat bell hanging from the lintel on the right. The bell served to announce visitors, not that he had encouraged such during his year's sojourn, fast coming to an end.

'Why do I do that?'

It was only another of the many questions posed by the house. Rhetorical they might as well be, as no definitive answers had revealed themselves.

Closing the main gates he turned right down the hill, past Agios Nektarios on the right, specially open for the occasion. Usually it only opened for the saint's name day, the celebration of the moving of his bones or the baptism of children named for the saint.

This was the bell that had woken him so abruptly that morning. There were no celebrants about and the bell now hung silent.

Left at the chickens with the high-walled house on the right. He recalled the time he'd passed and seen Panayiotis collecting the poisoned bodies of his cats. Not in any way a cat lover - he hated the way they insinuated themselves – even Kenneth was repulsed by this action. Some jealous neighbour? A grudge?

A few yards and he had a choice. Go straight on or turn to the right. The former meant the barking dog which always resulted in him taking several steps to the left, to avoid the lunge the dog invariably made. Its restraint looked frail enough for one more lunge to set the beast free. It would also take him past the gymnasio - the middle school. The litter pushed through the playground railings, piling up at the roadside never failed to produce a 'pshaw' or 'tut' from him.

Although a school day the three schools on the island were closed and had been the day previous. Kenneth had heard the bugles and drums as the children practised their marching. Not wishing to risk this being the day the dog's restraint failed he turned right - a short, slightly downhill walk and then left onto the main road, past the koutouki on the right. Signs of activity announced its expectation of a full house after the ceremony. The owner waved at him through the grilled window.

'Good morning, Mr Kenneth. Enjoy the celebration. See you later, maybe, yes?'

Kenneth lifted an arm in return, accompanied by a cursory nod of the head.

'Maybe.'

Kenneth passed down the road. The owner smiled. Now used to this man's apparent abruptness he no longer felt slighted by it. Kenneth turned left at the delicatessen. On the right he noticed the children's playground was deserted. They would already be lining up at the church for their march along the coast road to the Dapia, then round the harbour to Bouboulina Square where a service would be held.

He had now reached 'Horse-Buggy Hill'. At the Crossbows Restaurant, very popular with English tourists, the road to the left would lead him round the back of the town, cutting down to Clock Square and across to the Dapia. Deciding on the shorter route he bore right and slowed his step, listening for the clop of approaching horse or the engine of a motorised bike. The one would signal he was safe to keep on the side he'd chosen. The other would involve a swift, deft move to the other side.

Passing Kostas' closed bar - never open during the day, even on celebration days - he walked along the narrow street leading to the fish market. All the out-door tables of Klimis, the town hotel adjacent to the road, were already taken by people attired in their best and brightest summer clothes. As he neared the harbour the crowds became denser as they jostled for the best view.

He had hoped for the same viewing point as for the Armata but the steps of the Dolphin office were already full. Maybe he could find a spot the other side of the Dapia.

'Kenneth.'

He recognised the voice but couldn't see her. Where was she?

'Here, here.'

This time he saw her, standing, waving her arms and smiling. He made his way through the press of tables to one overlooking the Dapia, with a panoramic view of both sides.

'Welcome, welcome.'

Demi smiled and Alexandros rose to shake hands.

'We saved a seat. Kyria said you would come.'

'Did she indeed.'

Did Kyria have the temerity to blush or was the slight sea breeze causing the pinkness of her cheeks? Alexandros waved for a waiter. 'Coffee?

'Kenneth doesn't drink coffee in cafes.'

Kyria was teasing him again and Kenneth realised he enjoyed it. It showed she cared.

The waiter appeared. Kenneth held Kyria's eyes as he ordered a fresh orange.

'They are coming. I can hear the band.'

Kenneth was somewhat taken aback as Demi's excitement was mirrored throughout the crowd but then it was a very special day. He had heard the story from Kostas.

'Ochi' (No) Day, October 28th celebrated the Greek refusal, in 1940, to allow Italian occupation during WWII. The Italian army was repulsed. This resistance brought Greece into the war on the side of the allies.

The sound of the band and the less melodious tones of kazoos being enthusiastically blown increased in volume. The vanguard rounded the furthest corner of the Dapia. As soon as the Greek flag was seen people stood in respect. Three priests in full, colourful, ecclesiastical regalia with young boys, clad in similar garb and swinging censors were followed by representatives of the armed forces, politicians from Athens and local dignitaries. The musical sounds were replaced by intoning cantors. The procession snaked round the Dapia to Bouboulina Square. The children from Lykio, Gymnasio and Demotico marching, not completely in step, completed the procession and joined the important people in the Square. A religious ceremony was conducted after which everyone dispersed to the café-bars and tavernas, many opening for the last time before the winter closures. Alexandros and Demi politely turned down Kyria's invitation to lunch.

'We have friends from Athens who are preparing a barbecue. Why don't you join us?'

'That's very kind but I've reserved a table at 'Green Doors.''

Kyria hugged Demi and Kenneth shook hands with Alexandros. The two couples parted company.

'And where is 'Green Doors'? I don't believe I've heard of it before.'

'Not far from here, towards Agia Mama. It's the restaurant painted blue and white.'

'With green doors?'

'No, it's got blue doors but it's a long story. Don't worry about it. We'd better be getting along as I asked them to save us portions of the lamb fricassée. This is the last day they'll be cooking it, although they do stay open during winter. One of the few.'

Over a very good fricassée and some ice-cold beer Kenneth heard of the other significance of October 28th.

'Ochi' day marked the end of the official season. Kostas had had his 'final night' when all drinks were free. Other bars, restaurants, tourist shops would begin to close down. Outside furniture was stored inside and shutters tight closed against the winter gales to come. The houses of the Athenians would be similarly closed. Some would come for weekends should an Indian summer ensue but most would not risk being stranded. The weather could be cruel without warning. The workers only here for the summer were leaving. Few stayed for the winter these days. The summer season no longer afforded them enough to stay. Winter jobs were needed somewhere else. But they would return next year.

Diary Entry (early November)

Pleasant day again. Do enjoy her company. Must start thinking about packing. Tomorrow, maybe. Why this lethargy? Some travellers still around. Older, more robust type, wanting to see 'real' island. Here nearly six months. Still don't know 'real' island.

Kenneth was aware of a change of atmosphere. It wasn't only the lack of crowds and tourist jollity. It was becoming a different island but he was hard-pressed to express exactly how. Was it that people had more time to smile and say 'Hello'? Was it they could now get on with their lives in some sort of normality?

He sat on the front balcony staring at the empty china cup wondering why he was doing nothing. It had been over an hour since he had savoured the Blue Mountain he so relished. It was most unlike him - to sit doing nothing. Doing nothing in his childhood had been positively frowned upon by his parents if not actually thought sacrilegious and a portent of future and unproductive indolence.

He thought of an incident when in Jamaica some years earlier. He had accepted, from a former school chum, the offer of a bungalow where he could write in a more salubrious clime, away from all the distractions of London. As he was writing on his balcony, in the warmth of the sun but without the intense glare it would later become, he'd observed a local man in the garden of a near-by bungalow, sitting with his back to a tree. After a light lunch and a late afternoon siesta Kenneth had returned to his writing in the cool of the evening. The man appeared not to have moved.

Later, deciding his quota had been fulfilled for the day, Kenneth had carefully replaced the cap on his fountain pen, picked up the sheaf of papers and turned to go inside. The man had now disappeared. Kenneth observed this scenario on several subsequent days. Eventually he asked the lady who brought his groceries and changed the bedding why this man was doing nothing all day long. Her reply both surprised and shocked him.

'He ain't 'doing nothing', Sir. He's sitting.'

At the time the word 'lazy' had flashed through Kenneth's mind. Now, as he sat doing nothing, that scene and the lady's reply made sense. Here, on the island he had the time to do nothing and to value it. The realisation made him sit up. What had caused this change of attitude? Kenneth wasn't sure. The island? No, surely an island could never exert such influence. It was an enigma. Maybe it was the Ice Queen.

The sound of an engine in low gear interrupted these thoughts. Looking over the wall, down the hill, he could not see anything machine-driven, only a crowd of some thirty people walking slowly up the hill. His eyes moved to the garden gates just in time to see a small white van crawl past, its rear doors wide open. A man sat in the van with legs dangling out, with a hand on the end of the coffin resting in the back of the van, as if that were enough to prevent the coffin slipping out.

Kenneth stood in respect, suppressing the smile of black humour as he envisaged the scene if the coffin did slip out of the van and slide down the hill. The van passed out of sight, followed by the crowd, many carrying flowers, garden and wild. Several nodded acknowledgement of Kenneth's show of respect. He saw the woman of his recent thoughts walking past. She did not look his way. Her head was down, her shoulders slumped. Had she known the deceased?

The whole procession now vanished from sight, only to re-appear in seconds as it rounded the corner where Panayiotis' horses were tethered. The horses lifted their heads at the approach but, sensing no threat, quickly returned to their interrupted grazing.

Kenneth paused, turned and entered the house. He walked onto the side balcony where he saw the cortège take the road to the monastery, cross the bridge over the dry river bed and turn left into the small church of Agia Barbara. It might be some while before the final journey to the cemetery so he decided he would spend no more time doing nothing. Sitting at the desk he removed the top from his fountain pen and reached for a sheet of pristine paper.

He hardly noticed the time as the neat italicised writing covered several pages. Only the murmur of voices caused him to stop. The funeral was over. The people were moving down the hill. Kenneth walked to the side balcony and saw the Ice Queen amongst them. Straightening the hand-written sheets so they aligned with the blotter he replaced the top on the pen, the pen on its stand.

The funeral party was out of sight as he left the house but he followed the murmur. The sound told him they had taken the back road into the town. Not wishing to intrude at this stage he decided to take the longer, more circuitous main road. When he finally arrived at the Agia Mama beach he saw they were already seated at the Green Doors' restaurant some hundred metres further on. As he passed, several of the group acknowledged him with a nod, the Ice Queen with a sad but not unkind smile.

He walked on to the Dapia and the corner cafenion, sitting outside of which gave him a full view of all the goings-on around the harbour. He enjoyed the freshness of the sea air but was less enamoured of the smell of petrol that swirled around as the sea-taxis plied their trade.

Not feeling particularly hungry he decided to have an ouzo meze. The measure was generous and accompanied by a glass of water. Kenneth had not yet become accustomed to drinking the fire water neat. Adding water to the ouzo, which gave it a smoky-grey appearance, he took a sip and then added more water. He watched the kaikis bobbing in the harbour, near to the periptero. As each one filled with tourists the boats took off to the various destinations on the mainland shore across the narrow stretch. The waiter brought the meze, small portions of tarama, skordalia, crumbly feta and olives, with the ubiquitous quarter lemon on the side. He finished the meze and reached for the glass, now mostly water.

'May I sit with you a while?'

Kenneth stood up and pulled out the chair next to him. She sat down. Kenneth called a waiter.

'Ena elliniko café, parakalo, sketo.'

'Amesos.'

She rarely spoke Greek so Kenneth was somewhat surprised. Neither spoke as they waited for the coffee. The silence continued as she stared down into the black gunge which had never appealed to Kenneth.

'Was it someone you knew well? The funeral...'

'Hardly at all. An old man who had no-one. The island takes care of its own.'

The silence continued for a while and then she spoke again.

'But I won't go to the lifting of his bones. I'll leave that part to the nuns.'

Kenneth managed to stop himself choking on his ouzo. He thought he had misheard.

'Pardon?'

'Oh, sorry, you're probably not familiar with the custom. In Greece the bodies aren't left in the ground. After a while the bones are lifted and usually put into family crypts.'

'You mean the skeleton is removed from the grave and reburied?'

'Well, not actually a skeleton as such. Just... bones. A dismembered skeleton, in fact.'

She went on to explain whilst Kenneth sat in stunned disbelief. The burial of a loved one was not the final act of laying them to rest. It was a custom which often generated quite horrific stories of what the removal involved.

'Looks as he did when we buried him two years ago.'

'It was only a year and he wasn't ready. We had to re-bury him.'

The latter comment referred to the removal of the body on a sort of wheelbarrow, for re-burial in the hallowed ground reserved for just such an event. The relatives of the deceased followed, one laughing at this grotesque whilst another alternatively laughed and cried.

And the aged crone, who, during the 'lifting' of her husband's remains, decided to help with the disinterment by scrabbling in the earth and then shouting, almost gleefully.

'I've got the skull!' She held it up for all to see. This caused her daughter-in-law, a foreigner, to disgrace herself with inappropriate, if nervous, laughter.

'She was never forgiven.'

Kenneth watched the woman sitting next to him with incredulity as she paused to take a sip of the gunge in front of her. There was no sign she was being anything but serious. He felt it incumbent upon him to make a comment.

'I'm sure she wouldn't be. Might one ask what 'not ready' actually entails?'

'Some bodies are not ready. Modern drug treatment tends to preserve the flesh - especially in the case of cancer patients. But a small bit of flesh on the bones is all right. That will fall from the bones during the cleaning process.'

Kenneth refrained from asking for an explanation of the cleaning process, contenting himself with a slight inclination of his head and a large swallow of ouzo. However, his companion had paused again.

'Mm. When does this bone ceremony take place exactly?'

'Any time from one year after the initial committal. It depends on two things. First, the climate - a lot of rain helps for an 'early' lift. Second is the need for space. Severe winters can lead to an upsurge in demand.'

'Yes, I see. That would have a definite influence on things. And after the bones have been cleaned?'

'They are put into a box before being placed in the family vault.'

'The man this morning. Does he have a family vault?'

'No, he will be placed in the little chapel in the corner of the cemetery. The nuns will look after him.'

'If there's a shortage of land for burial why don't they just cremate and scatter or bury the ashes?'

'It's not allowed by the Church.'

Kenneth decided he had had enough of funereal customs.

'Would you like another coffee?'

'Thank you, no. I have some lesson preparation to do. Thank you for your company.'

For the first time in his life Kenneth did not rise as a lady left the table. But he did summon the waiter to request another ouzo, without the water.

Diary Entry (early November)

Damned strange, not so much custom - ossuaries/charnel houses etc - but matter-of-fact way she spoke about whole business. Just accepted as normal. Must have been here too long. Won't happen to me. Still time to be home for Christmas. Woken this a.m. about 6. Damned awful noise of discordant bell of Church next door. Loads of bike engines, even car or two. Went out on side balcony in dressing gown - see what all fuss about.

Kenneth's appearance in his somewhat, for the island, strange attire caused some laughter. Many of the assembled populous waved.

'It's the ninth. The name day of Nektarios. Special service.'

Not waiting to see who had shouted Kenneth quickly withdrew from the balcony. He decided to have an early breakfast and then… What would he do? He had no specific plans. Writing? Reading? A walk? Sitting? The island seemed to be dictating his life. Leading him on. Leading him on to where?

On his way to the kitchen he noticed a small, white envelope had been pushed under the front door. The envelope itself was blank but the note inside, written in a neat roundhand, caused a stirring in Kenneth.

'If free, meet me 17th at Roumani's, 11am. K.'

If free! Kenneth didn't know what he was doing after breakfast never mind the 17th.

What he was sure of now was that, on the seventeenth, at 11 am, he would be at Roumani's. He closed his eyes for a moment, conjuring up a scene of idyllic bliss. The stirring became stronger. He decided a shower might be in order before breakfast.

Loosening the tie of his dressing gown he turned towards the bathroom. He avoided looking into the mirror. He was afraid of what he would see there.

Diary Entry (mid November)

Tomorrow is the 17th. Have discovered it's Polytechneio Day. Student uprising against Junta. Mustn't be late… or too early.

Kenneth heard the sound of breaking glass. It seemed to come from the hallway. Getting out of bed he reached for his dressing gown. There was no broken glass but he heard a woman's voice, an angry, sneering voice, issuing from the balcony.

'Where's your flag?'

Opening the door he saw, halfway down the balcony, Kyria wrapped in a blue and white flag. She held a small rock in each hand. Her lip curled, the rocks clacked to the ground. She turned to leave. Outside the gate the red bike, no longer tangled in greenery, purred mockingly. The blue eyes of the man on the bike bored through Kenneth, making him shiver. Kyria mounted the bike, wrapped her arms round the man and gently laid her cheek on his back. Bike and couple headed up the hill.

Kenneth woke after a disturbed sleep. Would these dreams disappear if he no longer showed interest in Kyria. He knew the dreams were connected with their relationship, however innocent that relationship might be for the present. He often felt a strong male presence in the house, the cigarette smoke, the smell of aftershave, the shadowy appearances in the mirror. It was as if this man were warning him to back away. He remembered Joanna's words, 'She can never be yours.' What did the island know? What wasn't it telling him?

He was apprehensive of the forthcoming meeting but looking forward to it.

After all he was still planning to leave before Christmas so there was little time left to spend with Kyria.

* * *

As Kenneth passed the children's playground he saw it was busy with families and children of all ages, but no men. The shops all around were open. Builders were at work in the area. Many buildings sported the Greek flag. Some had a crown in its centre.

'Must ask about that.'

As he walked through the town he saw little in the way of a 'celebration' day apart from the abundance of flags and the fact that there were many children of school age in evidence.

He walked up the steps to Roumani's just as the town clock struck eleven. Several people were having coffee. Most were wearing coats in deference to the weather. Kyria, wearing an Arran sweater, was sitting at a table overlooking the harbour. She saw him, smiled and waved. All Kenneth's misgivings dissipated.

'I hope you haven't been waiting long.'

'Just got here myself. I haven't ordered but they do a really lovely hot chocolate here. And I'm going to indulge in a galaktovoureka, hot with ice-cream.'

'It sounds rather indulgent, just the sound of it. What exactly is it?'

'A semolina custard in filo pastry, dripping in syrup. It's the sweet you had on the Classical Tour. That was without ice-cream. We'll have that first, then the hot chocolate.'

Within minutes the two of them were scooping up the dessert.

'It is quite delicious. Wouldn't do to eat too much of this. I have noticed the Greeks love their sweets and the more calories the better, it seems. Whilst we drink our hot chocolate perhaps you could tell me about November 17th. It doesn't seem as if everyone observes it as a holiday.'

'It isn't an official bank holiday which is why the shops are open. It's more a recognition of the events of that day in 1973. An opportunity for all Greeks to display their patriotism regardless of political affiliations.'

'But the schools are closed?'

'Out of respect for the students who were involved. That's why I'm not giving lessons today.'

'What actually happened?'

'In the late 60s, early 70s Greece was ruled by a Junta, sometimes referred to as the Rule of the Colonels. In protest against draconian laws the students barricaded themselves into the law school. Thousands of Athenians gathered outside in support.

There were clashes with the police. A lot of injuries. Police brutality was the norm then.'

'What happened to the students inside the university?'

'The police brought in armoured cars. Shots and tear gas were fired. In the early hours of the 17th tanks were brought in. Despite students clinging to the gates a tank drove through the gates. The demonstration was over.'

'Were many killed?'

'I've heard varying accounts from none killed, although many badly beaten, to double figures being killed. It seems to depend on your political leanings.'

'Talking of political leanings I've seen flags with a gold crown in the centre.'

'Oh, Kenneth, haven't you realised yet? Spetses is predominately a royalist island. Try looking up at the chimney pots on your way home. Now, it's just after one. Shall we wander along to Green Doors for lunch. Unless you've something else to do.'

Kenneth couldn't think of a single thing he should be doing.

'That sounds like a very good idea but this time it's on me.'

'Fair enough but there won't be any fricassée.'

As they left Roumani's Kyria took his arm. For Kenneth November 17th was a good day.

Diary Entry (mid November)

Looked at chimney pots. Most had plain cowls. Some in shape of bird, crow like. Many with a crown. Good day with Kyria. Sweater she was wearing obviously hand knitted but too big for her. Was it knitted for Him. Am I getting paranoid! No mention of future meetings. Will persevere with writing. The Bitch hasn't been in touch for a while.

Will need to have something to give her when get home - before Christmas.

It was nearing the end of November. Despite the temperature often being in the high teens or low twenties Mrs Eleni was in winter mode, having switched from black cotton to black wool. Kenneth wondered how she didn't collapse with the heat. For the past two weeks she had come and gone, preparing meals, bringing in shopping, stocking the 'fridge. And this all without disturbing him whilst he was working. Certainly the muse seemed to be flowing and he'd had no disturbing dreams or occurrences. After so many continuous writing days Kenneth needed a break. He would go to the popular Ermione market. He had left a note with Esther to be passed to Kyria, inviting her to join him but had received no reply.

He wasn't entirely sure how to get there. Mrs Eleni had told him 'Morning ferry, still dark, bus Kranidi, bus Ermione. Follow people.' He thought the last piece of advice the best as many Spetsiots travelled weekly to the market where everything was cheaper.

It was still dark when he approached the Dapia. He could see no ferry waiting.

Had he missed it? He looked at his watch. Fifteen minutes to expected departure. Bikes and three-wheelers passed him taking a road that led round the cafes and restaurants on the Dapia to re-emerge on the other side and disappear into the Square.

'Jump in. You'll lose the ferry.'

A door-less three wheeler had stopped. The driver was unknown to Kenneth but he readily accepted the lift. As the vehicle careered round corners he began to doubt the intelligence of his acceptance. However they arrived safely at the ferry which was anchored at the other side of Bouboulina Square. Kenneth got out of his 'taxi'. Before he could thank the driver the three-wheeler had shot off back the way it had come. So the driver wasn't going to Ermione!

Kenneth boarded the ferry. A siren sounded and there was a flurry of late arrivals. The stern door began to rise and the ship moved into open water for the short crossing to the mainland. Having bought his ticket Kenneth leaned on the side of the boat watching his island slowly emerging from the darkness.

'Good morning.'

He turned.

'Sorry I didn't reply to your note. Only got it late yesterday.'

'No need to apologise. My decision to go to Ermione was a last minute one. Needed a break from writing.'

'Mm, I'd heard you were busy writing and shouldn't be disturbed.'

'Mrs Eleni?'

'The initial 'order' came from her, yes.'

'And then spread rapidly.'

'You're getting to understand the island. There are no secrets here.'

'I beg to differ. I believe the island has many secrets that she guards jealously.'

'Maybe…'

The change in the drone of the engine announced the ferry's imminent arrival at the mainland. The stern door safely down the foot passengers disembarked before any wheeled vehicles.

'Will we be using your friend's car today?'

'No, I didn't have time to get it checked so we'll be taking the bus.'

They followed the crowd along the path running by the side of the beach to where the main road started. There a bus waited. A queue formed whilst the driver sold tickets. A short wait and the 'bus set off.

'I noticed you got a lift in this morning.'

'Only from the other side of the Dapia. I was not expecting the ferry to be leaving from somewhere else.'

'It usually leaves from there in the winter. It's more sheltered.'

'Mrs Eleni spoke of two buses. Is it a long drive?'

'Not at all. It's just the way it's organised. But the second 'bus will be waiting for us so there won't be any delay.'

Kenneth refrained from asking why one 'bus wasn't used to complete the entire journey. He was sure there would be some Greek logic behind it.

* * *

The market was much bigger than Kenneth had imagined. It was thronged, with good business being done by most of the stalls. There were fruit and vegetable stalls, shoes and clothes for men, women and children, curtains and material, kitchen and bathroom wares, gardening and general tools, bric-a-brac as well as the food stalls. The plant stall in particular had crowds round it. Kyria had gone first to that stall and was standing in front of some poinsettia plants of varying sizes.

'Quite lovely, aren't they? Thinking of buying one?'

'Yes, we usually… I normally get one for Christmas but wonder if it's too early. I may not get over to the market again before Christmas and the ones on the island are always so expensive.'

'You could think about it and buy it on the way back if you decide you'd like one.'

'I need to decide now as they'll be snapped up by the time we leave.'

An hour later the two were sitting at a coffee shop overlooking Ermione Harbour. A bag of fruit and vegetables lay under the table. A poinsettia stood by Kenneth's chair.

'It's often called a Jamaican Christmas tree.'

'So I believe, although that's something of a misnomer as the plant is actually native to Mexico.'

'Jamaican has a much more romantic ring to it. Have you ever been to Jamaica?'

As Kenneth related stories of his time spent in Jamaica he saw a bus draw up in the nearby square. Most of the people from the morning ferry were boarding. As it left Kenneth interrupted his narration.

'Should we by any chance have been on that 'bus?'

'Don't worry. We'll get the later one which will allow us to be in time for the one thirty ferry. I thought we might have a light lunch before leaving. There's a small taverna just up the way from here.'

The light lunch over, a few small plates of mezethes, and the two were walking back to the square. Kyria carried the bag of fruit and vegetables whilst Kenneth carried the poinsettia.

'Are you sure there's a mid-day 'bus? Maybe we should enquire?'

'There always has been but….'

'Yes?'

'I haven't been for a while. You stay here. I'll go ask in the Dolphin office.'

Kyria returned, looking somewhat abashed.

'I'm sorry. The timetable has changed. The next bus is four o'clock.'

'So, what happens now?'

'I really don't want to hang around until the last ferry so I suggest we get a taxi to Kranidi where we'll be in time for the 'bus to the mid-day ferry. We'll be back on the island by two o'clock.'

Kenneth held the poinsettia, which he silently referred to now as that bloody plant, on his knee in both taxi and 'bus. He was tempted to drop it accidently overboard during the ferry crossing but believed that would cause Kyria some distress. The ferry docked once more at Bouboulina's Square. Kenneth had hoped to be allowed to carry the plant home for her. He had never been to her house. Wasn't even sure where she lived. His hopes were dashed when she said goodbye before climbing into a three wheeler, the bloody plant having been deposited in the back.

Kenneth decided to call for a large brandy at Klimis before his walk home.

Diary Entry (early December)

Enjoyed Ermione day. Did notice slip of 'we' although quickly covered it up. The poinsettia of great import to her. Secrets. No-one telling. Another note/invite to dinner 8pm in Old Harbour on Dec 6th. Sketch map of how to find eatery. St Nick's Day?

As it was a moonlit night Kenneth found the place quite easily. He was early but Kyria was already waiting with a half empty glass of beer in front of her. She smiled as he came to her table. There were four other tables. Each of them had people, several of whom acknowledged Kenneth's arrival. A log fire blazed away throwing out considerable heat. A large beer appeared in front of Kenneth. He raised his eyebrows. Kyria grinned,

'I hope you don't mind. I've taken the liberty of pre-ordering. We're going to have the traditional dish for today.'

'And that is?'

'Cod and garlic sauce. Have you had it before?'

'Once or twice, of varying standards but none bad.'

'I think you'll find this is the best ever.'

'Is St Nicholaos celebrated widely in Greece?'

'Yes, he's a national saint. But he's especially important here as he's the patron saint of sea-farers. Many of the local boats carry his icon. There will have been special celebrations at the navy establishments today. Many families with connections to the sea will have a decorated boat, instead of a tree, at Christmas.'

The meal arrived with a plate of greens and more beer. Kenneth acknowledged the fish was the best ever. Of course it was. He was eating it with this woman.

'How are your plans progressing to return to England before Christmas?' The question took him by surprise.

'Decided to stay on. Haven't quite finished the book.'

Kyria merely smiled and the meal was completed in silence.

'I thought we might walk along the front to the town. Is that all right with you?'

Walking round the island would be all right, with her.

'Fine.'

The walk was over all too soon for Kenneth. They reached the bridge that would take them to the town road.

'This is where we part company. Thank you for a lovely evening. And I'm glad the fish was the best ever.'

After brushing his cheek with her lips she smiled her sad smile and turned to continue her walk along the front to wherever it was she lived. Holding his hand to his cheek as though to retain the kiss Kenneth crossed the bridge and turned left to go home.

He heard footsteps behind him, a steady measured tread. He stopped and turned. He saw no-one and could no longer hear the footsteps. He was approaching the turn at Panayiotis' house when a red bike swerved past him. It drove up the hill and disappeared.

The driver was a big man, wearing an Arran sweater. Kenneth shut the metal gates behind him. The red bike seemed more overgrown than ever. But the engine, as he expected, was warm.

He moved slowly down the walkway. He saw the door opening. He wanted to turn and run away from whatever it was waited for him.

Kenneth woke, his hand on his cheek. It was still dark but he didn't want to go back to sleep. He got up and waited for the dawn.

Diary Entry (mid December)

Kyria busy with pupil exams. No plans to meet. Weather variable. Last few weeks atrocious. Didn't associate Greece with inclement weather. Tremendous storm recently. Thunder/lightning/torrents. Water coming under front door. Drainage pipes blocked. Had to don driz-a-bone/green wellies at 2am to sweep water down walkway before it flooded house. Did wonder why wellies in cupboard in dressing room. Colour a clue to previous occupant. Size eleven. Must have been a big fellow. Had to wear two pairs socks to keep them on. Still felt uncomfortable. Stepping into someone else's shoes! Next day like summer. Getting on reasonably well with writing. Bitch rang requesting drafts.

Tell her waiting to send/bring full manuscript. Assuring her all on track.

Kenneth decided to take advantage of some good weather for a constitutional. He could go to the town and stock up on brandy in case the weather turned wild again. Mrs Eleni had completely taken over the buying and deliveries of groceries. Likewise the replacement of the gaz bottles. She had also insisted he stocked up on bottled water and candles. More than he thought necessary but he didn't wish to question Mrs Eleni's rationale. He had learned there was an island lore which never did anything without reason.

Having arranged for four bottles of Courvoisier to be delivered Kenneth stood wondering if he should have lunch. He felt a hand on his shoulder. A shudder of pleasure travelled through him.

'I'm just off to Green Doors for lunch. Care to join me?'

'I was actually heading there myself so, yes, I would care.'

The short walk to Green Doors was quickly completed.

'In or out, Kenneth?'

'I think out. It is actually quite warm.'

They chose a table in the centre, away from the passage of traffic on one side and that of people on the other. Both ordered pork chop, green salad and chips with small beers.

'How are the exams going?'

'Oh, they're over. Just a matter of waiting for the results now.'

'So you'll have more time for yourself?'

'I still have students. Some even want lessons over the Christmas break.'

'And will you oblige them?'

'Certainly not. I need a break.'

Kenneth's hopes rose but were quickly dashed.

'I'm going away for Christmas, possibly New Year.'

'Anywhere nice?'

'Just friends. Oh, look there's a Dolphin so the sea must be calm. I expect you've realised by now the weather can change very quickly.'

Once again she had deflected any possible revelations of her private life.

Diary Entry (late December)

Usually spend Christmas with folks. Sort of duty. Mater very keen on getting everyone together once in a while. This Christmas rather different. Seven months still no nearer fathoming Ice Queen. Nothing much happening on Island. Crib of sorts near Bouboulina. Assorted, scattered lights. Ex-pats gathered in Dave's Bar few days pre-Christmas for carol singing. She asked me to go. Last time I saw her.

Seemed somewhat banal to me. Banal wrong word. Seemed to be air/suspicion of sadness. Got to spend time with her so didn't mind too much. Why did Dimitris, only Greek guy there, sing the Ave Maria? Beautiful, clear voice - very emotional. Not particularly Christmas material. A strange, sombre moment. Followed by toast to absent friends. Almost certain saw Ice Queen's eyes moisten but someone broke in with 'Ding, Dong, Merrily on High'- moment gone. Any event she isn't available for company so no excuse for not putting pen to paper.

Kenneth's hand flew over the paper. Occasionally he paused to consult one of the many notebooks which contained jottings as ideas had come to him. He wondered what The Bitch was up to now? Probably on the endless rounds of pre-Christmas lunches and dinners. Just how many Christmas dinners could one enjoy? She'd be pleased he was writing but what would she think of the content? It was of no matter.

A log fire burned in the fireplace. Once he had given up the idea of a return home before Christmas he had asked Esther about heating the house. She had arranged a delivery of logs for him. The ones in the wood store were insufficient for the Winter. She had shown him how to stack the logs so that they wouldn't collapse. They were on the front balcony in easy reach should the weather not be conducive to venturing down to the wood store.

Mrs Eleni kept him supplied with pine cones to use as kindling. They also gave off a pleasant fragrance. He had tried to persuade Mrs Eleni to use a taxi when the weather was bad but she had steadfastly refused. Her elderly beau brought and collected her in a very old, rusted three wheeler but Kenneth was pleased it kept her dry and out of the wind. There were fewer salads about. Meals were now soups, stews and casseroles, although fish appeared frequently once Mrs Eleni had realised Kenneth had a preference for fish. She often brought him home-made sweets and Kenneth was pleased he did not take weight easily.

There were halcyon days and on such he would leave his writing and go for walks, enjoying the winter quiet. From a deserted beach he watched the sea roll in, finding it very comforting.

He returned to his writing. The clang of the metal gates caused him to pause. A shiver ran through him as he heard steps coming down the walkway. A slow, measured tread. They stopped at the door. The goat bell remained quiet but there was an imperious knock. He didn't want to go to the door but felt compelled. Taking a deep breath he opened the door. As half-expected there was no-one but the smell of cigarette hung in the air. Surely someone was having a joke. He walked slowly around the garden. He looked up and down the road. Esther's house was already shuttered against the falling darkness. He took the key from its hook, locked the door behind him and closed the shutters.

Diary Entry (Christmas Eve)

Family over way preparing to spend Christmas in Epidavros. Due to leave Christmas Eve afternoon. In the morning Esther sent children with homemade sweets/biscuits, all elegantly packaged. Kind thought. Very enthusiastic lady - always busy. Children well-behaved. Violent winds meant cancelled car ferry and sea-taxis so plans quickly re- arranged. Invited to join them for meal. Churlish to refuse. Fortunately have decent French wine to take.

Although it was only a matter of a few yards to Esther's house Kenneth wore his dark navy, lamb's wool overcoat, with matching gloves and scarf. The wind tore the metal gate from his hands and it clanged shut. The noise had obviously alerted Esther to his imminent arrival as the door was opened before he had time to knock.

'Come in. Welcome, Happy Christmas. Let me take your coat and things.'

'Thank you. Some wine for the table.'

'That wasn't necessary, but thank you. Go into the living room. Christos is there. The children are helping me in the kitchen.'

Christos was crouched to one side of the log fire holding a hinged gridiron containing lamb chops, turning it whilst he sprayed a mist of olive oil on the chops.

'Welcome, Mr Kenneth. There is wine on the table. It's from my village. Very good.'

Kenneth reluctantly headed towards the jug of warm wine. His palate had still not completely accustomed itself to Greek wine, no matter where it came from, each area purporting to be 'the best'. A temporary rescue came in the form of Esther as she and the three girls entered the living room carrying a variety of salads and a wide assortment of vegetables. These were placed on the festively dressed table. Esther returned to the kitchen. The three children sat and looked nervously at Kenneth. He had never felt comfortable in the company of children despite his many nieces and nephews, but he felt he should make an effort.

'Were you disappointed you couldn't get to Epidavros?'

Irene, the oldest, and Constantina, the youngest, looked at Sylvia.

'No, Mr Kenneth. This happens often. We just go tomorrow, or the next day.'

Her sisters giggled. Another rescue, this time from further conversation with the children, as Esther appeared with a mountain of chips. Placing the mountain on the table she picked up an empty plate and went to the fire allowing her husband to transfer the chops to the plate.

The meal passed pleasantly with all the conversation conducted in English, the children joining in more readily. With the naivety of youth they proceeded to ask Kenneth personal questions. Did he have children? Was he married? Why not?

Esther intervened, saving Kenneth the embarrassment of answer. The main meal over Esther collected the plates, the children the remains of the salads and vegetables.

'That was lovely, Esther. Thank you.'

Christos re-filled Kenneth's glass.

'It's good, yes?'

'Oh, yes, certainly, yes, very good. Most unusual bouquet. Yes, very nice.'

A large choice of homemade sweets and biskwits followed. Kenneth was offered a cognac which he gratefully accepted. Then came the present exchange. Each of the girls received her chosen gift. Irene a wristwatch, Sylvia the latest Harry Potter and Constantina a novelty bedroom wall clock. The children's gifts to their parents had all been handmade. Dad's was a pipe stand made from stiff card and painted to resemble wood. Mum's was a round mirror rescued from the tip. It had been cleaned and was now resplendent in a colourful frame of homemade paper flowers. Kenneth's was a small picture frame made of corrugated paper with a decorative surround of broken mosaics in shades of pinks and mauves. From its centre three young faces smiled out at him. Not a man given to any display of emotion he felt moved by this token.

'How kind. Thank you. It will remind me of my stay here when I go home.'

'Maybe you'll stay forever. Like Mama.'

Sylvia was definitely the most forthright of the trio.

Diary Entry (Boxing Day)

Makes one think - never really have before - real meaning of Christmas. Go to church with Mater et al, a formality. Local populous expect landed gentry attending requisite services. One present each. Wouldn't get away with that with my grasping nieces and nephews. Could try it next year...

Kenneth rose early as usual on Christmas Day, surprised at the bright sunlight forcing its way into his tightly shuttered bedroom. The storm that had prevented people leaving the island the previous day had blown itself out. He could hear the silence as he opened the door and stepped out on to the front balcony. Looking across to Esther's house he realised they had left, probably on the first Dolphin at 6 am. He had breakfast and then wrote awhile before showering and dressing to go into the town where he had reluctantly agreed to support the event taking place.

The day was exceptionally warm, yet the locals thronging the bars and cafes along the front were wrapped as for the middle of Winter. And it was indeed Winter, the 25th of December. A small group of people dressed in more summer attire announced themselves as non-indigenous. This was their big celebration of the year and they would shortly return to their homes to celebrate in their own fashion. But this morning they had gathered at the town beach for a special event. One of many events being held to raise money for handicapped children in Athens.

A young man spending his first, and only, winter on the island had offered to do a sponsored swim on Christmas Day. Only after the event had been publicised and sponsors recruited did he reveal the fact he couldn't swim. But he did intend to learn.

With only two months to go, several ex-pats took on the roles of swimming instructors.

The sea was calm and inviting. Locals shook their heads in disbelief as the young man and his two 'life-guards' stripped to trunks and entered the sea, the foreign group shouting encouragement. Having swum one hundred meters unaided it was agreed the young man had earned his sponsorship. He returned to the beach to be rewarded with an embrace by one of the ladies who sensuously removed the fur coat she had been wearing to reveal a striking figure in swimwear. The soft leather, thigh length boots proclaimed she had no intention of entering the water.

Kenneth, standing apart from the main group allowed himself a smile at the scene before going to make his donation. He then turned for home.

'You will join us in Dave's Bar, won't you? He's got some mulled wine ready and there are homemade mince pies.'

It was the lady in the fur coat and boots. Kenneth turned to face her. In reply he crooked his arm. She slid her arm through his.

'Thank you, kind Sir. I'm Chrissie.'

The voice teased but it was full of promise. Perhaps Kenneth's Christmas Day wasn't going to be lonely after all.

Diary Entry (late December)

A very pleasant day, all in all. Just the sort of woman with whom to pass a convivial time. No strings, jolly good time all round. Why then feel guilty? Have no commitment to anyone. No-one has commitment to me. Pleased didn't stay the night.

Wonder how long before Ice Queen hears of it!

A rumbling sound woke Kenneth. It rolled nearer, reached a crescendo, then exploded overhead. Kenneth opened the bedroom shutters, shutting them almost immediately as a deluge of rain blew in. He reached for the light switch. Nothing happened. He flicked it up and down. Nothing. He tried switches in the other rooms before acknowledging there was no electricity. He opened the window in the door. He could barely make out the house opposite through the density of the rain. A bolt of forked lightning caused him to close the window hurriedly.

Although there was a modicum of light filtering through the shutters Kenneth decided to retrieve candles and matches from the drawer in the kitchen. Placing the candles in holders thoughtfully left by Mrs Eleni, they were ready for the evening should the electricity not be restored by then. He did not expect Mrs Eleni to venture out that day and was suddenly grateful for the gas driven camping stove. That would furnish him with hot food and drinks.

He went into the living room. The log from the previous day was still smouldering. He had been taught what to do. He took the poker and hit the log. The burnt pieces fell away. Cupping his hands over his mouth he picked up the bamboo stick propped next to the fireplace. Placing it over the log he blew hard into the hollow until the log glowed red. He blew harder and the log sprang into life. He threw a few pine cones into the flames and was grateful for Esther's advice. Always keep some dry logs in the house. There were three in the hallway.

Once dressed and breakfast over Kenneth settled down to the only thing to do that day. Write.

Diary Entry (early January)

Have never really celebrated New Year before. Couldn't be doing with all the enforced jollity. This year different. Thanks to Ice Queen.

The storm had blown itself out. The electricity was back, the candles carefully stored away for the next time. Kenneth looked at the garden in amazement. He had expected something resembling chaos but, apart from a few twigs and a sodden ground, there was little to show of the storm that had hit the day before.

Despite his good intentions there had been little writing. He had spent most of the day sitting in an armchair gazing into the flames. The face of the Ice Queen appeared several times but had given him no answers. Strangely he had slept well that night, to be woken by sounds of the arrival home of Esther's family so the car ferry was obviously operating. He hadn't expected them, thinking they would stay in their country home for the New Year.

He had gathered the New Year was a much bigger celebration than Christmas, usually extended family affairs where all ages got together for a party. At midnight St Vassilis, the Greek Father Christmas who has many of the attributes of St Nicholaos, arrives with presents for the children, one each. After this the adults start playing cards, continue all night and often the rest of New Year's Day. Although apparently illegal a blind eye is turned for the occasion.

On the morning of New Year's Eve Kenneth had found a note from Kyria asking if he would like to join her at a friend's house, about 9 o'clock. Very informal. An attached sketch-map showed it was a five minute walk away.

Carrying a bottle of wine Kenneth left the house at ten minutes to nine. He was greeted at his destination by Kyria who was wearing a long sleeved, black wool dress, fitted until the hips when it flared down to mid-calf.

The house belonged to a Greek-English couple, Spiros and Carol. Spiros' uncle, Michalis, was the only other person present. The meal was simple but tasty. A macaroni cheese base with bacon, mushrooms and spinach. Fresh fruit salad in Cointreau followed. The dishes were cleared away and conversation ensued until midnight. Michalis spoke no English and Kenneth little Greek so much translating was needed.

'When did you get back, Kyria?'

'Luckily just before the storm broke. Got the last Dolphin before all the ports were closed. A bit choppy but I've travelled in worse.'

Midnight came. The company toasted and wished each other well. Carol produced a pack of new cards with the seal intact.

'Just to be fair all round,' she joked. 'We're going to play thirty-one, Kenneth. Do you know it?'

'It sounds similar to twenty-one.'

'More a combination of that and rummy.'

Carol then deposited ramekins of one drachma coins next to each player.

'Just for fun. We'll play a few hands first so Kenneth gets some idea of the rules.'

Dawn was breaking when the game finished. Drachma were counted and Kenneth was surprised to have won.

'I hope I don't have to carry all these coins home.'

'No, I save them for next year but there is a prize for you.'

Spiros then produced a bottle of Chivas Regal.

'I couldn't possibly.'

'It's OK. We drink one night at your house.'

The party ended with scrambled eggs on toast with tea for the English and paximathi and coffee for the Greeks.

As Kenneth walked home carrying his prize he suddenly realised he was committed to having guests one night. He did not relish the thought.

Diary Entry (early January)

What a thought, another Christmas. This for people twelve days behind! Had only seen ceremony on film. Nubile young men showing off prowess. Bit different here.

Wonder about Petros' comment. A side of the island I haven't seen?

Esther's children had been to wish Kenneth Happy New Year and to remind him of the celebration of Epiphany. Kenneth had been aware of the importance of this ceremony for the sea-faring nation of Greeks and the islands in particular. He felt he should attend but also found himself wanting to be a part of such an important event.

Although the sixth was bright and sunny, there was a cold wind so Kenneth wore his cashmere. There was a steady throng of people and vehicles making their way down to the Dapia. Kenneth was aware of how many of them acknowledged his presence.

Arriving at the Dapia he looked for the Ice Queen but couldn't see her through the crowds. The whole island must have turned out, dressed in their finest warm clothes. Some had come early to secure seats at the coffee shops which had put out tables and chairs for the day was crisp and clear, if quite cold by Greek sensibilities. He positioned himself on the steps of the bank giving him a good view of all the proceedings.

Kenneth had heard of this 'second' Christmas when those who followed the 'old' Julian calendar celebrated the birth of Christ. Indeed he had a vague memory of a grainy black and white film in which virile young men braved freezing waters to reclaim a cross from the bed of the sea. Why they did so he could not remember. The males he saw at the other side of the Dapia were certainly no virile young men but boys in their early to mid-teens. No girls he observed. Probably not traditional.

He had been told a religious service would be held in St Nicholaos' Church near the Old Harbour after which the priest, local dignitaries and icons would process across the island, through the town round the Dapia to the side of the harbour adjoining Bouboulina Square. About 11.15 this procession arrived, no bands this time, just the intoning of the priests and cantors. As the icons passed men bared their heads. Nearly all crossed themselves. People in the coffee shops rose to their feet and more crossing took place. The procession reached the far side of the Dapia.

After another brief service, blessing the water and the boats, asking for the protection of their patron, Nicholaos, the boys entered the water. Some more stalwart souls had entered the water before the blessings. There were boats on hand in the event of rescue being required.

The Priest threw the Cross, securely attached to a piece of string Kenneth noted, into the water. In a comparatively short while one of the divers emerged, holding the Cross on high and receiving enthusiastic applause, with loud cries of 'oraio' informing all present of the family to which the holder of the Cross belonged. His reward was a gold cross and chain, a special blessing of good fortune for the coming year. A memento.

No doubt worn for life. Kenneth had noticed several men of all ages wearing these crosses. Had they all won them this way? The crowds began to disperse, some to tavernas and restaurants to have an early lunch, others for coffee.

Kenneth had been invited to join some ex-pats in Dave's Bar, a very small room but with a good selection of drinks, reasonably priced. Dave also advertised something called 'Smidgeon Coffee'. Kenneth was intrigued. He asked Dave about this coffee and was informed a regular female customer would ask for a coffee and then request a 'smidgeon' of Irish whiskey.

'That lady sitting over there.'

He indicated the Ice Queen, sitting with friends. One of those friends was Petros, the buggy driver. It was the first time Kenneth had ever seen him freshly shaved and dressed very smartly in sporting jacket, collar and tie and slacks. He was looking out through the window at the crowds passing by. Petros called him over.

'Look at them. You can smell the 'naphthalene'.'

This was a reference to the 'best' clothes that were only brought out on special occasions and smelled strongly of mothballs. He went on to draw attention to the amount of make-up worn by some of the more mature ladies, equating it with 'stucco'. He had chosen his imagery carefully as his final words made clear.

'They greet each other today with kisses and good wishes but last week they were stabbing each other in the back and will be again next week.'

Kenneth wanted to ask Kyria to have lunch but everyone sent out to the chicken shop and had a 'picnic' lunch in the bar. The company were obviously set for a long session and the Ice Queen appeared happy to stay. Kenneth muttered something about having to meet a deadline and left. As he walked home he felt strangely hurt that she hadn't invited him to meet her for this important ceremony.

Diary Entry (mid January)

Invited to join Esther's family for Protopitta - cutting of New Year cake. Seems a bit late. Enjoyed last visit so looking forward to it. No word from Ice Queen. Have I offended in some way?

'Let me take your coat. Go and sit by the fire. Christos is cooking the burgers. The children helped me make them. Everything fresh.'

The children waited with plates on which lay bread cakes still warm from the oven. Esther broke the bread cakes open; Christos popped a burger on one half. Sylvia offered the first to Kenneth.

'Our guest must have the first.'

Esther pointed to a huge bowl of green salad on the coffee table.

'Help yourself. We are all family tonight and will eat from our knees.'

Kenneth bit into his burger. The words 'out of this world' came to mind. As well as meat it contained minced vegetables with just a hint of garlic. Christos brought glasses of beer to the table.

'Beer is best with burgers. We will have a whisky with the cake.'

'Do tell me about the cake, Christos.'

'It's an old Byzantine custom. It's often called the Vassilopitta, the basil cake. Hidden inside it is a small charm. The person who finds it in his slice has good luck for all the year.'

'Then it's like the Christmas pudding eaten at home. A silver sixpence is baked inside. Again the person finding it has good luck for the next year.'

'Poof, I don't believe any of that. But the children like to do it.'

Silently Kenneth agreed with Esther.

Diary Entry (late January)

Sylvia got charm. Very excited. Decided this tradition good way of getting over invites to drink Chivas. Contacted Kyria via Esther. Mrs Eleni cooked cake/even provided charm. Invited Demi, Alexandros, Spiros, Carol and Michalis. (Esther and family away for w/e). Just drinks/cake cutting. Went well. Kyria won charm, head of Alexander the Great. Strange, everyone automatically accepted Kyria as hostess. Because we're now 'a couple' or is there more sinister explanation? Fell asleep in front of fire. Too much Chivas... Good job smelled burning.

Everyone had gone home. Only embers left in the fireplace. The two lay entwined on the sofa. Gently stroking, cuddling. Relaxed, enjoying the physical contact. She had chosen an LP. Someone he didn't know. An unusual voice. A new track started. A flame sprang up and threw a spark onto the rug. Kenneth jumped up to stamp on the smoldering rug. The music stopped. He turned but she was gone. The arm still rested on the LP. The track was 'Back to the Island.'

Diary Entry (end January)

Daily water boat interrupted due high seas/storms. Shops out of bottled water. Never thought would have to collect rain water to flush toilet. Nearest neighbour offered use of well, dug for this contingency. Why buy water when such an abundance on island. Economic? Quaint just doesn't fit bill here. Refrigerated lorries returned Athens. Crossing impossible. Could see them when rain abated. Butcher's freezer bare of all stock. Only meat available on show. Assured families will kill sheep or wring chicken's neck if necessary! May resort to vegetarianism. Prefer my meat neatly prepared, preferably packed. Less it looks like animal the better. The Bitch is a vegan. Sanctimonious/terrible bore/comments re 'dead flesh eaters'. Not worried as I deliciously masticate my rarish steak in her presence. Got carried away there. Back to island crisis. No-one unduly concerned. Has given opportunity to get on with writing. Wonder how Ice Queen coping... this weather probably suits her.

Kenneth walked briskly across the Dapia. It was a bright day with a clear sky but a cold wind. He was wearing his cashmere coat and felt grudgingly grateful to The Bitch's foresight in sending it. He had intended to walk as far as Zorba's, the other side of the Dapia, and have a light lunch. Zorba's was a good bar, with 'clean' drinks and tasty food. He had called there on several of his perambulations.

The bar next door he had always avoided as it was generally packed with tourists having a good time. Today the sound of laughter caused him to retrace his steps. The bar was full of locals with a smattering of ex-pats. The laughter was centred on a dart board to the right of the bar. He was about to resume his walk when a woman approached the throwing area. It was Kyria. Kenneth quickly revised his plans. As he entered the bar Kyria was about to throw her third dart. Silence descended as she narrowed her eyes, lining up the dart. Kenneth was hardly aware of the actual flight but heard a dull thud as it settled firmly in double nineteen. Followed by loud cheers. The ex-pats had beaten the locals.

'She's done it again. We'll do well on the Heli trip. Beat 'em sound.'

'Not bad for a woman.'

'Watch it, laddie. She never misses with them darts.'

'Well done, lass. What'll you be having?'

Kyria was obviously popular. There was a lot of banter but no over familiarity. She turned to the bar to accept her congratulatory drink and spotted Kenneth.

'Oh, I didn't expect to see you here. Would never have associated you with darts.'

'I was intending to go to Zorba's.'

'I'll join you. It'll be quieter there.'

Zorba's was quite full but did not have the raucous noise of the bar next door. There were two bar stools free at the end of the bar so they took those.

'I didn't realize you were a darts player and a good one it seems.'

'Why should you? I used to be in a darts team. Did quite well, most of them time. I've always carried my darts in case there's ever a chance of a game.'

'I heard mention of a trip and beating someone.'

'Oh, that. We've arranged a match with a Greek team who play in Porto Heli. It's next Monday. Why don't you come? Give us some support.'

'Well, if you're sure the team won't mind?'

'Course not. We're sharing the cost of the water taxi but it won't be much. We're meeting at the periptero on the Dapia at 7.30.'

'Thank you. I'll see you there.'

'Good. I'll leave you to enjoy your lunch. I'm off to practise my throwing.'

* * *

There was a very relaxed atmosphere on the water-taxi taking them to Kosta. Once again the driver was Apostolis who was also going to support the team. The Porto Heli team were waiting with a fleet of cars. They were soon at the bar where priorities were first observed, a drink on the house. While the drinks were being imbibed the partners were assigned by lot. Kyria was the only woman playing and she drew the captain of the Heli team. Kenneth felt a slight twinge of jealousy when he saw the two acknowledge each other with a shake of the hand.

'Does your husband not play?'

'No, and he's not my husband.'

Kenneth heard the exchange and had mixed feelings about the assumption. Did others think they were 'a couple'?

Kenneth had little knowledge of the game but heard an agreement made that they would all go straight off but end on a double. Again the order of pairs was decided by lot. Kyria and partner would be the last to throw. By watching the first pairs throw Kenneth soon got the idea.

The score was even. Now it was the final pairing. This would decide the match. Both wanted a double to finish. There were cheers as her dart hit double two. She was congratulated by her losing partner. She had pipped him at the post. But when she went to retrieve her dart she called him over to show her dart was just the wrong side of the wire in double fifteen. He won with his next throw. They went to the bar for Kyria to buy him a drink. Kenneth didn't enjoy seeing them share a joke together.

The evening was over. The fleet of cars, notwithstanding the amounts of alcohol consumed, took them back to the water-taxi. Apostolis was in a good mood as he reversed the taxi to turn towards Spetses. He turned on the radio and traditional music ensued.

'Very bad luck but good sportsmanship.'

'I was off form tonight. Maybe it was you watching me.'

'Oh, I do hope not. I wouldn't have come if I'd thought...'

'Kenneth...'

'I see, you're teasing me again. I did enjoy the evening. Quite unexpected. Thank you for asking me.'

The water-taxi moored and each went their separate ways.

Diary Entry (early February)

Surprise. Snow. Only a flurry although lots on mountains over on mainland. Heard main road to Athens blocked. Children very excited. Some never seen snow. Imagine. Esther and children went up to Prophet Elias. Enough snow for 'fight'. Not enough for snowman. Weather very changeable. Sky pale blue, watery sun, fluffy white clouds. Temp up to 15 degrees some days. Some days take coffee on balcony.

Kenneth woke earlier than usual. He opened the bedroom shutters. It was still dark. Feeling fully awake he made his first cup of tea of the day and opened the kitchen door to the balcony that looked towards the highest parts of the island. He stared towards the horizon and saw a faint light. For the first time he truly experienced Homer's rosy-fingered dawn and knew the poet had not been taking poetic licence. Kenneth was seeing what the poet had described so eloquently. The faint pink, almost imperceptibly turning to lilac and then deepening to mauve, red, orange, heralding the arrival of the sun.

The sound of an engine interrupted Kenneth's contemplations. He looked at his watch. It was early, far too early, even for the local populous to be abroad for either Dolphin or work. But he could definitely hear a motor-bike making its way up the slope towards the house. He felt cold. Was it another of his imaginings. He heard the engine cut out and then the clang of the garden gates. He heard steps so there was a visitor. The steps were slow, measured and determined. So this time there was a real visitor.

Kenneth passed through the kitchen to the front door to receive his visitor, wondering what was so urgent to justify such an early morning call. He waited for the knock or the jangle of the goat bell. Nothing. Kenneth opened the door. The birds were beginning their dawn chorus. The air felt fresh but with a slight smell of cigarette smoke. There was no-one there.

Puzzled, Kenneth checked over each balustrade in case his visitor had chosen to stroll round the garden. Perhaps merely popped in to help themselves to the horta so beloved by the indigenous population. He had never previously thought of weeds as a culinary delicacy but was now developing a taste.

There was no-one there. He looked towards the gates. They were closed. He walked slowly down the walkway. Opening the gates he looked up and down the road. Nothing. No bike, no people. Had he imagined the noise?

As he closed the gates his eyes again alighted on the red motor-bike which rested against the balustrade near the steps to the walkway. The tyres were still flat. The frame entwined in the encroaching foliage surrounding it. Kenneth shuddered. Not again. He didn't want to touch the engine.

'Good morning, Mr Kenneth. Up early today.'

It was Esther, hanging out washing. Kenneth turned.

'Good morning.'

Did that woman never sleep? But he was grateful for the air of normality.

Diary Entry (early February)

Children another day off school. Saw Esther's having fun climbing the fig tree. Wandered over to ask what celebration this time. The three saints of Spetses! Esther invited me to stay for coffee. She made good Italian. Also wanted some homemade 'biskwits'. Wasn't disappointed with either. Learned three saints nebulous people. General story three brothers from Spetses, martyred Chios 1822 after refusing to convert to Islam. Feb 14th passed uneventfully for me. Have never sent such a card. Have received several though. Understand Apokries/Carnival starts soon. Frowned on by priests as Dionysian in origin. Just a bit of fun.

There seemed to a lot going on before the onset of Lent. Esther and her children had been practising for a concert to be held in the Kapodistriaki theatre. Kyria had asked Kenneth to go with her. He was pleasantly surprised when they arrived at the theatre. Although in the traditional style with the stage at one end and the seats arranged in rows in front, the building was fairly modern and had been named after the first head of a newly liberated Greece, with the title of Governor.

The programme began with the children's dancing, first Demotico, followed by Gymnasio and then Lykeio. All were in very colourful traditional costumes and were most proficient. Kenneth did observe the majority of dancers were female. Next was a Bulgarian guitarist who sang folk songs from his own land. When adult dancers took the stage Kenneth recognised Esther and noted there were a few males in the group.

The evening concluded with a selection of traditional songs from an adult choir.

More males this time. Must have done a quick change, thought Kenneth as he saw Esther singing enthusiastically among the sopranos.

The audience filtered out. People stopped for a while to chat, discuss the concert and talk about the forthcoming play. Kenneth had missed the first production of Demi's 'Peace' as he was in Athens but now realised he would have a chance to see it.

'Quite a lot of talent on the island.'

'Why do you sound so surprised?'

'I meant no disparagement. It was a compliment. I thought the adult dancers showed more enjoyment than the children.'

'Maybe they were concentrating on just getting it right.'

'Possibly. Will you be coming to Demi's production?'

'Of course. You?'

'I would like to. Perhaps we could have dinner afterwards?'

'That would be nice. Look forward to it. I'll meet you here.'

As she said 'Goodnight' she touched his arm gently before disappearing into the crowd.

Diary Entry (mid February)

Enjoyed production. Well done Demi and children. Good to see old Greek drama still in vogue here. Pleasant meal at Green Doors after. Still didn't get to see K. home. Suspect she lives other side of square. Maybe should follow her.

She raked her red fingernails down his back. He gasped in pain and pleasure as the sharpened points, painted red for the occasion, penetrated his flesh. The legs encircled him. He felt the stiletto heels of the red, patent leather shoes cut into his buttocks. He cried out again in pain and pleasure. Sun streamed through the lathes of the shutters. The sheet on which he lay was drenched from the sweat dripping from him. He felt possessed. His dreams were becoming more vivid, more intense. Should he cease his attempts to connect with her? Would that bring him peace?

* * *

It was Tsiknopempti, the Thursday burning of the meats and they had been invited to a barbecue at Demi's house. They were to meet there but he wondered if he should give it a miss.

The smell of smoke and meat being barbecued hung heavily in the air as Kenneth made his way down to the Old Harbour. He was still unsure about whether he would go to the barbecue. The decision was made for him.

'Hi there, Kenneth.'

She was approaching from the opposite direction. She took his arm and they arrived at Demi's together. There were quite a few people already present. The wine and beer were flowing freely. Alexandros, dressed in chef's hat and apron, was busy at the barbecue on which lay an inordinate amount of meat, pork and lamb chops, several kinds of sausage, chicken legs and breasts, homemade burgers packed with vegetables. More meat peeped out from a nearby tray.

On a table lay baskets of fresh bread, various salad dishes and dips - tzatziki, aubergine, garlic, hummus. An awning stretched over a large wooden table and chairs.

'In case it rains,' explained Demi who had just come down the steps from the house carrying a huge bowl of chips. Alexandros removed the cooked meat from the barbecue onto plates which also went on the table. The barbecue was then replenished and flared up as Alexandros sprayed olive oil over the meat.

Kyria was deep in conversation so taking a lamb chop, a sausage and some salad Kenneth went to sit at the table.

'You must be the author from England.'

Kenneth put down his plate to shake the hand proffered.

'My name's Lukas. I'm a friend of Demi, from Athens. I understand you've come to live here for a year to write a book. Spetses attracts a lot of artist of all kinds. Some stay. Others leave. We wonder which you will do.'

Kenneth was saved from giving an answer as Kyria and others came to the table.

Later, after more wine and beer, the dancing began and continued until late. On his way home Kenneth thought of what the man had said. 'Some stay, others leave. We wonder what you will do.'

It hadn't been a question. It had been a statement. As he approached his house Kenneth himself wondered, would he stay or would he leave?

Lifting the key from its hook on the door jamb - he would never understood that one - he inserted it in the lock, thinking of the symbolism as his thoughts turned to what might, one day, lie beyond that door. The door closed with an almost imperceptible click. Removing his jacket he placed it carefully over one of the eight chairs that stood in perfect arrangement around the glass topped, oval table in the dining area.

His hand slid into the inside pocket of the jacket. He paused before removing a silver cigarette lighter. He softly fingered the embossed crest as he turned to the desk that gave him a view of garden overlooking the sea. A slight sigh as he lifted the lid of a wooden box that lay squarely on the desk. He had bought the box many years ago, admiring the intricate Arabic carving on the lid, its shape resembling an upturned boat. The box had not been made to house cigarettes but he took one of the small cigars that lay inside - an occasional treat despite his aversion to cigarettes. He poured himself a large Courvoisier and went over to the fireplace. He poked the dying embers, threw on some pine cones and sat to watch the flames take hold.

In the flames he saw a man and a woman. They were both naked. He was sure the woman was Kyria but the man not himself. The man's tongue moved over the softly closed eyelids, lightly brushed the partly separated lips, trailed down to the nipples which displayed their expectation. The navel waited implacably, the pubic hair accepted its being overlooked as the tongue continued its downward journey. The woman's body stiffened and arched in response to the tongue's assault as it reached its destination.

Kenneth shook his head, the fire had died. Had he fallen asleep? He threw the cigar stub into the ashes, downed the remains of the brandy and retired to a fitful sleep.

Diary Entry (late February)

Was invited to join barbecue group to watch carnival procession. Decided not to go. Telephone call from Kyria asking where I was. Claimed slight indisposition. She didn't enquire further. Thought heard disappointment in voice. Imagined? Said she'd see me the next day if I felt up to it.

Kyria had asked him to go for a walk, telling him to wear warm clothes. She had waited for him to join her outside the gates of his house.

'You seem to be over your indisposition.'

'It was nothing serious. Where shall we walk?'

'We will soon be celebrating Lent so I thought I would show you the last piece of frivolity before the austerity kicks in.'

'That's very kind of you. It's a pleasant break away from my writing.'

'Yes, you don't have long left to finish your book.'

There was no inflection, no emphasis. The statement was difficult to interpret. They were at the bottom of the slope. Kenneth paused.

'Which way?'

'The Old Harbour but we're taking a different route.'

'Any special reason?'

'Wait and see.'

They walked on in silence, past the hotel, the taverna with signs of preparations being made for the spring openings. A short way along the Agia Marina road Kyria turned left down a dirt road. Kenneth was convinced they had cut through someone's garden and out the back gate but Kyria assured him it wasn't really trespassing. Some way along the road outside they came across a grassy area where a group of men were working on a framework. Kyria stopped.

'This is what I wanted you to see. Hi, Dimitris. How's it going?'

'Fine, Kyria.'

'But will it fly?'

'Of course it will fly.'

'We'll wait for it to appear in the sky next Monday.'

There was much laughter from the group as Kyria and Kenneth walked on to the Old Harbour.

'I take it they were building a kite. But why? And why so big?'

'Next Monday is Clean Monday. It's a day of picnics, weather permitting. In the afternoon kites are flown although no-one appears to know why. Traditionally the kites are homemade and there is much competition to produce the biggest flyable kite. That's what those men were doing. I don't think men ever really grow up.'

They decided to walk across the island as it was more sheltered than the coast road. Arriving in the town they parted company, arranging to meet for Clean Monday and see if the biggest kite would fly.

Diary Entry (early March)

Quite breezy on the Monday. Some kites made it up. Sad to see so many shop-bought ones. No big kite. Heard it never made it. Definitely getting warmer. Bright, sunny. One can almost feel the island drying out. Almond trees in garden in full bloom. Whole island seems to be waking up. Greenery/buds everywhere. Been here 10 months. Tempus fugit. Winter officially over. A different island in Winter. Quite a lot of activity about. Lots of painting. Pleased I shelved the writing and took constitutional.

Kenneth woke and instantly felt different. He rose, not quite comprehending. Opening the shutters a stronger sun streamed in, a warm breeze bringing with it the smell of almond blossom. Spring had officially arrived despite the very unsettled weather of late.

Kenneth thought of the previous Monday when he had woken to a blizzard. Beyond a battered Peter Pan he had observed a sea so frenzied he had not ventured out at all. The blizzard abated but left behind a covering of snow. In minutes the snow had gone.

He breathed in the warm air, hoping last Monday had been an aberration, that the winter weather he had found so hard was finally over. Donning his silk dressing robe, he took his coffee and croissants on to the side balcony, enjoying a leisurely breakfast. He showered and dressed before settling down to write. The crested fountain pen flew across the page. Thoughts came more quickly than he could get them down coherently. He knew there were mistakes but he didn't stop for corrections as he normally did. He needed to record his ideas. They had never flowed so easily. He suddenly felt exhausted. A pile of hand-written sheets lay scattered on the floor where he had thrown them in his frenzy of writing. He leaned back in his chair, looked at his watch. It was just after noon. Screwing the top on his pen and replacing it on its rest he stood up. He went to the window and breathed deeply.

Although it looked warm the sun was deceptive so Kenneth donned a jacket but dispensed with the hat. The bougainvillea round the entry to the deserted hotel opposite his house was profuse. The bar area was also bursting with a similar beauty, and would soon provide much needed shade from the heat of the summer. He decided to walk up towards the monastery but branch off to the right. It led upwards. Although he had climbed halfway to visit Joanna he had never been to the top of the mountain. Several motorbikes, on their way to the monastery, overtook him. He returned their acknowledgements with a raise of the arm. He no longer jumped to the side on hearing their approach.

He came to the fork in the road, the left leading to the monastery, the right leading, he hoped, to the top of the mountain. As he passed the sparsely spaced houses he noticed summer clothes airing on lines or spread on the fences and bushes. Other lines held winter clothes that had obviously been washed. He smiled. He knew what was going on here. The reverse of what he had observed in the autumn. The winter clothes were being packed away and the summer clothes unpacked in the certainty they would be required, not the winter ones. How different from his homeland where there was no distinction between the seasons as far as clothes were concerned.

He eventually left the houses behind. He was surprised the birdsong was only intermittent. He heard the wind rustling in the fresh leafage. He heard strange scurrying sounds in the undergrowth. He was pleased he had chosen the stout walking boots found in the balcony cupboard. The path became rougher, smaller. He was not even sure he was heading in the right direction. He just headed upwards. He came to a recognisable road. The right had a definite descent incline so Kenneth turned left. A short walk and there, set in a clearing, was the church dedicated to the Prophet Elias.

Kenneth had heard the story of when a fire had swept over the island the church had been spared as the flames parted on reaching the building and then re-joined on the other side. Kenneth thought the 'miracle' had more to do with the clearing being a fire break rather than due to divine intervention.

The door to the church lay open but Kenneth first walked around the outside. He looked down to the sea below. The houses stretched out so they seemed to reach the sea itself. Everywhere he saw the signs of Spring - the island awakening from its winter sleep. The island was awash with colours of wild flowers - sedges, daisies, margaritas, wild cyclamen, blossoms of fruit trees - almond, apple, orange, lemon, quince, fig, olive. He felt conflicted. He had never meant to stay the year his agent had intended but now that year was almost spent. In a little over two months he would be returning home. Returning to what? He felt he didn't know any more but couldn't put it into words. With a sigh he turned to the church.

It comprised one main room. A lot of modern wood carving adorned with signs of extensive woodworm infestation. He wondered if anyone had done, or was doing, anything about it before it all crumbled to dust. He was surprised at how modern the structure seemed, imagining it would be much older in architectural style.

A paint-splattered, plastic chair stood on the hardened ground outside. Kenneth sat to enjoy the silence and try to work out his feelings, about the island, about her.

His eyes caught a flash of silver-blue, iridescent in the spring sun. He didn't move. He watched this light fluttering amongst the tangled growth. The light settled for a fleeting moment, long enough to see that the light was actually a butterfly. Marvelling at its beauty and delicacy he tried hard to remember when, in his life before the island, he had had time to sit and admire anything in nature. He discounted the galleries and museums with their man-made beauty. This was real. No man could recreate such exquisite frailness. The silver-blue light took to the air again, fluttered, settled.

Kenneth watched, transfixed. It was hypnotic, watching the light flitting from leaf to leaf. He wanted to retain the moment, not wanting it to end. He knew that at any sudden movement the light would disappear. He would have to return to reality and the decisions that needed to be made. The light disappeared. Kenneth left the church and thoughts behind.

He came to the path he had followed on his ascent. He thought of Robert Frost's 'The Road Not Taken'. He chose not to take the right turn which would have retraced his steps. Continuing straight along the road he hoped it would lead him somewhere he recognised. Kenneth had learned you only had to follow slopes down and you would eventually arrive at the coast road. This would take you to the town whichever way you walked, although one way would inevitably be longer than the other. Were it the longer, he had been assured, a bike would at some point come along and offer a lift.

Kenneth found he was enjoying the leisurely walking. The relative quiet of the sounds of nature, the sound of the sea gently rolling in, the birds busy with mating and nest-building, the wind rustling, whispering, an overall tranquillity. A fleeting thought of should he stay but he pushed it away. It wasn't to be contemplated. The open scrub and natural vegetation gave way to more formalised, ordered arrangements of land tended by human hand. Gardens round houses of a much older style than those nearer the town. Houses deliberately built up the mountain, away from the shoreline and marauding pirates. Many of the gardens sported mature trees with branches hanging precariously over stone walls which now bordered a more kept road.

Passing one such tree Kenneth was conscious of an apparent shadow falling from the tree, brushing his shoulder. He froze as the shadow revealed itself to be a snake of intricate design, before it disappeared over the wall to bury itself in a dense hedge.

Kenneth moved a few steps to his right, choosing to complete his downward journey nearer the centre of the road. He knew he was approaching the town as the area became more built-up. Built-up for Spetses, he thought wryly. To his surprise he suddenly found himself in the centre of the town, quite close to the Dapia. He took a taxi home.

Diary Entry (mid-March)

Haven't been out much of late. Getting on with writing. Conscious of time passing. Ignoring letters from The Bitch. She'll get a book. Just need to get it finished before May.

Kenneth walked slowly round the garden. Daffodils, crocuses, irises, freesias in an old bath at the back of the house, firefly, wild coffee, hedges of geraniums, hibiscus, a grape vine, lemon tree, all in various stages of growth. He had wondered at the strange sequence but had been told, 'They grow when they want.'

He looked at his watch. Time to meet Kyria at the ten o'clock car ferry. She had suggested they went over to Porto Heli 'just to get away for a few hours.' Although passing the town several times Kenneth had not stopped there since the Classical tour, his first encounter with her. Could that be significant? After ten months he still could not 'read' this woman.

'I knew you'd be early.'

She jumped down from the sea wall. They boarded the ferry and she suggested they stood outside. The ferry began its short journey.

'I always feel sad watching the island receding, even though I know I'll be returning. There was always a fear I wouldn't come back.'

Kenneth remained silent. He couldn't make sense of her words. Was she talking about now? Another time? He wanted to ask but she continued, almost talking to herself.

'How will you feel, do you think? When you leave the island behind. Will you want to come back?'

A sudden gust of wind seemed to carry her words away. Kenneth realized he didn't know.

There was a slight bump as the ferry docked and the stern door was lowered. They walked along the sea side to where the 'bus waited. The same 'bus, the same driver as when they went to Ermione. The 'bus approached the roundabout.

'We'll get off at this stop and then we can walk the whole length of the town. Won't take long.'

Although she had restored a more relaxed air Kenneth felt this day was going to be different from other time spent with Kyria.

'I suspect we both had early breakfasts but it's too early for lunch. There's a very nice coffee shop at the other end of the town where we could sit and admire the view. I suspect you don't want to explore the shops so we'll cross over to the sea side.'

The sea was quiet, with an occasional ripple. The yachts at anchor scarcely moved.

A Dolphin appeared as if from the land and moved slowly to a mooring, took on one passenger and then moved on in the direction of Spetses.

'You must be wondering where it came from. There's an inlet where the Dolphin anchors overnight. It's safe there if a storm blows up. The name Heli reflects the presence of the inlet which is supposedly shaped like an eel. Ah, here's the coffee shop.'

The coffee shop in question had an outside area protected from wind and rain by stout plastic walls at the sides. It wasn't very busy so they were able to take a table giving them an uninterrupted view of the island they had just left. Without asking Kyria ordered two hot chocolates. These were duly brought with two small chocolates.

'You never thought you'd stay a year but now a year has almost gone by. Are you surprised?'

'I never really wanted to come. Then I thought I could come, write the book, enjoy the summer and go home.'

'Home. What is home? Is it just where we live, where we have always lived or is it more?'

'I always thought London, my life there, my work, my flat, all that was my home. I don't know.'

'A home is more than a place. It's love, friendship, companionship. If all that is taken away it isn't home anymore.' Kyria was staring intently towards the island.

'Do you feel the island is your home, Kyria.'

'Yes, no, once. Oh, I don't know any more. We're getting far too serious. We came to have a few hours away from the island.'

'Can one ever be away from the island?'

'So you feel it too.'

Kenneth felt he was saying 'I don't know' more than he felt comfortable with so stayed silent. In any case 'So you feel it too' was a statement, not a question.

The mood was lightened with Kyria's suggestion they walk further along. Leaving the main town behind the way became greener with trees and bushes growing at the water's edge. They passed a taverna with outdoor seating overlooking the water. It too was protected from the wind by staunch plastic.

'That's where we'll be having lunch later.'

Diary Entry (late March)

Porto Heli. A strange day. Nearest she's come to revealing her past, yet said little. Must be connected with this house. 'He left'. Did a man desert her? Did she live here, with him? Knows a lot about the house. What happened? Why won't anyone tell me? I don't know anything anymore.

It was March 25th, the most important secular day of the year for all Greeks. It celebrated the rising, in 1821, against four hundred years of Turkish rule. Spetses was the first to raise its flag which proudly proclaimed 'Freedom or Death'. The island would be full of visitors and there would be a big parade. So Kenneth had learned the previous night when Kostas' Bar had re-opened after its winter break. Kyria had told him it was customary to go to establishments on their re-openings to buy a drink and wish them well for the coming season. Kenneth was only too willing to comply with the custom as it afforded more time with Kyria, conscious of his year fast coming to its close.

For this parade Kyria had chosen a sea side table at Klimis.

'We'll hear the procession, then see it as it turns the corner and come right past us. They'll be at the Church in the Old Harbour now. After the service the procession will form.'

Their conversation was interrupted by the sound of a band. The military style music gradually became louder. The head of the procession rounded the corner. As usual the clergy were in front with icons paraded behind them. Lots of decorated uniforms represented all the armed forces. Next came the Greek flag carried proudly by a girl. The top student in Lykeio Kostas had informed Kenneth. A great honour. As they reached Agia Mamas everyone stood. There was much crossing of breasts, applause and cheers as the flag drew near and passed on. All the pupils from the three schools followed as they had on October 28th. Kenneth noticed several surreptitious waves and grins from some of the children as they passed their teacher of English. He also noticed Kyria's hand, by her side. The fingers were wiggling in acknowledgment.

Although many restaurants were now open in readiness for Easter they ate at Green Doors. There was no more conversation about home, staying, going, but Kenneth had much to ponder on his walk home.

Diary Entry (early April)

Pleased winter over. Not quite idyllic island of summer! Flight ticket arrived from Bitch. Dated second week in May. No note. Tempted to send it back, no note, just to imagine her reaction. Suppose have to think about packing. What do I make of snippet gleaned in Kostas' last night. Ice Queen once lived here, in this house. Her partner didn't go away. He died. Suddenly. Kept that quiet - all of them. What else don't I know - or should I know? The island drunk clammed up - realised he'd said too much. Was hustled away. What's to do? More transpires on this island than meets proverbial eye. She grows ever more desirable, damn her...

Kenneth was in that state of not quite awake but not fully asleep. He thought he was dreaming for he could hear singing although more of a sort of tra laa-ing, usually associated with snow-capped mountains and goat-herds, a cross between 'Heidi' and 'The Sound of Music'. The singing conjured up melodious cowbells and cuckoo clock chalets. As he woke to full consciousness he could still hear the singing. The dreamlike scene that had been conjured up was not far from the truth for, as he looked through the half open shutters, he espied his neighbour, Esther. Balanced on one hip and held in place by an outstretched arm was a basket full of the washing generated by the two adults and three daughters of Esther's household.

Dressed in a long, white, cotton night dress, buttoned to the neck, Kenneth thought she could give quite a good audition for the role of Mrs Rochester - although an obviously much happier one and possibly much saner. Had Kenneth not been already acquainted with the lady in question he may well have doubted the latter. She spotted him and waved cheerfully as though wandering round in a night-dress was quite normal.

As Kenneth turned to retrieve his dressing gown he realised that he had not found this occurrence at all strange as he might once have done.

Diary Entry (mid April)

Easter movable here as other places. Late this year. Quite looking forward to it. Never experienced Orthodox celebrations before. Good for travel article.

It was Big Monday, the first day of Big Week. Kostas had kindly taken him through the customs so there were no surprises. He would hear a lot of church bells calling the faithful and believers to services. It was a long time since Kenneth had attended church, the marriage of a younger sibling who had teenage children now.

Kenneth heard the clang of the main gate. There was a tentative knock at the door. He heard giggling and opened the door.

'Kyria said it was all right to come.'

Several young children apprehensively stared at him. Kenneth recognised Esther's two younger children. A somewhat crude mock-up of what he construed was a representation of the rising of Lazarus was thrust at him. After his questioning of 'Who?' 'What?' 'Why?' all answered by Silvia, Kenneth gave then a generous handful of drachma and a box of sweets which Mrs Eleni had left, saying only,

'Maybe you want.'

He watched them as they walked down the walkway, carefully shutting the metal gates behind them. He saw Esther on her balcony. She waved.

'Coffee?'

There wouldn't be many more coffees with Esther so he closed his door and went over. The kitchen was full of the delicious smell of baking. Trays of sweets and biskwits cooling. Trays of unbaked items waiting their turn. Esther thrust her hands into a huge bowl of dough.

'Help yourself to coffee. Pot on the stove, cup in that cupboard there. Don't touch the baking. The children will bring a selection before we leave for the village.'

'You're not staying here for Easter?'

'No. Most people try to get home for Easter. Just like you do for Christmas. It is the biggest celebration of the year.'

Kenneth was drinking his coffee, looking at the temptations before him.

'Ok. You just have one, but no more. I'm watching you.'

Kenneth smiled. He loved the way his friendship with Esther had developed. They were very relaxed together, less formal than when he first came.

'That's it, you've had coffee. I'm busy. Come Thursday morning. I'm baking tsoureki. You can help us paint the eggs.'

Kenneth took no offence at this directness. He found it quite refreshing. He was quite looking forward to Thursday. But what was tsoureki and why would he want to paint eggs. Kostas hadn't mentioned either.

* * *

Irene answered the door.

'Come in Mr Kenneth. We're all in the kitchen.'

All the paraphernalia of Kenneth's earlier visit had been replaced by bowls of eggs. There was also an assortment of leaves, what looked like pieces of a lady's stocking, a paint box and several small brushes.

'We boiled some eggs yesterday. The tsoureki is in the oven so we can paint the eggs.'

Sylvia was in charge of three pans of boiling water. Each pan had a wooden spoon. She stirred each pan in turn.

'They're ready now.'

'Turn the heat down but not off and put four eggs in the yellow and green pans and six in the red. We'll prepare the others.'

Esther explained what was to be done.

'We dye the eggs with food dye. Mostly red, some green, some yellow. On some we like to put a pattern.'

Sylvia removed the coloured eggs using a slotted spoon and placed them into a sieve so cold water could be run over then. Constantina dried them before placing them on a rack to cool. More eggs were added to the pans.

'Some we'll leave plain. Others we decorate.'

She picked up a brush, dipped it into the paint box. It seemed only seconds before a chick appeared, on the outside of the egg.

'Mama is very artistic.'

'Poof. It's easy.'

Not so thought Kenneth, hoping he wouldn't be asked to produce anything so perfect.

The children had obviously done this before and set about their tasks without further ado. Esther took two undyed eggs and gave one to Kenneth.

'Just do like me.'

He was shown how to place a leaf onto the egg and tie it in position with one of the stocking pieces. The egg was placed into a pan to take the colour. When cooled the stocking was removed, leaving a leaf pattern and the mesh pattern of the stocking. Different leaves produced different patterns. Leaving Kenneth and the children to their mass production she attended to the tsoureki. This turned out to be a plaited semi-sweet bread with a red egg in the centre.

'Red eggs seem to figure a lot.'

'An ancient symbol of life. Then some Christians took it over as representing the blood of Christ.'

'As they did so many things.'

'Whatever you believe, take a walk to the cemetery tonight. At dusk. You will see something quite moving. But maybe you will feel nothing.'

Clutching his bowl of decorated eggs Kenneth crossed the road to his house wondering what he would find moving, or not.

* * *

Kenneth joined a trickle of people making their way to the cemetery. More passed on bikes or in three wheelers, some taxis. As he approached the gates of the cemetery he was aware of eerie glows coming from within. Once through the gates he saw that every grave had a red egg nestling in a glass of fine sand with a white candle. Many of the candles were already lit. People arriving were lighting others.

Moving was not the word he would have used. He thought atmospheric more suited. He also felt as though he were intruding so left. He would go to Seven Islands for his G&T and eat there. He had just finished his meal when he saw Kyria pass. She must have been at the cemetery but he hadn't seen her. Maybe for the old man who had no-one. He called but she merely waved and continued on her way.

* * *

He was woken early by the tolling of the bell at the church next door. It seemed exceptionally loud today. Realisation told him there was more than one bell and not all in unison. Kostas had warned him that some would toll all day. He would immerse himself in his writing. He could usually cut out extraneous noises when writing. And he had some serious writing to do if it was to be finished before he left the island. He became so engrossed it was mid-afternoon before he felt the pangs of hunger. Having had a light lunch he took an early siesta.

Although there was no arrangement to meet Kyria, he was sure she wouldn't miss this event. He showered, shaved and dressed. Only one bell tolling now. Somewhere in the Old Harbour.

There were no tables out as yet at Kostas' so he sat inside hoping Kyria would pass by.

'She's gone to join the crowd outside the Armata church. She'll follow the procession.'

Kenneth nodded. The procession was that of the Epitaphios. An ark-like structure which represented the tomb of Christ, decorated with flowers on the Thursday night by unmarried girls. On Big Friday, after dusk and a two to three hour service, the Epitaphios would be carried out on four long poles held by men specially chosen for this honour.

The tread of many feet in unison could be heard approaching the bar. Kostas immediately switched off the lights and the music. Everyone went outside. The whole town was now in darkness, the silence deafening. The procession began to pass. First the acolytes swinging censers of smoky aromatic incense, carrying banners or icons of saints. Next the priest in full, very ornate, ceremonial vestments. A crowd of some two hundred followed, each person carrying a slender, brown, lit candle about fifteen inches long. The procession stopped. He saw Kyria and made as if to join her. She shook her head and he stepped back.

From the sea road another procession wended its way whilst a third was coming down the side road from behind the town. Kenneth watched the processions merge. They would meet up with other processions from the far side of the island. A service would be held at Bouboulina Square and then the crowds would disperse. Some to follow the tombs back to the churches, others to bars and restaurants. Lights and music back on, Kostas placed a Courvoisier in front of Kenneth.

'She left a message. She'll meet you at St Nicholaos' Church at half past eleven tomorrow night.'

'Thank you. I'll have another Courvoisier. Make it a double.'

* * *

She had been moved by the sombre, almost mediæval atmosphere of the Big Friday procession. By the eeriness of shadows, the whispering of the tree. After the service she had joined him at Kostas'. They left soon after.

Tears ran down her cheek. He wiped them away with his hands, gently cradling her cheeks. There, on the balcony, he made love to her in a way she had never before experienced, strong, passionate, feverish, urgent and somehow gentle. They lay comfortable in each other's arms. No need for words. The balm of the night turned to a golden dawn.

Kenneth woke up from the sun lounge where he had collapsed in a drunken stupor in the early hours of the morning. His head hurt. Dragging himself to the bathroom he turned the cold tap to full blast and held the shower over his head until it felt anæsthetised. He hoped he could sleep it off before the night's assignation.

* * *

He finally came round about eight o'clock in the evening. The head no longer felt disconnected from his body but he did feel slightly sick. He went to the 'fridge and found some cold chicken. This, with a small salad and two cans of lemonade, helped restore his equilibrium. By eleven o'clock he felt he was able to meet Kyria without her suspecting him being 'in his cups' the previous night.

'I thought you might not make it after your session last night.'

He should have known by now. How could she not have been aware of the condition in which he had left the bar.

'Did overdo it but not too bad.'

'That's not what I heard. Kostas had to get a taxi driver out of bed to drive you home. Said he left you on the balcony. I'm pleased to see you recovered.'

She handed over a white candle. The crowd outside the church fell silent as all the lights in the area were extinguished. The service continued inside. The Eternal Flame the only light, brought by military jet from Constantinople and circulated round the country to every church. The bell struck twelve for the midnight hour. All the lights came on and the priest emerged carrying a white, lighted candle.

'Christ is risen.' He then allowed the people nearest him to light their candles. 'He is truly risen'.

In this way the light was passed on to everyone waiting.

'What happens now?'

'Most families will return home to burn a cross on the lintel of their front doors with the smoke of the candle, for protection.'

'And us?'

'We're going to Green Doors to eat the traditional meal. We'll keep the candles lit till we get there. You can keep them as a souvenir.'

Diary Entry (Big Sunday)

Not so keen on the traditional soup. Lamb entrails – no! Salads just what my stomach needed. Enjoyed the egg-tapping. Bit like conkers. Suspect some cheating going on. Not sure staying at Kostas' till five o'clock a good idea but very lively. Kyria relaxed, enjoying herself. Apparently have been invited to house in Old Harbour for the traditional lamb barbecue. Meeting at the children's swings at one o'clock.

The smell of lamb being barbecued seemed to be the only smell around as Kenneth walked down to the swings to meet Kyria. He saw traditional spits being turned by hand. Those people must have been up early. Other people had opted for electric spits, not so traditional but quicker and less labour intensive.

They walked past the church, down the steps, took the left turn and came out in the Old Harbour near the house of Demi and Alexandros. Kyria pointed out the house on the other side of the harbour.

'That's where we're going. Nice family, from Athens.'

'But I know them. At least I know one of them, Rania.'

'Yes, that's right, Rania. How do you know her?'

'I met her once in Seven Islands. Charming lady, very knowledgeable and a wicked sense of humour.'

'She never told me she had met you.'

Did Kyria sound a little peeved?

'Why should she? It was a very brief encounter. Do you know her well?'

'Quite well. I stay with her when I go to Athens. She lives in Ambelokipi. We can go straight to their garden this way, rather than the front entrance. It's quicker.'

There was a lot of activity that ceased when the couple arrived. Introductions were made to Rania's sister and mother.

Snacks and salads were brought out and placed on a large stone table built in situ under a permanent wooden awning. Half a lamb was turning in an electric oven, a kitchen one being operated via a long extension. There was quite an assortment of drinks on the table and crates of beer under it. Rania offered drinks. Kyria took a soft drink and Kenneth a small beer. Rania was drinking tsipouro. They sat watching the continued activity.

'You didn't tell me you'd met Kenneth, Rania.'

'Didn't I? Must have slipped my mind. Probably there was nothing to tell.'

'How many people are you expecting?' Kenneth decided to change the subject.

'Don't really know. No official invitations today. People just turn up, call in. I'd better go and see if mother needs any help. Do help yourself to drinks and food. The lamb will be ready shortly.'

People began to arrive, had drinks, ate some lamb and salad and left. A doctor and his wife stayed a tad longer. Kenneth felt they wanted to practise speaking English as they attempted to engage him in deep discussion about political situations round the world. Why did they assume he was an expert? Rania rescued him by asking about the man's new practice in Athens.

It was growing dark. The outside lights were lit and the mosquitoes arrived.

Coils were produced and lit. They were only partly successful. Kyria and Kenneth thanked their hosts and left. They made their way round the other side of the harbour. The bars were filling with young people and the music was loud and raucous.

'Shall we go to Kostas' for a drink?'

'We'll be lucky to get a seat. But we can try.'

Kostas' was full so they stood outside the open window, using the sill as a table.

'I don't want to stand for long, Kenneth, so I'll go home after this drink.'

'I quite agree. It's been a busy week. Maybe we should have an earlyish night.'

'The celebrations aren't quite finished yet. There's Kounoupitsa tomorrow. That's the official end of Easter, when an effigy of Judas Iscariot is burned. The people of Kounoupitsa invite the whole island. The food is provided by the inhabitants and the alcohol by one of the wealthier occupants. There's usually fireworks and dancing which can go on to the early hours.'

'What time does it start?'

'Mid-afternoon so we wouldn't have to get up so early. You needn't come if you'd rather not.'

'No, no. I'd love to come but maybe for a couple of hours only. I could leave if you wish to stay late.'

'A couple of hours sounds just fine. I'll see you at the other side of the harbour about threeish.'

She reached up, lightly kissed his lips and was gone. A kiss, a real kiss if only brief. His thoughts raced as he walked home. Was the Ice Queen finally melting? They were friends but did that kiss tell him more than friends. Was he reading too much into it? There was a bond, of sorts, but she still kept a distance. He had always walked away from long-term commitments, keeping relationships superficial. This was different. Something disturbed him. Something about her? Or was it the island?

* * *

They made love slowly, exploring each other's body, each responding with pleasure to the other's touch. It was as if their souls had merged, become one. This was how he'd always believed, hoped it would be. Kenneth had never felt so fulfilled, physically, emotionally. She ran her hand through his hair. The hands moved gently over his face. He looked in horror as they morphed into the strong hands of a man. The long fingers encircled his neck and began to squeeze till he could no longer breathe. He heard the woman laughing. Kenneth woke gasping for breath. He was cold and trembling. He could still hear laughing but recognised the voices of Esther's children playing outside.

Diary Entry (late April)
Kounoupitsa very relaxed, friendly. Stayed just over two hours. Walked to Dapia. As usual parted company there. Everyone getting ready for influx of tourists. Yearly cycle begins. An ending for me, or a beginning? Which do I want? Which does she want?

Have strong feeling she'll never leave island. Me? I don't know...

The fireplace had been cleared of its winter fires, the pots and urns replaced for the summer. The envelope containing the ticket home lay propped up on the mantelpiece. Kenneth thought of the conversation about what was 'home'. Could the island ever be 'home' for him? The island wanted Kyria to stay, of that he was certain. She belonged to the island but did he? He stared down at the open suitcases, still empty.

'I don't know. I don't know.'

Mrs Eleni knocked at the dressing room door.

'What you want. Problem?'

Kenneth hadn't realised he'd shouted.

'It's OK. It's nothing, thank you.'

He heard her return to the kitchen. He opened the wardrobe door and began to take clothes off the hangers. He couldn't continue. He needed to think. Yet he had been thinking and he still hadn't found an answer. He felt he couldn't stay on the island. He didn't fit. His life lay elsewhere but could it be without her? His soul felt it was one half of her but he couldn't hold her. He felt they could be soul mates but something nebulous held her back, he was sure of it. If only he could break through that barrier then everything would be all right. Joanna, he would go find Joanna.

Mrs Eleni watched him stride away from the house. She put her hands together.

'He is a good man, Lord. If he can't have her, then give him peace.'

Kenneth approached the place where he had last seen Joanna. There was no smoke or smell of burning wood. Although he called her name there was no apparition this time.

He slid to his knees, hands covering his face. He heard Joanna's voice, 'She can never be yours.' His own cry was only heard by the trees.

'Why? Why? Why?'

The trees gave no answer and Kenneth cried.

Diary Entry (early May)

A bitter-sweet May Day. Supposed to be jolly, a day for lovers. Did I lose my chance? Was that kiss an invitation? Or was it just goodbye?

One case was packed, locked, labelled. It now stood in the dressing room. The other waited but Kenneth was reluctant to complete its packing. It seemed so final. It would mean he was leaving. Would he ever come back? He felt he would. The island had decided that for him. But when and why? He didn't know. He pushed such thoughts away as he prepared for his last celebration on the island.

It was a non-religious one, May Day, a celebration of Spring and nature. The Ancient Greeks had dedicated the entire fifth month to Demeter, goddess of agriculture and her daughter, Persephone. This was the month the daughter returned to her mother after a dark Winter with Hades in the Underworld. Temples and sanctuaries were bedecked with flowers.

Kenneth was to spend the day with Kyria. She had told him she would arrange everything. He was to meet her on the Dapia at eleven in the morning. He chose off-white linen trousers, a matching shirt and deck shoes. Knowing the sun could be hot in the afternoon he lifted his Panama from its peg near the door and placed it in his bag with his Carreras and the usual bottle of water. He opened the door and was surprised to find a wreath made of grasses and wild flowers hanging from the metal grill. He recognised the selection. They were all from the garden. He had heard nothing.

* * *

She was waiting at the spot they had met on their first 'date', so long ago. She was wearing the same dress. Petros was there, his horse and buggy decorated with flowers and ribbons. The horse's ears poked through a straw hat and the bells on his harness shone bright.

'Petros is going to take us all round the island. We'll stop on the way for a picnic.'

'What about Petros?'

'He'll have his own picnic with the horse and probably a siesta.'

Kenneth helped her into the buggy. Petros clicked his horse into action and they were on their way, round the Dapia, through the town and along the Agia Marina road. The town was soon left behind. Paradise, Anargyri and Paraskevi beaches were busy. Traffic became sparser. The road followed the coast-line for some way and then veered right.

'Do you have a particular place in mind, Kyria?'

'I thought we'd avoid all the popular places. Zogeria may be busy as the kaikis offer trips there. But not far from there are some good spots for our picnic. Petros knows the places.'

Petros pulled the horse to a halt. He jumped down and left the reins hanging. He lifted down two rucksacks that had been nestling under his seat.

'All right here, Kyria?'

'Here's fine, thank you. Will you take the blue rucksack, Kenneth? It's the heavier. See you in two hours Petros.'

Petros drove on to the beach whilst Kyria led Kenneth to the trees some way from the road.

The cloth was spread, the cold mezethes set out and the wine removed from the cool box in the blue rucksack. She smiled sadly.

'This could be our last meal together before you leave the island. Maybe our last meal together.'

'Surely not. There are a few more days. We have some time left.'

'There is time left but is it time for us? Could it ever be our time?'

Kenneth opened the wine, filling two small tumblers and passing one to Kyria.

'Maybe I could come back later. Arrange things at home and then...'

'At home. So you've decided this is not your home.'

'I don't know. Sometimes I think I should stay, other times... I just don't know.

Are you going to stay here forever, Kyria? Would you consider leaving? If there was someone or something to leave for?'

'Not at the moment. For now my destiny lies with the island. Maybe sometime in the future. Who knows?'

The meal was completed, the wine finished. The rucksacks were packed and ready to go. They heard the clop of a horse coming nearer, stop. Kenneth held out his hand, pulling her to her feet. She did not let go but drew close. Standing on tiptoes she kissed him on the lips. Kenneth felt the pressure and his heart ached. She broke away, lifted a rucksack and headed for the road. Picking up the other rucksack Kenneth followed.

* * *

The house felt oppressive. Kenneth was restless. In a state of not awake, not asleep he heard music coming from the living room. He got out of bed to investigate. In the living room a cassette tape had finished but the reel still turned. He switched the machine off. As he fell asleep he remembered imperfectly the words of the song he had heard - something about checking out but never being able to leave. He dreamed he was in a hotel, searching for Kyria, but every time he opened a door there was no one there.

* * *

It was Kenneth's last night on the island. He had not seen, or heard from Kyria since May Day. He had said goodbye to a tearful Mrs Eleni, slipping a monetary present in her bag as she wiped her eyes. He had called on the family over the way and had a pleasant glass of wine. He had walked down to Kostas' for a final drink, hoping she would be there. He downed the beer and ordered a Courvoisier.

'Just popping out for some fresh air, Kostas. Back in a minute.'

Kenneth crossed the road to the beach. Stepping over the sea wall he slid down onto the sand until his back made contact with the wall, stretching out his long legs. The smell of the sea enveloped him. The noise of the bar and bikes faded. He could hear only the sea breaking on the shoreline. She must have seen and followed him. As her hands explored his body he remained silent, eyes still shut. She moved closer.

The clanging of a horse buggy announcing its passage broke the moment and she was gone. He returned to the bar and asked if she had been in that night. The reply confounded him.

'She's gone to Athens. She'll be back tomorrow.'

* * *

Kenneth stared at the handwritten manuscript in front of him. He carefully put the last full stop with a sigh of satisfaction before rescrewing the cap on the fountain pen that had eventually done such sterling work in his hand. He put the pen in his inside pocket, feeling the touch of the envelope with his ticket. The stand went in his brief case. He straightened the pile of A4 sheets and tied them together with the ribbon specially bought from the sewing shop in the town. The owner had looked at him enquiringly but Kenneth had refrained from offering an explanation. Too complicated. Gazing at the completed 'book' he smiled. His final edit unless his agent decided otherwise. He wondered what The Bitch would think of it but she had demanded a book and she'd got it.

He put his finished work in a box folder purchased from the newspaper shop which sold an eclectic mix of stationery. He would carry the manuscript in his brief case. He couldn't risk losing it. It was far too valuable - to him. He had destroyed all his notes but had retained his diary. That he would keep. He looked out of the window above his desk as if to commit the scene to memory. A slight breeze bowed Peter Pan in a farewell salute. Kenneth rose and gave a slight nod of the head in return.

Outside the metal gates his suitcases awaited his departure. A trunk was already on its way to Athens and thence to his home. He heard the toot of the taxi. He picked up his briefcase, walked through the door locking it for the final time. He hung the keys on the hook from which he had removed them a year earlier. As he passed the red bike he paused.

'It's all yours.'

The breeze whispered, then was silent.

The cases were already in the boot of the taxi. Kenneth did not look back.

He did not look back when the Dolphin left the Dapia. A lone figure watched the Dolphin until it was a dot on the horizon, and then turned back to the island.

* * *

Epilogue

Kenneth rose shortly after dawn. His sleep had been fitful. He now knew that, whatever happened today, he could never stay on the island. He sat in the garden, enjoying the freshness, the coolness and quiet of the early morning. He realized he had missed this. There was something special about this island. It, not the people, drew you in. It was the island itself. There was something, a spirituality that had nothing to do with organized religion of any description. It was much, much deeper than that. An ancient magic in which the island decided your meera. And he believed even now the island was weaving its thread, that only the island knew his fate, that it was the island that had prevented him from finding her until now.

He had learned from Rhea the lady had left the island suddenly, quietly. She had gone to the bar, had a drink, told Kostas she was leaving early the next day. Two trunks were to be collected from the house and sent to Athens where they would be stored. Rhea didn't know if they had ever been collected or to where they may have been forwarded. Some islanders believed she had returned to England. No-one knew for sure. She returned from time to time, arriving without fuss or announcement, re-tracing what she called her special places, always visiting the monastery before she left.

Her last visit was very sad because she had died. She just died. Because her death was sudden her body had to be taken to Athens for… Rhea had paused here searching for the word but Kenneth had understood.

'No matter, go on.' The result had surprised everyone. No cause of death could be found. The islanders said she died of sadness. The body had been returned to the island, its magic at work again, and buried in the cemetery next to the Monastery. Some years later, as was local custom, her bones had been lifted, cleaned and placed in a box in what Rhea had described as 'a little house' in the corner of the cemetery.

'You may go and see, if you wish.'

Kenneth re-played Rhea's words. Of course he wished. He left the garden and started the walk towards the Monastery. Right out of the hotel, up the slope, left where the slope met the road, left at the fork, over the bridge. The incline became steeper. It was a short walk physically but the longest walk emotionally Kenneth had ever taken. Past the church of Agia Barbara on the left. The Monastery loomed before him. He walked slowly, leaning heavily on his cane. The island was exerting its power, drawing him towards his destiny. Up the avenue of trees, the carpet of wild cyclamen between them. The wind rustled the leaves as it gently whispered her name. The gates of the cemetery were slightly to the right. He paused as he felt a heaviness in his heart, not knowing whether it was physical or emotional. He had to go on. The island demanded it. Walking through the graves he came to seven steps which led up to the 'the little house'. The door was locked. He left the cemetery by the nearby side gate which opened onto steps leading to the Monastery doors. His legs felt heavy as he pulled the iron ring that signalled a visitor.

A small door set in one of the larger ones opened and a petite, bespectacled nun appeared. Kenneth explained he was a friend from England and wished to pay his respects to a lady whose bones now rested in the chapel next to the Monastery. The nun smiled understandingly and produced the key. Kenneth's heart was pounding as he followed the nun into the small room. It was almost full, floor to ceiling, with silver coloured boxes, each inscribed in Greek with what he presumed were names. He saw the nun indicate two boxes with Roman lettering.

He stretched out his hand to touch the box which bore her name but withdrew it quickly to clutch at the band that grew ever tighter round his heart. His eyes moved towards the name on the other box but it became blurred. The last thing he heard was the nun's soft voice.

'We thought she would want to be next to him. They were always together.'

Another voice came back but he didn't hear it.

'She can never be yours.'

Outside the wind whispered her name one last time then carried it away on its never-ending journey. The island was once more at peace.

Acknowledgments

Linda - for all the hours, Mike for photos and advice
For their help, support, permission, hospitality

Esther, Joanna, Demi and Alexandros, Frankie, Costas, Maroula of the Spetses
Archives, Sister Salome - for her kindness and serenity

Tim Severin for permission to quote from his book 'The Jason Voyage'

Most of all the people of Spetses who helped not only in the writing of this book
but who gave me support when it was greatly needed. You know who you are...

Other unsung heroes
    Catriona
    Members of the Leven Litts Writers
    The 'Old Brigade' of the Helensburgh Writers' Workshop

Finally for my family who put up with me...

Lightning Source UK Ltd.
Milton Keynes UK
UKHW010755201020
371905UK00001B/54